IRONIC SACRIFICE

BRIDES OF PROPHECY

Book 2

BROOKLYN ANN

Copyright

Cover art by Brooklyn Ann and Kent Butler

Published by Broken Angels, an imprint by Brooklyn Smith

https://BrooklynannAuthor.com

Dedication

Dedicated to Karen Ann
6~11~62 – 2~14 ~09
You were the best mom that I could ever wish for.
I'll never stop missing you.
Thanks for believing in me.

And in memory of Bill Kieffer.
I'll always miss our fun conversations about
books, horror movies, and heavy metal.
You were a great friend.

Acknowledgements

Thanks to all the people who read this book and helped make Razvan shine: Erica Chapman, Jamie DeBree, Rissa Watkins, Shelley Martin, Bonnie Paulson, Michel King, Millie McClaine, Layna Pimental, Jess Haines, Shona Husk, and Laurie Schneider.

Thanks to Kent Butler for taking an awesome background photo and helping me create the cover.

Thanks to my friends at Gus's Cigar Pub for your enthusiastic support.

And thanks to my friends and family for being there for me on this crazy journey.

Chapter One

Spokane, Washington

"Oh God, please, make them stop!" Jayden dug her fingertips into her temples as if she could tear the horrid visions out of her skull.

Long after the police officer left, the imprint of him invading his daughter's room every night and the sound of her terrified whimpers was irrevocably burned in her memory. For the rest of her life, along with her worst visions, it would flash behind her eyes like a bad commercial, leaving behind a chill in her soul and a bitter taste in her mouth.

Again the temptation beckoned to end it all, to climb over the Division Street barrier to the dam churning the waters of the Spokane River and jump, drowning the visions permanently.

Oblivious to curious onlookers, Jayden sank to her knees on the cracked sidewalk.

The visions were getting stronger. The cop's hand barely grazed hers when she handed him her driver's license after he checked her ID. Immediately, she'd been pelted with vile images. It had been agony for her to keep a straight face as he interrogated her. She wanted to hit him— no. She wanted to tear his balls off and make him suffer a thousand-fold for what he did to that innocent child.

But there was nothing she could do. He was a man of the law while she was just a crazy homeless twenty-four-year-old woman. Once he confirmed her age and finished harassing her, the policeman left, free to rape and molest again while Jayden Leigh was trapped with terrible revelations of suffering that she could do nothing to prevent or free herself from.

"Are you all right, dear?" A gentle hand touched her shoulder and for once Jayden didn't get a vision. Although for a moment it seemed she could smell fresh baked bread.

Jayden looked up into the compassionate blue eyes of an elderly woman.

"Yeah," she croaked, licking dry lips. "It's just a…migraine." She fell back on the usual excuse for these situations, though she was tempted to shriek the horrible transgressions she witnessed.

The woman nodded, brushing a snowy lock from her forehead. "Don't you fret, dearie. I've just the thing for that!" she declared, reaching into her gargantuan red leather purse.

Jayden began to protest, but the matron cackled, "Ah-ha! Here you are, dear. Keep the bottle. My doctor gives me plenty of pills as it is."

Jayden smiled at the Excedrin. If only a little pill would cure her problem. Or perhaps it could, if she took the whole bottle.

"And take this too. It looks like you've fallen on hard times." The kindness in the woman's voice was enough to make Jayden's throat tighten with humble gratitude and the barely suppressed desire to cry on the stranger's shoulders and pour out her sorrow.

"Oh no, Ma'am, I couldn't." She tried to return the twenty-dollar bill, but the woman had already walked off and was getting into her Buick.

Her eyes brimmed with tears at the generosity. She pocketed the pills and money, picked up her bottle of cheap Chardonnay and resumed walking to her car, where she lived. She could always jump into the dam tomorrow. After all, it wouldn't do to waste the wine.

Sleep came hard that night. It wasn't the wailing of police sirens, or the rumble of semi-trucks on the freeway, or even the sounds of a couple screaming at each other a block away. Something else drowned those incessant city noises. A voice in her head sobbed despairingly, *"Why? Why? Why!"*

That voice had grown so loud that she could barely hear anything else. And still the keening cry rose higher... *"Why? Why? Why!"*

A real headache was dangerously close.

"Why indeed?" she murmured as she uncapped the wine bottle and took a deep drink. She knew perfectly well what the voice was asking.

Why have I been reduced to this pathetic state?

Jayden still did not have an answer.

Only three months ago things had been normal. *Or had they?* She'd had a decent job that fit with her college schedule, taking care of people with developmental disabilities. It fulfilled her hungered spirit and was a step closer to becoming a counselor, a secret dream she'd nursed since childhood. Jayden had been working in the group homes for almost a year when she began having the visions. They were quick and faint at first, making her blame her imagination even though her instinct argued furiously. *Just too much work,* she would tell herself. *All I need is a break. Things will get better when the semester ends.*

But the next day the visions would come back stronger and soon the breaks did little to hold them off. Jayden became convinced that she was losing her mind. It was beginning to look as if she was going to end up like her mother after all. Stark raving mad in a psychiatric ward, heavily medicated in a padded room until, unable to take it any longer, she died a slow painful death of a broken heart and shattered mind.

Shortly after summer break began, Jayden's supervisor fired her for being unproductive and upsetting the clients.

The next month, her landlord evicted her from her apartment. By then Jayden was half-insane from the severity of the visions, so she didn't really care.

Mechanically, she'd packed what little belongings that would fit in her little Toyota and left the apartment. She then withdrew the rest of her money from the bank and closed the account. Going back to school in the fall was not an option.

Besides the hassle of showering, going to the bathroom and having to move to a different location every night, living in her car was kind of liberating. She didn't have to pay bills or work or answer to anyone. The self-delusion only lasted a week when Jayden saw how quickly she was running out of money. She tried a few times to get a job, but every place she walked into and every person she encountered gave her such a cacophony of visions that she soon gave up, realizing that she would probably never be able to exist with the rest of humanity ever again.

Now it was early October and she almost froze to death every night.

"Why? Why? Why?" the voice cried again, despite all the wine she drank to muffle it.

"I told you already, I don't know!" Jayden growled. "Besides, *why* doesn't matter anymore. What I need to figure out is *what* the hell am I going to do?"

She put on her headphones and turned the volume up on her MP3 player, seeking solace in the music of her favorite band. For a blissful half hour, Rage of Angels' latest album blocked out the voices until she turned it off, mindful to conserve her batteries.

Her heavy eyelids drifted closed.

Glowing eyes...Blood-dripping fangs...A dark shadow closes over the figure of a woman, about to drain away her life. Jayden's voice screams, "No! Take me instead! I want to die, I need to die." Mocking laughter rings in her ears, "An ironic sacrifice I do say. Very well, a life for a life."

The shadow gently engulfs her and she begins to drown in thick velvet blackness. The sinister voice echoes, "A life for a life...A life for a life...A life for a life."

The piercing trill of a car alarm shunted Jayden from the dream.

"Damn it," she groaned and pulled the blankets over her head. Even nightmares were preferable to her miserable consciousness.

As she shifted in a fruitless attempt to seek comfort, Jayden realized that she had to pee. Cursing again under her breath, she sat up and pulled her shoes on. It was freezing cold outside. She shivered and her breath came out in big puffs of steam. She hurried into the alley to find a safe spot to relieve herself. When the street was out of view she crouched and unzipped her pants.

Just when she finished, a scream of terror tore the air close by, making her jump. Jayden yanked her pants up, zipper forgotten, skin prickling with acute alertness.

"No. Don't you *dare* touch me!" a woman demanded haughtily. She had to be only twenty feet away.

Jayden knew she should get the hell out of there and drive as far as her near empty gas tank would take her, but her legs propelled her relentlessly forward. Her heart pounded with a heady mixture of terror and anticipation as she came upon a scene that had only before existed in her dreams.

The woman was a tall leggy blonde in designer clothes. Jayden fleetingly wondered what such a classy lady was doing in a dark seedy alley. But then a vision assailed her. This woman had been so spoiled all her life that it was sickening. Her love for herself and utter scorn for all others rose up more noxious than the scent of her expensive perfume. Scenes of her temper tantrums flitted through Jayden's mind. She didn't really start to hate the woman until she saw her kick a bum on the street.

"H-how did I get here?" the woman demanded shrilly, trying to hide her fear. "I don't belong in this filth!"

"As a matter of fact, this is *exactly* where you belong," another voice replied. His voice was deep, smooth as velvet and faintly accented.

Jayden's eyes shifted to the dark form looming before the woman. It looked like a man, but it wasn't a man. This thing was far older and far more terrifying than a mere mugger. She started to take another step closer, but then it spoke again. His voice was so rich and enchanting that it held her motionless.

"I have brought you here, Charise, because it is time for judgment to be passed upon you."

Charise's eyes widened in terror. She gasped and put a dainty hand to her throat as if she were rehearsing for Broadway.

The creature nodded. "Yes. I know of your crimes. I know everything. And it is I who will decide your fate. In fact, I already have."

"What is it then?" she whispered.

"Death."

Slowly, he cupped her face in his hands. She shrieked and tried to scratch out his eyes with her long, manicured nails, but the man easily restrained her, seizing her anorexic-thin wrists with one hand, and tilting her neck to the side. His eyes began to glow with an unholy light, reflecting on his bared fangs.

Jayden saw the monster for what he was immediately, and at the moment, she didn't take the time to examine the impossibility of it all. She just flat out accepted it. *Vampire.*

"Wait!" she cried out, surprising herself.

Those glowing eyes now turned upon her, freezing her heart. Jayden stumbled back with an icy intake of breath.

"Yes?" The whisper was silky, invoking tendrils of fire in her belly despite the chill of the night and its events.

"D-don't k-kill her," she found herself stammering. "T-take me in-instead. I *want* to die."

The vampire laughed. Its mocking tone struck a sharp chord within her soul. This laughter had haunted her dreams many times before.

"You know what I am, don't you?" he asked, amusement lacing his voice like spun sugar.

Jayden nodded.

"And you know this woman for the foul selfish creature she is too, don't you… Jayden?"

She had felt his mind whispering against hers since their eyes met, but the shock of his learning her name almost stole her breath… or perhaps it was the intimate way in which he spoke it.

"Y-yes. I saw," she admitted, unwilling to show her fear of him.

"She deserves to die. Surely you cannot argue with that."

"I am not one to pass judgment," Jayden stated plainly. "Nor, do I think are you…Razvan." The ancient, foreign-sounding name came to her like a curveball.

The woman stared at them both dumbly. Her gaping lips opened and closed like those of a dying fish. She didn't even bother struggling in her captor's grip.

Razvan chuckled and twirled his short black goatee with one long finger, regarding Jayden like she was an amusing new toy. "And you offer yourself in her place, you say?"

"Yes," she whispered.

Again, the rich mocking laughter rippled across her body, touching her in places that should never be touched.

"A very powerful psychic I have come across," he said musingly, and crooked a finger, gesturing her to come forward.

Unbidden, her feet carried her forward. It was a powerful mind trick. Jayden realized with trepidation that the vampire could probably make her do anything he wanted against her will, as if she were a puppet. When she was inches away from him, he raised a hand and lifted a lock of her dirty hair, then let it drop.

"A poor girl for a rich one, a vagabond for a socialite, a truth for a lie," he murmured in a voice that brought goose bumps all over her flesh. "An ironic sacrifice, I do say. Very well, then. A life for a life."

Those familiar words made her heart jump into her throat.

The vampire turned his attention to the other woman, whose wrists he still held. "You know that this woman is sacrificing herself for your worthless hide, right?" he asked her.

The blonde nodded rapidly; her relief apparent as the vampire released his grip.

"And you are grateful, yes?" Razvan prodded. His tone oozed with false sincerity as he circled around her like a stalking wolf.

She nodded again. Her facial muscles twitched strangely. Jayden realized he must be now immobilizing her with his preternatural power.

"Then say it!" he ordered harshly.

Cerise flinched, but obeyed. "I-I'm grateful!" she half-shouted.

"No, you stupid bitch, I don't want or need your gratitude, but *she* does." He inclined his head to Jayden. "Now thank her."

The woman slowly approached Jayden, eyes full of awe. "Th-thank you."

Jayden nodded.

"Now kiss her hand." The icy command was irrefutable.

Charise took Jayden's hand, face screwed up in disgust at the dirt and grime that covered the flesh, and quickly brushed her lips across it. Jayden was confused about Razvan's motives for such a pointless demand. Maybe he just wanted to be cruel. One glance at the wicked glee in his eyes confirmed her suspicion.

"Very good, Charise," he said in a way a teacher congratulates a pupil.

Then, quick as lightning he pinned her against the brick wall. Jayden thought he had changed his mind about letting Charise go, but it appeared she was wrong.

"Now you are going to redeem yourself, yes?" he whispered. "I am certain you will, Charise. I am certain you will treat every person you encounter from this day forward with respect and dignity. Do you know how I know this?"

"H-how?" she stammered.

"Because, my dear, if you don't…if you remain the same self-centered trollop that I summoned into this alley, I will know and I will bring you here again. And trust me, you will not be so lucky as to survive the encounter. Now go!"

She didn't move, only stared dumbly.

"Quickly!" he growled, "before I change my mind. I am getting very hungry."

Charise ran. The sound of her clacking high heels echoed down the alley long after she was out of sight.

"Now, Jayden, where were we?" Razvan turned to her.

Oh God, she was going to die now. Jayden gazed up at the vampire, desperate to study the last thing she would ever see.

Razvan was taller than she, about six feet. His hair was long and dark and fell in rich waves to his shoulders. His eyes were like perfectly carved onyxes and when she met them it was like looking into eternity and slowly slipping over the edge. She shook herself, unwilling to fall under his spell, which he was surely trying to exert upon her, and turned her attention to the rest of his face. It was all harsh masculine planes and angles, with a firm jaw under a goatee and high, almost hollow cheekbones. The brows were thick and arched in such a way that he would always look malevolent. It was the same with his lips; they were so sharply sculpted and tinged with cynicism under a rakish mustache, it was doubtful that they could ever portray a smile of joy or honesty.

"What is the matter, Jayden?" Razvan asked suddenly. "Don't tell me I've now frightened you speechless. Not after you so boldly confronted me."

"No. Nothing's wrong," she said too quickly. "Well, besides the fact that I'm about to die. It's kind of a large thing to grasp, if you don't mind."

His smile faded, eyes turned serious. "Don't worry. I will give you time." He held out a hand. "Come."

She frowned in confusion. Was he toying with her? Unease trickled down her spine like rivulets of ice water. "What do you mean? Aren't you going to kill me now?"

Razvan shook his head. “No, I think not. You amuse me too much right now. And I would at least prefer to have you fed and bathed first.”

Her cheeks grew hot with embarrassment. She didn’t think about how badly she must smell to him, having not bathed in a week.

“Well?” He raised a brow.

Shivering in apprehension with a touch of excitement, she placed her hand in his. It was cool to the touch, but not as cold as she had expected of an undead creature. His other hand clamped about her waist as he pulled her body against his. The shocking intimacy made her tremble.

Suddenly, they both began to rise up into the air. Jayden clung to him in support, but as their ascent quickened, the wine, malnutrition, lack of sleep and shock got to be too much for her. Blackness closed over her as she slipped into unconsciousness.

Chapter Two

Coeur d'Alene, Idaho

Razvan shook his head in incredulous mirth as he laid the unconscious woman down on the hotel bed. Why did he make such a ridiculous bargain? He could have easily fed on both women or spared Jayden by washing all she had seen from her memory. But he had not.

Her offer to sacrifice her life for a stranger had both intrigued him and struck a chord within his blackened soul that he had thought long dead and buried. What had spurred her to such a rash action? Was she truly so noble, so selfless that she would die for a stranger? Or did she feel that her own life had no value? He had to know.

And then there was her incredible psychic power. He hadn't encountered a mortal with such strong abilities before in his near millennium of existence. It amazed him, this power. Her clairvoyance could be a near match to his prodigy, Silas's, and he was well over five centuries old.

Usually, his kind stayed far away from any human with even a scrap of psychic power, for their abilities were dangerous to vampires for obvious reasons. Razvan, however, used to seek them out to help him find his missing brother. All had failed...but this woman...Dare he hope?

He looked at her again. She was so dirty and wrapped up in faded, worn clothing that it was hard to determine her appearance. It didn't matter. There was something about this one, something that drew him more than his previous pet psychics.

Before he could think any further, Razvan bit his finger and coaxed her lips open to receive his blood as he recited the words that would Mark her as his property. "I, Razvan Nicolae, Lord of Spokane, Mark this mortal, Jayden Leigh, as mine and mine alone. With this Mark, I give Jayden my undying protection. Let all others, immortal and mortal alike, who crosses her path sense my Mark and know that to act against her is to act against myself and thus set forth my wrath, as I will avenge what is mine."

The Mark flared between them with an electric blast of hot energy. Razvan stumbled backward, eyes wide. Was this a normal reaction? He had no way of knowing, for he'd never Marked a mortal before, not even the only one he'd felt a smattering of affection for and later, to his undying regret, Changed. What the hell had possessed him to do this thing, and with such a pitiful scrap of humanity that lay before him? The more he thought about it, the more his chest tightened in near panic. Shaking his head, he forced the disturbing question away. The deed was finished.

With that settled, Razvan went into the bathroom and started running bathwater. Amusement curved his lips as he recalled the resort staff's shocked expressions at the well-dressed gentleman carrying in a vagrant from the streets. When she was bathed, fed, and dressed in new clothes, they wouldn't recognize her.

His amusement faded. A hotel was not the best place, but Razvan couldn't think of anywhere else to take his new possession. His home wasn't suitable, especially for one in her malnourished and mentally unstable condition. And, of course, when immediate necessities were taken care of, there were other things that needed to be done.

When the bath was full, Razvan returned to the bed and began to undress Jayden. Whether from exhaustion or malnourishment, she had not yet awakened. His breath caught in surprise when he felt a tremor of desire at the sight of her naked flesh. She was much too thin, but he appreciated the sight of her small pert breasts and narrow, yet still feminine hips. Her legs were long and graceful as a dancer's, and her stomach was smooth and flat.

Again, the sense of irony struck him. Though he was a vampire, he still had a man's needs, but not quite so often or intensely. He rarely bedded mortal women, for not only were they food, but their ignorance and frivolousness annoyed him. Instead, he found his release with females of his own kind. But this woman…even dirty and half-starved…She ignited his lust more with every second he looked upon her.

She began to stir, moaning softly when he lowered her into the steaming bathwater. As he gently began to scrub her with a soapy washcloth, her eyes snapped open, and for what felt like an eternity, their gazes locked in what seemed a violent battle of wills.

The spell broke. Jayden's mouth opened in a silent scream of terror, and she began to squirm desperately out of his grasp. Hot water sloshed in the tub, splashing him.

"Shh…" he whispered in a placating tone he didn't know he had. "It's all right. I am only trying to help."

"Oh, God…Oh God!" she gasped over and over again, arms crossed over her breasts in an age-old feminine gesture of defensiveness. "It wasn't a dream!"

There was a long moment of silence in which Razvan stood up and watched the emotions play across her sculpted features, dancing within eyes that were so dark and deep a green they were nearly as black as his own. Then she lowered her head so that her hair covered her face and her shoulders began to shake as a soft gasping sound came from her lips. *Damn it.* She was crying. The only time he dealt with crying women was when they were pleading for their lives and all he had to do was sink his fangs into their throats to resolve the matter. What was he supposed to do now? He didn't want to kill her. She was too interesting.

Then, her face lifted. To Razvan's shock Jayden was laughing. She looked up at him and laughed harder. His brow creased. Was she having hysterics?

Tears of mirth streamed down her cheeks. "You're a real live honest-to-God *vampire!* And...and I *asked* you to kill me."

"My apologies, but I fail to see the humor in this situation," Razvan replied. Why did he always end up with the mad ones?

"Don't you get it?" she cried in a choked voice. "Every time I touch somebody, I see their darkest secrets in living color, and *I can't take it anymore!* And then...*you* come."

This time the tears were of pain, not laughter. "I don't belong with people anymore. And the pain of my warped existence is becoming unbearable. Thank you so much for taking me, Razvan. But please, *please* end it soon."

Razvan stared at her in stunned awe of her passionate, painful declaration. He wanted to tell her that her powers were a blessing, that she could use them to fulfill her most unimaginable desires, she only needed to learn how to control them, and that he was going to take her to get help. But now was not the time, not when she was in such an overemotional state.

Instead, he said, "That will come later, Jayden. Now finish your bath, and I will order you something to eat."

With that, he left the bathroom to call room service and ponder the woman's outstanding power and courage and what he was going to do about it. Everything with Razvan Nicolae had a means to an end.

When she came out bundled in an overlarge terry cloth robe, skin pink, freshly scrubbed, and smelling of feminine arousal, he felt another tremor of desire.

And he still had no idea what that end would be.

Jayden stared at the exquisite furnishings of the hotel suite in awe. Never before had she seen so much luxury in her life. The bed, which suddenly appeared intimidating, was large enough for five people to sleep in.

Remembering her odd situation, she pulled the lapels of the terry-cloth robe tighter around her body and fixed her gaze upon the vampire, death incarnate who was to take her pain away. A verse from a John Keats poem flitted through her mind.

"I've been half in love with easeful death.
"Call'd him soft names in many a mused rhyme
"To take into the air my quiet breath."

Not only was Death easeful, but he was beautiful as well. Her knees trembled, and her lower body quivered at the sight of him. His black eyes locked on hers, glittering with dark knowledge and wicked promise. She opened her mouth to say something—she didn't know what— anything to break the awkward silence, but was saved by a knock on the door.

Razvan rose from the bed with enviable grace. "Your meal is here, my pet."

He opened the door and a boy came in with a covered tray. *Coeur d' Alene Resort* was embroidered above his nametag. So that was where she was. She'd read about the place and driven by it a few times. Only rich tourists stayed here. It struck her as odd that he'd take her across the state line to a fancy lakeside resort in Idaho to kill her. But here she was… On her last night alive. The strangeness nearly brought back another burst of maniacal laughter. Razvan took the food, paid the boy, and set the tray on a table across the room. He gestured languidly for her to come to the table.

My last meal, she thought, and her amusement dissipated.

She sat at the table, lifting the cover from the tray. Fettuccine Alfredo, calamari, and glazed vegetables graced the plate like an expensive sculpture. She hadn't eaten in at least two days, and the scent of the food made her stomach growl. She blushed in embarrassment, but Razvan merely smiled, fangs concealed, and gestured for her to eat.

Tentatively, she took her first bite. It tasted so good that she was lost since then and devoured the meal like a ravenous animal.

When the plate was clean, Razvan presented her with a glass of red wine, which she polished off in seconds. Once her belly was warm and full, the vampire stood, and reality sank in once again.

Jayden rose from the table and slowly walked to Razvan. She was so close to him that she had to tilt her head upward to meet his eyes.

"Well, now what?" she asked with more bravado than she felt.

For the longest time, he was silent, trapping her eyes with his, making her feel she was falling into their blackness. He raised a pale hand, and she flinched, but he only touched her hair.

"Your hair reminds me of spun rubies," he whispered.

"Um… yours is pretty too," she said awkwardly. He was so frightening, so beautiful, that it made it difficult for her to think.

"Remove your robe," he commanded softly.

It was time, she realized. Now she would fall into the arms of this exquisite creature, and he would sink his fangs into her throat and slowly drain the pain that was her life away into oblivion. Solemnly she untied the belt and slipped the robe from her shoulders, allowing it to fall into a fluffy puddle on the floor. Some part of her recoiled at being naked in front of a stranger, but the rest quivered with desire.

His cool hands reached out. One caressed her breasts; the other ran lightly down her hip, drawing a tremulous gasp from her lips. He pulled her against him, and the feel of his body against hers made her heart pound even harder. Surprisingly, with her ear against his chest, she heard his heartbeat in answer. Funny, she didn't think a vampire would have a pulse. Her thoughts were banished when he cupped her chin and tilted her head to meet his obsidian eyes. The Keats poem sang once more in her mind.

Now more than ever seems it rich to die.
To cease upon the midnight with no pain.
While thou art pouring forth thy soul abroad
In such an ecstasy…

"You are beautiful, Jayden Leigh," Razvan whispered in a voice that made her shiver from the top of her head to the tips of her toes.

His lips lowered to capture hers, and she began to shake even harder. Jayden wrapped her arms around him as the power of his kiss washed over her, filling her with electrifying sensations. His tongue caressed her lower lip before plunging in to dance against hers. Her knees weakened, and she collapsed against him.

God, she'd never dreamed it would be this good.

Razvan lifted her and lowered her onto the bed, all the while continuing the kiss. The weight of his body on hers felt so delicious that a low moan escaped her lips. His hair tumbled down to rest against her shoulder, and her hand rose to tangle in those rich, long tresses. It was softer than it looked. His mouth trailed from her lips down her jaw, and when he began to kiss her neck, she gasped loudly and ground her hips against his. Suddenly, his body broke contact with hers, and he sat up. Jayden whimpered, audibly bereft. But he was only removing his black silk shirt.

Not only was Death beautiful of face, he was exquisite of form as well. His sculpted chest was reminiscent of Michelangelo's *David.* She couldn't believe that this satiny flesh was being pressed against hers. *If only all women could die like this...*

Then, he kissed her again, and all coherent thoughts dashed away. His hips moved against hers with demanding force, and Jayden reveled in the intoxicating spell this so-called monster wove around her.

His hands caressed her all over, making her feel cherished, even prized. After what seemed like an eternity, Razvan's lips once again trailed from her now swollen lips to her throat. This time, she felt the sharp prick of his fangs piercing her flesh. The sensation was painful, but there was a poignant undertone of pleasure that seemed to expand as her blood flowed out of her veins and into his mouth. *Dying feels so wonderful*. Desperately, she clung to him, for already dizziness was taking her over, and delicious blackness was hovering near, waiting to close its welcome arms over her.

The vampire made a low, dangerous sound, pulling her from the brink of darkness. His fangs withdrew from her throat, and his body lifted from hers. She could hear the rustle of his pants as he removed them.

His weight settled back onto her body, and suddenly he thrust inside her. Jayden cried out in surprise and overwhelming pleasure. His fangs plunged into her neck again. Her hips writhed against his until they were both undulating in a mindless dance of ecstasy. Razvan's arms tightened around her as the climax overtook her with unfathomable insanity. She shook and trembled beneath him, feeling as if she were struck by multiple blasts of lightning.

The last sight Jayden beheld before the blackness claimed her was glowing eyes and blood-dripping fangs set within a visage whose beauty took her breath away. The last thing she heard was a masculine growl of pleasure that pulled at her heartstrings. Then there was nothing.

Razvan withdrew from Jayden's exquisite body, still panting with ecstasy. Immediately, he checked her pulse. It was a little weaker than he would like, and there were dark circles under her eyes. An unpleasant sensation built in his gut, overcoming the pleasure still singing in his loins. He'd only felt this particular sensation a few times before, but he was quick to identify the feeling: guilt.

Slowly he got out of the bed and bit his finger, smearing his blood across the puncture wounds on Jayden's neck to heal them, fighting off this new and alien urge to leave them displayed to the world.

He tucked the blankets around his new charge before burying his face in his hands. What had come over him? First, he took a crazy woman off the streets, then he Marked her, *then* he had sex with her despite her weak condition and his policy about not fucking his food. What was it about this woman that made him lose his mind?

He sent her a mental command to sleep through the day, feeling an uncomfortable twinge at how easy it was in her weakened state. The Mark flared between them again with its unsettling yet pleasurable electric heat. Razvan sighed. At least he would have plenty of time to figure out this enigma. He had seen the woman's memories. She truly was alone in the world without family or a mate to be concerned with her fate. *But did that make what he was doing right?* He shook off the disconcerting thought with a growl.

As he left the resort to return to Spokane for the day, he pulled out his phone and called the Lord of the city.

"Hello, Razvan," the vampire immediately answered.

"*Lord of Coeur d'Alene, I beg permission for a short visit. Also, I have brought something interesting.*"

Immediately came the reply: "*Was it so interesting as to delay your announcement of your arrival in my territory? If we were not friends, Nicolae...*"

Razvan chuckled and broke the connection before Lord McNaught could build up to a full tangent. It was good to keep the man on his toes.

Chapter Three

When Jayden awoke, the vampire was gone. She would have thought all that happened was a dream, but for the luxurious room that she was in.

"Oh my God!" Her voice seemed loud in the emptiness but not as overwhelming as her memories of the previous night.

She'd given herself to a *vampire*. Not only had he drank her blood, but he'd also made love to her. On the heels of that realization, another intruded.

I am still alive; he didn't kill me.

Those surreal facts took a while to absorb. It was all she could do not to tear at her hair and scream like a maniac. Then she looked at the clock and realized it was six pm. A whole night had passed. Her darting gaze settled on the door, and her mind was momentarily cleansed with a goal.

Jayden slid out of the bed and stood up, pausing as a wave of dizziness threatened to drop her. How much blood did he take? When she regained composure, she searched the room and the bathroom for her clothes. They were gone. Why the hell had he taken her clothes?

At least he left the robe. She put it on, tied the belt securely, and crept to the door. The knob was cool on her sweaty palms. It turned easily. She'd expected it to be locked. She opened it and tiptoed into the hallway, praying no one was around to see her in nothing but a robe. Maybe she could steal some clothes from the lockers in the pool area.

The corridor was empty and quiet besides the tinny sound of Mozart playing from the ceiling speakers. So far, so good. Jayden took a deep breath and continued walking. The plush royal blue carpet muted her footsteps. Then dizziness struck again, making her head swim and spots flash before her eyes, but she kept going, determined to escape.

She was just rounding the corner when she came face to face with the vampire.

"Going somewhere?" Razvan's lips curved into a malevolent grin.

Her breath caught in her throat as she gazed up at him. All he had done with her last night flashed in her mind with startling clarity as his midnight eyes threatened to trap her in their depths. Her gaze darted frantically to avoid them, focusing instead on the old-fashioned black frock coat that he wore. An urge to run her fingers along the folds, to see if it was soft as it looked, made her hands ball up at her sides. When she looked up at the wavy mass of hair that caressed his shoulders, her stomach clenched painfully as she remembered the soft feel of it in her hands. Defeated, she dropped her gaze to the floor.

But Razvan was not so easily placated. His fingers grasped her chin and tilted her head to look up at him.

"You were trying to escape." His voice sounded amused but frightening all the same.

She nodded. There was no point in denying the obvious.

"But I thought we had a bargain, Jayden." His tone was now patient and gentle, like a parent with a recalcitrant child.

"But you didn't kill me." A triumphant smile touched her lips, and she met his eyes in challenge. "You're the one who didn't hold your end of the bargain first. So I guess the deal is off."

Surprised laughter echoed through the hallway. "That is indeed a good argument, but I'm afraid you're wrong."

"How so?" she asked with a small frown. Her bravado was replaced by confusion.

Again, he laughed. "You should dress and eat first. Then I will explain."

She frowned. "I don't have any clothes."

He held out a shopping bag, previously unnoticed. "You do now."

The vampire took her arm with his free hand as he steered her back into the room. "Come, let us see if one of these gowns do you justice."

As he opened the shopping bags and began pulling out impossibly expensive clothing, he said jovially, "By the way, that police officer who harassed you the other day…he made a delightful breakfast. His daughter will be safe now."

Jayden's heart thudded in her skull. How had he known about the cop who'd stopped her yesterday? And about the terrible things he'd done?

As inhuman as it may be, she couldn't help but be relieved that the vampire had stopped him from harming anyone ever again.

"Thanks," she murmured.

Razvan grinned and pulled two gowns from one of the shopping bags. "What do you think? The black or the green?"

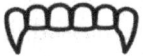

Jayden kept her eyes downcast as she nibbled on her dinner. Not only was it hard to eat in front of someone who wasn't doing so, but with all that had happened between them, especially the things he'd done to her body, she was terrified to look at him. Razvan didn't make things any easier. She'd hoped for immediate explanations, but he refused to speak to her until she ate.

"You are much too thin," he'd stated with a baleful glare.

The food was sumptuous, but she could barely choke it down. Her stomach felt like a cement mixer. Finally, with a curious stare at Razvan, the waitress took the plate away.

"I have never been on the boardwalk, have you?" the vampire asked.

She shook her head, eyes fixed to the lapels of his coat.

"Well, let's go."

He took her hand and led her outside. She shivered in the night air and buttoned her new fur coat…or faux fur anyway. She didn't know whether he was being cheap or if he cared about animal rights. The man—vampire—was the most puzzling being she'd ever met. Her heart pounded in anticipation of what he was going to do with her.

"My protégé and good friend is the Lord of this city," Razvan commented. "Beautiful, isn't it?"

She looked up and around. Everything was bathed in moonlight, from the smooth planks of the boardwalk to the gentle lapping waters of the lake.

"Yes." Her voice sounded harsh and alien in the still night.

He lapsed back into silence as he led her further down the path. She wondered if he'd brought her here, to a thin strip of wood surrounded by inky water, to further discourage her from escaping. A couple embraced on a bench nearby. A whisper of a vision struck her when she passed them. Quickly, she averted her eyes and willed her focus on the rippling water.

"You saw something." He nodded toward the couple.

It unnerved her that he could read her mind.

"The man is married to another woman," she replied.

His brows rose. "You did not touch him to see that."

She rolled her eyes. "He's reveling in his affair so much that I'm surprised the whole world doesn't know."

He laughed. She trembled.

"The point is, Jayden, you can see people's secrets without touching them. That makes you very powerful…and interesting."

They climbed a set of stairs and came upon a narrow arching bridge. Razvan leaned over the railing to peer down at the water. A slight breeze ruffled dark locks against his cheek. He was so beautiful.

"Why aren't you going to kill me, Razvan?" she whispered.

He smiled and scratched his beard. "Sometimes, my kind will keep a human companion. Some of us call them 'pet mortals.' I think you shall make a nice one."

"You want me for a pet?" She didn't know whether she was more shocked or outraged.

Uncomfortable with that subject, she moved on to another. "What made you change your mind about killing me?"

Razvan smiled wickedly. "I never said I was going to kill you. I just accepted the offer you made: your life for that woman's life. And I intend to keep you…and your life."

Waves of heat rushed through her body at his serious tone, even as her skin prickled as if chilled. He meant every word he said. Her stomach knotted at his trickery as her heart thudded at the possible implications of the situation. What would it mean for her? Would she become a mindless zombie, like in the Dracula movies? Or would he keep her as a regular food supply, locked up in a cold basement where no one could hear her screams?

Cautiously, she asked, "Were you going to do that with the other woman, Charise?"

He shook his head, still smiling in that unnerving manner. "No. She did not amuse me."

Jayden trembled with fear and confusion at his cavalier attitude at the prospect of making her his plaything. "Why do I amuse you?"

Razvan chuckled. "Come now, Jayden. You are a clairvoyant so powerful that you are half-mad with it. What's not amusing about that?"

She choked back a gasp. "You are evil."

He laughed low and sinisterly. "Only when I'm bored. Any more questions?"

"Plenty, but you kinda unnerve me, so I don't know what to ask." She sighed and turned away from him, leaning on the railing to stare out at the dark water. Maybe jumping in wouldn't be a bad idea. Wasn't there a myth about vampires and water?

The vampire leaned beside her on the railing, still laughing softly. "I am sure you will come up with something. Women never stop with their questions."

Jayden ignored the jibe and watched a boat pass under the bridge. Finally, she had a question. "Why don't I have visions when I touch you?"

"I have control over my thoughts." Something that almost sounded like respect tinged his voice. "You will not see what I do not wish you to. Don't worry, dear pet. I will get help for you to control your powers as well. That way, you will only have visions when you choose to."

"You can *do* that?" Tentative hope bloomed in her breast. Perhaps belonging to this creature wouldn't be so bad. She would give anything to have her sanity back. *Anything.*

"Of course," Razvan said. The arrogance and amusement returned to his tone. "I am a Lord Vampire."

No way! Not only did she end up with a vampire, but he was also a big boss vampire? "Is that a power thing or political?"

He inclined his head in a mock bow. "Are they not the same?"

"Well… I guess so, but I meant, what does being a Lord Vampire entail? How did you get the job?" She couldn't help her curiosity.

Razvan grinned. "I control the vampire community in my city. Any vampires who live and hunt there need my approval. If one wants to open a business, they must go through me. And if any want to enter my city, they must offer gifts and beg my approval."

"Vampires run businesses?" she asked in disbelief.

"Of course," he replied patiently. "We need money too. What did you think? That we skulk around cemeteries, sleep in sewers?" He turned to rest his back against the railing, a deceptively casual pose. "Power grows with age. Only centuries-old vampires can be Lords, and I am probably the oldest in the region…well, besides the Lord of Seattle. I don't know which of us is eldest."

Jayden chewed on a fingernail. "How old are you?"

"Nine hundred and fifty? Sixty? I cannot recall exactly."

The offhand manner of his grandiose statement made her feel as if she was in another dimension, but she didn't doubt his words. He reeked of power. Nine hundred years, what could one possibly learn and experience in that amount of time?

Razvan broke the silence. "Tonight, you shall meet the Lord of this city…and his pet. She is extraordinary. I may have claimed her for myself if Silas hadn't gotten her first."

Jayden fought off a surge of jealousy. *Don't be ridiculous.* She chided herself. *You're not supposed to want to be a pet!*

She turned to deliver a scathing retort, but he had pulled out his phone and was ordering a cab. The sight of the ancient vampire using a cell phone like a normal person added to the realization that Jayden was far out of her element.

"Well," he said after putting away his phone. "We had better get your bags packed."

The cab ride was over before she had a chance to worry much over meeting another vampire. They stopped at an auto-repair shop on the corner of 15th and Sherman. Jayden was perplexed. She'd expected a fancy mansion. The neon "Open" sign glowed a bright blue. She frowned. She'd also expected any auto shop to be closed at this hour.

Razvan winked at her. "Silas is out hunting. I don't believe you would like to witness that. For now, there is someone I would like you to meet."

Chapter Four

Jayden stared at the girl in grease-stained coveralls that entered the office of "Resurrection Wrenches." She couldn't be more than five feet tall. A mop of black ringlets framed a cherub-like face with amethyst eyes, a button nose, and Cupid's bow lips. Only the steely cynicism in her eyes and the curves of her breasts under the coveralls revealed the mechanic to be a grown woman.

Those lilac eyes met Jayden's and widened. For a moment, it looked like she would speak to her, but then she turned to Razvan.

"Whaddya want, asshole?" she demanded.

Jayden gasped, terrified that the vampire would destroy her for speaking to him so rudely. Razvan laughed and bowed to her.

"Akasha, fair Lady of this glorious city." His tone was all exaggerated formality with his signature touch of mockery. "I bring you the good tidings that I have finally found a pet mortal whose beauty comes close to matching yours. I beseech you to guard her whilst I seek your master."

Akasha's gaze whipped to Jayden. "No shit, really?" She turned back to Razvan with a glare. "He's not my master. He's my husband." Without waiting for a reply, she darted to the window and turned off the neon sign that said "Open."

"Let's go into the shop. You need to tell me what the fuck is going on." She tossed back her mass of curls and marched through the door.

Jayden blinked. This woman did not match her packaging.

Razvan bowed to Akasha and urged Jayden forward with a hand at the small of her back. She had never been in the service area of a car repair shop before. It struck her as odd that this one didn't have a waiting room. The smell of oil, grease, and metal was as overpowering as it was fascinating. Cars and trucks of various makes and years were up on hydraulic lifts with their hoods open and their guts exposed. A Siamese cat peered at them from a car window before disappearing from view.

Akasha pushed two wheeled stools their way and went to a mini-fridge next to a royal purple toolbox. "Do you want a beer…lady?"

"I'm Jayden. It's nice to meet you…and sure. I'll have one." She shot Razvan what she hoped was a defiant glare.

She didn't have time to gauge a reaction. Akasha pulled out two bottles of Kokanee, twisted the tops in an expert motion, and handed her one. When their fingers brushed, Jayden gasped and was thrown back, sucked into a vision.

A little girl screaming as bullets sliced up a man and a woman... running in the blood-stained snow...in an orphanage, can't speak...in a home filled with robotic children in matching uniforms reciting under a stern woman's eye...the woman beating Akasha with a bible...running away...starving, cold, alone... a man takes her in, she is happy for a while...she cries as the cops take him away...alone again...pinned on the hood of a Cadillac, a gun pressed to the back of her head as a man tears her body with his violent lust...beating the man...bashing his head into the pavement until his skull comes apart in her hands…throwing up…driving…

“Jayden!”

Strapped to an operating table…a scientist poking, and prodding…trying to make sense of the freak…going to kill her when it’s all over…

“Jayden!” Razvan’s command pulled her from the vision.

The beer bottle smashed on the floor, adding another mess to the concrete.

Her eyes met Akasha’s. “Oh, God, you were so young! And…and so much pain!” Jayden’s voice cracked as she was overcome with sympathy.

Akasha’s lower lip trembled as if she were about to cry, then her eyes narrowed to slits, and in a blur of speed, she backhanded Razvan.

He rocked back on his stool with the force of the blow and crashed to the floor. Jayden leapt up, heart in her mouth.

“I’m sorry!” she cried. “I can’t help it! Please, don’t fight.”

She couldn’t bear it if Razvan killed this woman who had suffered so much.

Akasha ignored her and hauled Razvan to his feet with a strength that shouldn’t be possible for her size. He spat blood on the concrete floor and laughed, fangs flashing. His cheek was already swelling and turning purple. She must have cracked the bone, and still, he laughed as though the mechanic had done the cutest thing in the world. As Akasha marched Razvan back to the parts room, Jayden didn’t know who to be more afraid of; the vampire or the girl who was strong enough to take one down. Who were these people? She shivered. Was it too late to escape?

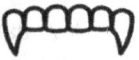

"What kind of sick game do you think you're playing?" Akasha demanded.

She'd had a bad feeling the second Razvan arrived with the statuesque redhead. They may have been all dolled up like a couple on a dinner date, but the girl looked like a frightened rabbit as she huddled in her faux fur coat and darted nervous glances around the shop as if looking for an escape route. Razvan, on the other hand, looked way too pleased with himself, like the villain who'd just tied the screaming damsel onto the railroad tracks. There was another look in his eyes, something she couldn't read…and it disturbed the hell out of her.

"Is she willing?" she whispered to him.

He avoided her eyes. "We had a bargain."

"That's not what I asked." She clenched her fists and stalked towards him. "Is. She. Willing?"

"You saw her power," he said, ignoring her question again.

It dawned on her. Centuries ago, Razvan's twin brother, also a vampire, disappeared, and he'd been using psychics to try to find him. Silas was the most powerful clairvoyant Razvan recruited, and even he failed. Jayden's detailed glimpse into Akasha's head implied that she may be even more powerful than her husband.

She glared at the vampire. "You may have used Silas in your quest, but hell if you're going to use this poor terrified woman."

Razvan drew himself up and opened his mouth, ready to fire back a smart-ass remark, then he slumped and sighed.

"She was going to kill herself, Akasha," he whispered, actually sounding sympathetic. "She even wanted me to kill her."

Her jaw dropped. "What?"

"Jayden is so powerful that she can't control her visions, and they've driven her insane." He gave an uncharacteristically helpless shrug. "She was reduced to living in her car, half-starved. She was going to jump off a bridge the next day, but instead, she found me in an alley with my prey and offered to take her place."

Akasha hugged herself as goosebumps crawled over her skin. "*Do* you kill your prey?" It was supposed to be illegal under vampire law, but she knew there were loopholes.

Razvan chuckled. "Not usually. I just like to play with them a little." He put his index finger to his lips in a hushing motion. "Now, don't go and destroy my reputation."

Akasha rolled her eyes at him before returning to the matter at hand. "Does she know you're not going to kill her now?"

"Yes," he replied impatiently. "Now would you please watch her so I can find Silas? Only he can teach her to control her powers so she can be well again."

She nodded reluctantly. "All right. But if she's unwilling, you know I'm going to help her escape and tell you where to stick it."

Razvan laughed, his sinister demeanor restored. "Help all you want. I have Marked her. She can never escape me."

Akasha gaped at him. His Mark meant that Jayden was under his protection for the rest of her life, and he would kill anyone who dared to hurt her. Either this wasn't a game to him, or it was one with very high stakes.

She followed him out and noticed that Jayden was sweeping up the broken glass from the floor. She watched in amazement as Razvan caressed Jayden's cheek with infinite tenderness.

His deep, gentle voice made her spine tingle. "Farewell, for now, my pet. I leave you in Akasha's capable hands. I will return soon."

After he left, Jayden stared at her with wide, fearful green eyes. Akasha glanced down to see that she still had blood on her knuckles. She reached for a shop rag, and the girl flinched as if expecting to be hit.

Akasha sighed. "Fuck. I need another drink."

Jayden watched warily as Akasha wiped the blood from her hand with a rag and returned to the mini-fridge. She pulled out two more beers, opened them, and slid one across the bench to Jayden, careful not to touch her this time. She lit a cigarette after a big swig of beer, then blew the smoke in the opposite direction.

"You can relax. I'm not going to hurt you. Razvan just has a way of pissing me off."

Jayden straightened and sipped her beer, humiliated that she was cowering before this tiny woman.

"How long have you known him?" she asked, curious about the nature of their relationship.

"A little over four years." Akasha laughed. "We kinda got off on the wrong foot when I threw him through a sliding-glass door."

"Why?" Jayden asked, thunderstruck.

"I thought he was threatening my man." Akasha smiled in remembrance.

"And why did you hit him this time?" she asked, hoping she wasn't going too far.

Akasha was silent for a while as she nursed her beer and smoked. Finally, she crushed out her cigarette into an overflowing ashtray.

"Razvan likes to toy with his prey. I didn't like the smug look on his face when he brought you here. He's a little more old-fashioned than Silas is with humans, and I didn't know if you were with him willingly or not."

"But you didn't get mad until I saw…your...um…past." Jayden trailed off lamely.

"Razvan especially likes psychics," Akasha said as if that was the point.

"Oh." She still didn't get it. "Why?"

Akasha sighed and lit another cigarette with the butt of her first one. "He's been searching for his missing brother for centuries, using psychics to help. When they fail, he throws them away. Now I'll ask you, are you with him willingly?"

Jayden was touched and perplexed that the woman cared so much about the fate of a stranger.

She shrugged. "We made a bargain."

"What kind of bargain?" Those amethyst eyes narrowed, making her want to squirm.

"I offered my life in exchange for another woman's." Jayden looked down at her lap. "I wanted him to kill me."

"So Razvan was telling the truth." Akasha's voice softened marginally. "Are your visions really that bad?"

Jayden refused to look at her. The pity would be unbearable. "Yes. They grew so strong and invasive that I lost my job and dropped out of college, and then when I couldn't get another job, I lost my apartment. I just want them to go away. I don't want to see any more terrible things!" she cried, choking on tears of frustration. "You can't know how awful it is for me."

Akasha got up and tossed her beer bottle in a trash barrel. The clang of glass against metal echoed in the shop. "You're right. I can't." Her tone was implacable. "But now that you know Razvan isn't going to put you out of your misery, doesn't it mean the bargain's off?"

Jayden shook her head. "No. He said that since I offered him my life, it is his to do with as he pleases."

Her new acquaintance snorted in outrage. "So, what, he owns you now? I don't fucking think so. This is the twenty-first century, and we aren't living in the feudal system he grew up in. If you want, I'll do what I can to help you. He Marked you, so he can find you wherever you go, but I have connections that can make him back off."

"No!" The shout tore from her throat.

Panic rose at the thought of losing the stability she felt around the vampire and being cast back to the chaos and perpetual visions of suffering on the streets.

She met Akasha's shocked stare defiantly. "I mean, I'm okay for now. Razvan's been kind to me, and I don't get visions from him when he touches me."

Her cheeks flushed as she remembered his tumultuous lovemaking. Akasha saw it right away and leaned forward in a flash, eyes narrow slits of accusation.

"He fucked you?" she demanded. "He actually thinks his 'owning' you goes that far?"

Jayden blushed harder. "It's okay… I mean, it was wonderful." She couldn't suppress a sigh.

"Oh damn, mental picture!" Akasha opened another beer as if trying to drink the images away. "But if you had said no, do you think he would've stopped?"

Jayden frowned. It was hard to imagine telling such a dark and powerful man "no." But Akasha had a point. It didn't matter how gorgeous he was or how good he was in the sack. She didn't want him to rape her.

"I don't know," she mumbled.

Akasha glared. "Well, you'd better find out; if you're going to stay with him. If he rapes you, I *will* hurt him…for real."

Jayden changed the subject. "What is your husband like?"

Akasha lit up with a dreamy smile, and her eyes overflowed with adoration. "He's a sweetie. You'll like him. He's going to help you control your powers."

"Really? Razvan didn't tell me." Surprised pleasure washed over her, and a tiny candle of hope ignited. Could there truly be help for her?

"Yeah, I'm not surprised. He likes being an enigmatic bastard." The mechanic put a flashlight on the bench. "Could you point that for me while I check out the wiring harness in that Dodge?"

"Sure." Jayden picked up the flashlight and followed her to the car.

"And Jayden?"

"Yeah?"

"Until you get your shit under control, don't fucking touch me again."

As he walked in search of Silas, Razvan pondered his intense fascination with Jayden. Never before had any of his pet psychics weighed so much on his thoughts. Perhaps it was because he'd enjoyed her body so much. He hadn't had a release with a woman for a long time. Or maybe her power brought him hope. Could she be the one to find Radu? His heart quickened at the thought, but something told him that there was more to his growing obsession. Either way, he couldn't ask her about Radu until her mind was healthy and strong again…if it ever would be. Besides, he'd given up on his quest to find his missing twin. His fists clenched as he reiterated the statement. He had given up.

Razvan spotted the other vampire behind a tavern on 2nd street. He hung back and watched his prodigy feed. Silas McNaught was a large warrior, with broad shoulders and powerful muscles. The physique remained from his practice with the sword, though he now directed most of his efforts to tedious matters of finance.

Silas touched his victim as little as possible. When he finished, he handed the young man some money and, as if on command, a taxi pulled up. Razvan chuckled at Silas's way of turning his meals into a virtue. Every night he fed he kept a drunk driver off the road. It seemed he was still covered with guilt over deeds long past. After Razvan had left McNaught to his own devices back in the sixteenth century, Silas had launched a bloodthirsty campaign against the English who had slaughtered his clan. According to rumor, he had killed at least one soldier a night…until the Elders had instituted their ban on killing humans.

Of course, there were always accidents. Razvan chuckled aloud at the thought, thinking to announce his presence.

Silas raised a brow at his laugh and crossed the street, meeting him on the cracked sidewalk. Dead leaves crunched under his polished shoes.

"Greetings, Razvan Nicolae, Lord of Spokane, Washington. How are you this fine evening?"

Razvan bowed. "Greetings, Silas McNaught, Lord of Coeur d'Alene, Idaho. I am well. I seek a favor from you."

Silas stared hard at him with his far-seeing peridot green eyes and ran a pale hand through long black hair that fell past his shoulders. "Might this have to do with the woman you found?"

Razvan was stunned. "You know about her? What did you see?"

Silas laughed. "Why do you presume I saw anything? I can smell her on you. I thought you did not advocate having sex with your food."

Razvan grunted noncommittally and shifted back and forth on the cracked sidewalk. "I generally do not."

Silas laughed harder. "Oh, you look so uncomfortable right now. I suppose I will take pity on you. I had a vision of you taking her from the streets last night, so I think it was intended."

"Intended? How so?" He hated the angst revealed in his tone.

Razvan had had centuries to get accustomed to the fact that things happened for a reason. Human beings had no idea how many prophecies and portents were being played out every second of their meager lives. Still, he'd never had awareness of being directly involved with one, despite his exposure to all the psychics he trafficked with. The idea that this fact could be changing made him wary.

"So, what was the favor you wanted to ask me?" Silas asked, ignoring the question, as they began walking down Lakeside Avenue.

Razvan measured his words carefully. "Jayden, my new pet mortal, is a psychic. A very powerful one."

McNaught raised a brow. "How powerful?"

"So powerful that she cannot function in normal human life. She sought death to escape the intensity of her visions." He hoped that his worry and guilt were concealed from the other vampire.

Silas blinked, then seemed to carefully compose his features. "And I suppose you came upon her as if by chance?"

"Yes. I was playing with my food, and she burst into the alley, brazenly offering her life in exchange for a spoilt woman's." He shook his head, still amazed at Jayden's brave, but pitiful demand. "She *begged* me to kill her."

Silas nodded with understanding and pity. "I often felt that way when the visions first came upon me. Where is the poor lass now?"

"At Akasha's shop."

"So that is what I happened to your face." Silas grinned. "I should have known her handiwork. Is anything broken?"

"I think she cracked my cheekbone."

The other vampire laughed. "That's my lass."

Chapter Five

Jayden smiled as Akasha's cat, Isuzu, butted his head against hers. "Your kitty is really affectionate."

Akasha grunted in what may have been agreement. It was hard to tell since she was under a car.

Jayden sighed and shifted on the shop stool, trying to get comfortable. In the growing silence, her nerves began to tic and jump, and her neck was sore from turning to the doorway at every sound. Razvan would return any minute and with him, Akasha's vampire husband, who was Razvan's psychic prodigy. Would he help her? And more importantly: would he be kind? The way his wife's frigid eyes warmed at his name indicated he wasn't a bad guy. On the other hand, even Hitler had a lady love.

She whipped around at the sound of a parking car. It was only someone getting gas across the street. Akasha rolled out from under a Dodge Stratus. Ears burning, Jayden twirled around on the stool, forcing her gaze everywhere but at the door. Her eyes lit on a photograph taped to the inside lid of Akasha's toolbox and widened in disbelief.

"No way," Jayden breathed, hoping her eyes weren't going to pop out of her head.

In the picture, Akasha was arm in arm with Jayden's favorite band, Rage of Angels. The lead singer, Xochitl Leonine, was holding out her hand in the classic devil horns gesture, and Sylvis Jagwolfe, the lead guitarist, was giving Akasha bunny ears. The bassist, Beau Thompson, was kissing the drummer, Aurora Lee, behind them even though the whole world knew Beau was gay. This was surreal.

"You *know* them?" she said.

Akasha followed the direction of Jayden's awed gaze. "They're my best friends," she said with a fond smile. "They practiced at my house back in high school. Silas and Razvan hooked them up with the owner of the club in Seattle, where they got their start."

Jayden nodded. "The Mortuary."

She'd read every scrap of info and gossip on the band since she'd first heard them on the radio. She usually wasn't the type to obsess over rock stars, but there was something about the music of Rage of Angels that set her heart aflame and made her imagination soar.

Akasha's grin widened. "When we get to my house, I'll show you more pictures and where they used to practice."

"I'd love that." Jayden tingled with excitement. Not only was she going to get help with her visions, but she would see where Rage of Angels started. "I used to fall asleep with their music playing. It gave me the most intense dreams! Some were a little scary; some were beautiful, far-off worlds and…"

She shut up, afraid she was sounding like an obsessed groupie. Akasha's eyes had turned speculative as if Jayden claimed that she held a map to buried treasure. "When they come here to visit next week, I'll introduce you if you're still around."

Jayden was too stunned to reply. *Meet the band*? She was spared by the sound of the front door opening. Razvan and Silas had returned.

"And how are ye lasses on this fine evening'?" A Scottish brogue intoned.

Akasha's face was breathtaking in its display of pure love. Jayden turned to see Silas McNaught, Lord Vampire of Coeur d'Alene. He was taller than Razvan by about four inches, and his shoulders were broader. Silky straight black hair caressed the lapels of his suit and framed a face that trumped Brad Pitt's. His emerald gaze focused on Akasha with infinite tenderness. *This must be what actors try to convey in romantic movies,* Jayden realized with a lump in her throat.

Unable to stop, her eyes darted to Razvan. He was watching the couple with an unreadable expression playing across his saturnine features. As if he sensed her perusal, his eyes, black as sin, locked on hers. Jayden hated being a redhead now more than ever. She knew every inch of her skin had turned crimson in an instant.

Razvan turned back to Silas. "If I can pull your attention from your bride for just a moment, McNaught, I would like to introduce you to my pet, Jayden Leigh."

Silas turned to her and bowed. "Ah yes, the seeress. It is a pleasure to make your acquaintance in person, Ms. Leigh."

He held out a hand, and she shook it, noting the open kindness in his eyes. No horrific visions assaulted her. She didn't expect them to, since Razvan had spoken of his powers, but it was nice to know the truth. *Please, God, let him be able to help me.*

Silas smiled. "It may take a wee bit of prayer, as you are indeed more powerful than I, but I think that if I teach you a few simple tricks, you'll be much better off."

Jayden's breath caught in amazement and indignation that he read her mind so easily. "Your accent is gone," she said.

His hand rubbed the back of his neck as if he was embarrassed. "I have lived in the States for almost two centuries, so it is gone for the most part, unless I am upset or…"

"How is Max doing?" Akasha interrupted.

Razvan turned to Jayden. "Max is Akasha's mentor and business partner. He suffered a minor heart attack last week."

Silas grinned. "The irascible devil is fine. It has been a trial, keeping him in the house and away from the cigarettes and beer. I very nearly had to restrain him to keep him from coming to work this evening. Dr. Greenbriar and I agree that he should take at least one more week off."

Akasha smiled. "I guess that means I'll be calling the college and letting the auto students intern again this week." She went to the sink and began washing her hands. "In light of all the shit that's come up tonight, I guess I'll close up early."

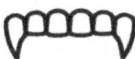

Sitting in the dark with Razvan in the backseat of Akasha's 1973 Plymouth Roadrunner reminded Jayden of the chaperoned dates she'd been on when she was fifteen. She didn't know whether to talk to him or if she was sitting too close. She remained rigid the whole ride, staring at nothing out the window. She was so focused on fighting her trepidation that at first, the castle on top of the hill seemed a product of her imagination…until they pulled in the garage.

Akasha got out and flipped the driver's seat forward so she could exit. "Welcome to castle McNaught. I'll order dinner and get the guest rooms ready."

"Room," Razvan said. "She'll sleep with me."

Akasha's eyes flared, but Silas, with Isuzu perched on his shoulder, put a hand on her arm and met her gaze. Some silent communication passed between them, and Akasha sighed. "Fine. Less work for me, then."

The castle resembled something out of one of those celebrity lifestyle shows with its plush carpeting, cherry wood furnishings, and expensive paintings adorning the walls. The only thing amiss was the odor of stale cigarettes emanating from the house. Razvan took her coat and hung it on an ornate hall tree in the foyer. They followed Akasha and Silas into the living room and were greeted by two people. The first, with the white coat and stethoscope, was obviously the doctor. The second, a huge man with a white and silver beard who looked like an aging biker had to be Max, Akasha's mentor and business partner. And the man who'd taken her in as a child…Jayden suddenly recalled from her vision. Max's blue eyes twinkled when he saw Akasha.

"Hey, Spark Plug," he said. "The doc here says I can have two cold ones a day now as long as I promise to cut back on the smoking."

"Right on!" Akasha replied. "Have you started yet?"

"Nope. Thought I'd wait and have one with you before heading back to bed."

"Cool, I'll grab 'em after I order some takeout." She flounced off to the kitchen. Max lumbered up from the couch and followed her. "You're not gonna order me any vegetarian crap, are you?" he groaned.

Silas shook hands with the doctor. "How is he really, Jonathon?"

The doctor ran a nervous hand through his brown hair. "Honestly, my lord, he is the most trying patient I've ever had. It has been agony to get him to take his medicine and rest properly. I really don't want him drinking or smoking at all, but I know if I say so, he'll rebel and get right back into the habits that landed him in this situation to begin with. Since he refused surgery, I've also been treating him with small doses of my blood in hopes that it will heal some of the damage to his heart. I'll have to have him come in for an EKG to see how well that has worked…Oh, hello, Lord Nicolae." The vampire doctor bowed to Razvan. "It is a pleasure to see you this evening."

"Greetings, Dr. Greenbriar," the vampire said. "Allow me to introduce you to my pet, Jayden Leigh."

The doctor's eyes widened for a minute, then his cheeks reddened, and he lowered his gaze. "It is a pleasure, Ms. Leigh." She caught a brief glimpse of fangs as he spoke.

Jayden smiled and inclined her head at his polite greeting. Shy vampires…she never would have guessed. The doctor conversed with Silas a little longer and left. The food arrived soon after, and Jayden did her best not to devour her fried rice, sweet and sour chicken, and crab Rangoon like a wild animal. Still, starvation was too familiar not to eat with gusto. Akasha gave her a knowing look, and she realized that her hostess had experienced more than a nodding acquaintance with hunger. Jayden suppressed a shudder as her glimpse of Akasha's memories came back. What the hell had the poor girl gone through that she'd been shot at, beaten, starved, raped, experimented on, and God knew what else?

She remained silent throughout the meal and listened to the conversations going on around her. Before her life fell apart, Jayden had many friends, or so she thought. Now, as she witnessed the closeness between these vampires and humans—though she had her doubts about Akasha being human—surrounding her, she realized that all her previous relationships were artificial. She sighed and set down her chopsticks, no longer hungry. If one of them were having problems, the others would stick around.

"It's going to be all right, lass," Silas said softly.

Jayden looked up at him sharply. Was he eavesdropping on her thoughts? Her shoulders slumped. Hell, she did the same all the time, even though she couldn't help it.

"Thanks."

She offered to help clear the table, but Akasha refused, obviously afraid that she'd touch her. In the end, she sat in silence as Akasha and Max drank their beer, and Silas and Razvan discussed vampire politics, which was a lot more boring than it sounded. They sounded more like corporate executives than powerful immortals.

Razvan withdrew a Sherlock Holmes-looking pipe from his breast pocket and lit it. As the scent of cherry-flavored tobacco filled the room, Jayden's eyes were drawn to his slender fingers and sculpted lips on the pipe's stem. She shivered as she remembered those hands and lips all over her body. Would he touch her again tonight? Could she refuse such intoxicating pleasure? She looked down at her hands, praying that no one was reading her internal struggle. She would have to refuse him. It was imperative that she know whether he truly thought of her as a toy or if he had the slightest regard for her as a human being.

As if he knew her thoughts, Razvan grasped a lock of her hair and twirled it about his fingers without breaking his conversation with Silas about quarterly taxes. Was this an omen? Akasha and Max gaped in obvious astonishment, but Silas merely blinked and rambled on about interest and capital gains. Apparently, Razvan was not one for casual touching.

Her scalp tingled at his touch, and an unbidden sigh escaped her lips. This was awkward. Akasha threw a pointed glance at her, at Razvan's hand, then back at her. Did she want him to stop?

Well, it wasn't like he publicly groped her…and his touch *did* feel good.

She shifted closer to Razvan to convey that she didn't need any interference. Akasha shrugged and asked Silas about annuities versus IRAs for a vampire's fake retirement. Jayden was surprised that the foul-mouthed, beer-swilling mechanic would have any interest in such a subject.

Shame knotted her belly at the judgment, as she remembered that Akasha owned her own business. Of course, she would know. Further humiliation ate at her as she realized that everyone around her was a success, except for her. Hell, Akasha looked to be in her early twenties, and she managed an auto shop. Akasha's friends were a world-renowned heavy metal band. And here Jayden was, homeless, half crazy, and at the mercy of all of them. Still, it was better than where she was yesterday. And they were all the most interesting individuals that she'd ever encountered.

She studied them one by one. What was the story behind Akasha? Where did she get her incredible strength? How did she meet Silas? And was their love as real as it looked? It sure seemed to be. The Scottish vampire held more kindness and gentleness in his eyes and voice than Jayden could imagine Razvan possessing. But could Silas help her? And if he did…if she managed to get back to normal, what then? Her mind shied from the question.

The combination of a full stomach and the boring conversations around her made Jayden drowsy. Her eyelids drooped, and she dozed off.

"I think it is bedtime for my pet," Razvan's voice rumbled in her ear. Jayden jolted awake and raised her head from his shoulder. The moment of truth was coming.

Silas stood up. "Very well, Akasha and I shall show you to your room."

As they followed Silas and Akasha down the stone steps to the secret chambers below, Jayden's heart tried to beat itself out of her chest. It was time to test Razvan's honor. As much as he fascinated and attracted her, she must be strong. When they reached their bedroom, and he tried to pull her into his arms and enslave her with his seduction, she would refuse him. *And then what? Will he rape me? What will it prove?* It seemed that with each step she took, a thousand questions screamed in her mind, the most frightening was: *what if he gets angry? Will he hurt me?* She did not doubt that, vampire or not, he could make her previous longing for death more paltry than a candy craving.

She bit back a startled gasp when Silas opened a door, jerking her back into reality. "I wish you both a good day's sleep. And Jayden?"

"Yes?" she did her best to sound casual.

"Your lessons will begin tomorrow."

"Oh. Okay."

Razvan led her down the hall into a room that put the Resort's suite to shame with its sumptuous carpet and California king-sized bed. A wall clock, framed with silver curlicues read 4:30 AM.

He set her bag on the bed. "I will be back shortly."

Jayden sat down on the mattress hard as the door shut. Where the hell was he going? Then it occurred to her. He needed to feed. He was going out to hunt. *Why didn't he feed on me?* She wondered. *And how often do vampires need blood?* Do they need it once, or is it three meals a night, like people? How much blood could she lose in a night? Jayden had no idea; she'd never donated blood before. It wasn't that she was selfish; she just wasn't at the right place at the right time.

She changed into one of her new nightgowns and brushed her teeth, all the while psyching herself up for what would happen when Razvan returned. She sat back on the bed and watched the clock slowly turn closer to five. What time did the sun come up this time of year? Five-thirty? Six? Just as she was about to slap herself for dozing off again, she heard his footsteps on the stairs. It was time to refute the vampire's advances. The door opened.

"You are still awake," Razvan said. "If I had known you meant to wait for me, I would have brought down some books from Silas's library."

He turned down the covers and patted the mattress. "Come, now. You have a busy evening ahead."

Cautiously, she lay down. He turned off the lamp and pulled the covers over them as he put his arm around her. *Now's the time.*

"Good rest, Jayden," he whispered.

And that was it.

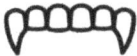

Razvan breathed in Jayden's delicious scent and congratulated himself on his restraint. Gently he whispered in her mind, coaxing her to relax and sleep. If only his body would heed the same command. He wanted her again, no. He hadn't stopped wanting her. Gritting his teeth against the raging desire, he contented himself with breathing in the sweet scent of her hair. Perhaps tomorrow, he would take her when she was better rested. He didn't know if he could wait any longer. And there was no place more restful than Silas's home.

A fond smile curved his lips as he remembered Jayden's courage when meeting his friends. She had seen Akasha at her worst, yet she did not flee. And best of all, she seemed to take to Silas well. Razvan was surprised at the well of gratitude that filled him for Silas's willingness to help. He only hoped that

McNaught's efforts would be a success. Jayden's mind was so fragile. Could she ever heal?

Chapter Six

The next evening, Jayden began her lessons with Silas. It was exceedingly hard to concentrate. *Why didn't Razvan want me?* She ached with disappointment, but couldn't tell if it was because she didn't get to test him, or because she wanted him to desire her.

"Jayden, you need to focus," Silas said again. "Now, try to read my thoughts."

"Okay, sorry," she replied. They had been at this ever since Akasha left for work. Razvan, Max, and one of Silas's subordinate vampires had gone back to Spokane to get Jayden's car. She was beginning to suspect that Razvan didn't know how to drive.

Already Silas had more than lived up to his promise to help her. She now knew what had triggered her visions. Unlike popular stories and myths, psychic powers did not usually manifest at puberty. Instead, they came with one's wisdom teeth. Silas believed that it was the cranial pressure from the new teeth that triggered the part of the brain responsible for psychic abilities.

Had that been why her mother had gone insane and ended up committed in a psych hospital when Jayden was five? Jayden had always thought it was because of the stress of becoming a mother in the tenth grade. Instead, maybe her mother began having visions too.

She had an insane urge to tell Razvan and see what he thought.

Silas watched her with an impatient look. “Are you even trying?”

She sighed. “I just don’t see how reading your thoughts will help me stop seeing other peoples’ secrets.”

Silas tapped his pen on the table. “Well, if you had been listening to me instead of thinking about Razvan, you would have heard me explaining that if you can sense the barrier on my thoughts, you would get a better sense of how to construct one of your own.”

“Oh, that makes sense,” Jayden began, and then the rest of his words sank in. “Wait, you read my thoughts?” Her eyes darted around the vast dining room, looking for a retreat.

Silas chuckled. “Only the subject, not the details, lass. Unlike you, I have to be touching a person for my powers to work efficiently. Now, try to read my thoughts.”

Jayden focused on him. Nothing happened.

“You’re just too good.” She spread her hands wide in surrender. “I can’t sense anything.”

Silas frowned. “I think it is mostly that I am more practiced, and you are still not concentrating enough. Your powers far exceed mine.” She gave him a doubtful look, and he sighed. “Fine, place your hand on mine and try again.”

She looked down at the appendage in question. His hands were large and looked more suited to wielding one of the huge swords that hung on the walls rather than flipping through tax forms. Jayden placed her hand atop his, marveling at the cool, rough texture of his skin. She couldn't help but wonder how he and the tiny Akasha were able to make love. Her fingers didn't even reach his wrist. She and Razvan, however, pulled it off wonderfully…

A vision of Silas lying in a field surrounded by corpses in chain mail and plaids slammed into her mind. A hooded figure approached him and blotted out the moon.

"Ah, 'tis the specter o' Death come for me now?" Silas croaked, "Come mon, finish this."

The figure did indeed resemble Death; his features were obscured in blackness. But his voice, achingly familiar, made her hair stand up on end.

"Not yet, far-sighted one," Razvan replied with a heavy Slavic-sounding accent, "I've others to attend to."

What felt like a steel wall slammed into place, throwing her back into her own mind like a backhanded slap.

"Well?" Silas said as she shook her head to clear it.

"I felt it!" she gasped. "It almost hurt."

The vampire nodded. "I'm sorry for that. For a moment, you got in. What did you see?"

"I think I saw the night you became a vampire," she said. "When did it happen?"

"In 1513, after the battle of Flodden Field. I would have died if Razvan had not found me. Was that all you saw?"

Jayden nodded. "Yes, then your shield forced me out."

Silas smiled in approval. "Do you think you can try to make one of your own?"

Doubt hardened in her stomach like a stone, but instead of protesting, she replied, "I think so."

It took a few tries for Jayden to build her own shield in her mind, but after a while, it seemed to be working. Her head ached from the strain, but Silas was a merciless taskmaster. He kept her at it until Max and Razvan returned with her car.

"It's got a bad C.V. joint, maybe two," Max said and held out her keys. Razvan took them before she could grab them. It appeared that she would not be able to come and go as she pleased.

She glared at him and his lips curved into the sinister smile that seemed to be his trademark. She was a prisoner here, but the people were kind to her, and she was getting help. Still, did that make it right? Her head ached from the quandary.

Max looked at them and shook his head before continuing as if nothing happened. "The fuel injectors need to be cleaned, and I'm sure she needs a tune-up. But I can get her purring like a kitten in no time."

"Thanks," she said weakly. What was the point if she couldn't drive anywhere?

Razvan took her chin in his hand and tilted her face up as if he were about to kiss her. "You look very pale, my sweet. Why?"

"I…uh, I've been working," she murmured. "It's harder than I thought."

Razvan turned to Silas. His black eyes glittered. "She will rest now and eat something."

"Think you can command me in ma 'ain house?" Silas's eyes flared neon green, and his brogue crept into his words, revealing his anger as he stalked forward.

Razvan held his ground.

"Actually, I am hungry," Jayden said quickly, hoping to avoid a fight. "If you don't mind, I would like a break."

"Go fetch a nibble and sit for a while, lass." Silas glared at Razvan, who seemed pleased at his ire. "You, old friend, are a pain in the arse."

Razvan laughed and stalked out of the room with predatory grace. As he passed Isuzu, the cat laid his ears flat and hissed at him. The Siamese then meowed and wound his way around Silas's legs before running to his empty food bowl, giving it a pointed glare.

Max chuckled and turned to Jayden, "Come on, girl. I make a mean grilled cheese."

The man wasn't kidding. As she bit into the sandwich, her taste buds seemed to moan in ecstasy.

"The secret is real butter…a lot of it." Max offered her a beer, but she refused, noticing with amusement that he was looking for an excuse to sneak in an extra one.

Silas glided into the kitchen on silent feet. "I am off to get sustenance as well. Max, may I ask a favor?"

Max nodded, not taking his eyes from the frying pan. "Anything, boss man."

"I think it would be best if Jayden were able to practice shielding her powers with a normal human," the vampire said. "Would you be willing?"

Max smiled. "I don't know if I'd exactly call myself *normal*, but sure. I got nothin' to hide." He yawned and stood up. "But not tonight, if you don't mind; I'm beat. Being out of work is getting me back onto daytime hours. Tell Akasha I'm sorry I couldn't wait up for her. Goodnight, y'all."

Silas nodded. "You did very well tonight, Jayden. I shall see you later."

Jayden got up and washed the dishes, wondering if Razvan went hunting with Silas. She was so distracted that she accidentally sprayed herself with the nozzle attached to the sink.

"Damn," she muttered, looking down at her dripping shirt. Hopefully, it wasn't made of any expensive fabric that was ruined easily.

She went downstairs and pulled a new top out of her suitcase. A shadow fell over her just as she removed the wet shirt.

"Well, Jayden, it seems we are alone now," the vampire said with deceptive civility.

As Razvan stalked towards her with predatory grace, Jayden resisted the urge to flee. Now her question would be answered.

Chapter Seven

Razvan's hands tangled in Jayden's hair, and his lips came down upon hers. She leaned into the kiss without thinking, yielding her mouth to his questing tongue. His scent teased her senses. Her knees went weak, and moisture seeped between her legs as she felt his hardness pressing against her. She was falling under his spell again. The thought cleared her head somewhat, and she raised her hand to his chest, pushing him away.

"No," she murmured when he lifted his mouth from hers.

Razvan's eyes narrowed. "Why not?"

A large part of her said, *yeah! Why not?* But she pushed the inner voice away. She must know if he had any respect for her as a person or if he truly believed that she was a toy for his amusement.

"I have the right to say no," she said, then ruined the declaration by adding, "don't I?"

"What sort of game is this?" he asked, stepping away from her.

His words irritated her, and the bereft feeling she had the moment he pulled away angered her further. "It's not a game!" she shouted. "My body is not a thing for your sole pleasure!"

His eyes raked her up and down. "I do not know about that, my dear, for it is a most pleasing sight," he said. "But your mouth is certainly not pleasing at this moment."

He grabbed his jacket from the chair and headed to the door. "If you are not inclined to share my company, I shall take myself off for now. Good night, Jayden."

Razvan left the room, and Jayden now knew one thing. The vampire who "owned" her life would not rape her. As for everything else, she was more confused than before.

"What's your problem?" Akasha asked when the vampire stomped into the living room.

Razvan plopped down in Silas's chair, poured a shot of whiskey, pounded it, slammed the glass down on the table hard enough to crack it, then lit his pipe. His black eyes glittered with rage.

"You're going to get indigestion if you keep that up," Akasha commented mildly. "So what's wrong?"

His expression softened slightly as he looked at her. "It's not something best discussed with a female." He raised a sardonic brow at her, unable to resist a taunt. "Not that you resemble such a creature at the moment."

Akasha looked down at her grimy coveralls and attempted to wipe a smudge of oil from her cheek, missing it completely. "Dude, I just got home from work, so it's not like I'd be wearing something pink and frilly." She leaned forward and met his gaze, completely undaunted with his vexation. "So Jayden cock-blocked you, then?"

The vulgar term made him choke on his smoke. When he had his coughing under control, he met her gaze again. "Your command of the vernacular never ceases to amaze me, little one." Then the meaning of her words appeared to sink in. "How did you reach that conclusion?"

She favored him with a mocking grin and took a deep drink of her beer. "I thought this wasn't a 'subject for females,' although I'm pretty sure the subject *is* a female."

"Don't try my patience tonight, woman," Razvan growled.

To his obvious ire, her amusement only increased. "But it's so fun!"

He sighed. "You women are all mad with your silly games. Now would you please tell me how you know that Jayden, ah, my pet, was unreceptive to my advances this evening?"

Akasha's eyes widened at the slip. "You see her as a person, don't you? It goes beyond her powers and her suicide attempt. You actually care about her." She polished off her beer and grabbed another from the mini-fridge under the end table. "And apparently, you didn't rape her."

"Rape her?" Razvan nearly spluttered in disbelief. "What in God's name are you talking about?" Akasha's attention suddenly focused on the fireplace. "Well?"

Her gaze crept back to his. "I had a talk with Jayden when you first brought her to my shop. I needed to confirm that she was with you willingly," she said quickly. "And well, she let it slip that you…um…did her and that she didn't exactly say yes, but she didn't say no either…and, well you made such a big deal about her being 'your pet' and 'owning' her life that I thought—"

"You thought I would rape her?" Razvan's voice was low and dangerous. "Do you truly believe that I would do something so despicable?"

"Well," Akasha said, studying the carpet. "You are kinda a prick."

He ignored her. "And I suppose that Jayden is under the same misapprehension…Damn it!" The coffee table shuddered under his fist before he stood up and strode out of the room, the tails of his silk shirt flapping ominously.

"Holy shit," Akasha breathed to the empty room. "I think that son of a bitch is falling in love." She chuckled and lit a cigarette. "And the poor bastard doesn't even know it."

Jayden jerked the covers to her chin as the door opened. Razvan flicked on the light and regarded her with a terrifying sneer. "Must you cower like a frightened rabbit? If I'd wanted to hurt you, my fangs would have been buried in your throat seconds ago."

"Oh, *that's* reassuring," she snapped before she could stop herself.

Razvan's eyes glowed like banked coals. Every step he took towards her was rife with impending violence. Jayden's eyes darted around searching for escape or at least a weapon. She found none and was filled with impotent anger at her helplessness.

"What did I do?" she asked, sounding like a little girl and hating herself for it.

He stopped at the foot of the bed, looking way taller than he really was. "I understand that Akasha gave you the impression that I would force ah…my affections on you."

Her cheeks flamed at his words, even as relief surged through her that his anger was not directed at her…or was it?

"I know now that you won't."

The vampire's eyes narrowed. "You would have known if you had simply *asked* me, rather than playing a silly game."

"I didn't know that I could ask you!" Jayden protested, tossing the sheet away in frustration. "I don't know how to act around you. I don't know anything about you besides that you're an ancient bloodsucker. I don't know what's going to happen to me!" She got up from the bed to face him. "Do *you*?"

He sighed and ran a hand through his hair, avoiding her gaze. "Well, you are going to learn to control your powers…"

"And then what?" she demanded, ire creeping back into her voice.

"I do not know." His tone was unreadable.

A bitter laugh escaped her lips as she stalked forward. "You don't know either. That's just great. Well, what about now, then?"

He raised a brow. "What do you mean?"

Jayden's head was spinning with desperation. "What am I now? Am I your slave, your snack, your girlfriend, or a burden you feel responsible for?" She stopped in touching distance of the vampire. Her spine tingled at the proximity, but she resisted the temptation to step backward.

Razvan's eyes had stopped their eerie glow, and he looked uncomfortable. "Must we have a specific label?"

Jayden fought back a groan. He may be centuries old, but he still sounded like a typical man. "I need to know where I stand. Not knowing is driving me crazy."

He sat down on the bed hard enough to make the headboard smack the wall. "I haven't been with a human woman in centuries. The rules have changed a lot since, although I suppose it wasn't any easier back then. Vampire females don't seem to need so many words."

She nodded, reassured a little by his clumsy apology. Still, jealousy surged up in her at the mention of other women, especially the vampire women. Surely they were better lovers, with all those years of practice.

"I'm just so confused," she whispered. "I don't know what to do."

He took her hand and gently pulled her down to sit beside him. His fingers caressed her wrist. Jayden gasped, amazed at the intensity of such a soft touch. The strap of her nightgown slipped off her shoulder, and he eyed her bare flesh like she was a prized treasure.

"What you can do, Jayden," he leaned in to whisper, "is stop your worrying and just enjoy things as they are." His other hand stroked her back in a soothing motion, even as his lips at her ear tantalized her. "Let me pleasure you. I can smell your arousal just as I did the other night. You wanted it then, and I know you want it now."

"That was different," she protested weakly. Every nerve ending in her body tingled.

"How is it different?" Razvan's voice was like rich chocolate. His tongue flicked over her neck, and she gasped in pleasure.

"Be-because," she stammered, trying to regain her senses, "I thought I was going to die that night, and I wanted to go out with pleasure."

Razvan's lips trailed up and down her neck and shoulder, making her weak with desire. "You want pleasure now."

He made a very good argument. His teeth grazed her neck, and she moaned.

"Please, Jayden, may I make love to you?"

"Yes…" The word escaped her lips a second before Razvan claimed them in a mind-bending kiss. They sank down onto the bed. His weight on top of her was filled with promise. She buried her hands in his hair, reveling in its texture and subtle spicy scent.

After what felt like a blissful eternity, the kiss ended. He gazed down at her with fathomless black eyes, and she was struck by his dark beauty.

"May I taste you, Jayden?" His deep voice rumbled through her body, making her tremble beneath him.

"Yes," she whispered and turned her head to the side, exposing her neck. His weight lifted from her, and she closed her eyes, preparing for the strike of his fangs.

That wasn't what he meant, she realized, as she felt his hands gripping the bottom of her nightgown, hiking the fabric up. He cupped her ass in his hands as he kissed the insides of her thighs. She cried out when he kissed her through her thin satin panties. Her core seemed to throb with excitement, and he hadn't even begun. Slowly his fingers grasped the cloth, sliding it down. Jayden gasped as the cool air caressed her moist heated flesh. Then his tongue flicked across her clit, and she bit back a scream at the powerful sensation.

Jayden gripped the blankets like a lifeline as her hips writhed beneath Razvan's mouth of their own accord. His tongue worked dark magic on her flesh, sending her into spasms of ecstasy.

"Mmmm, you are delicious." The vibration of his voice broke the tenuous hold on her senses.

The climax rushed through her, tearing a scream from her throat. It was too intense. She squirmed to get away, but he held her hips firmly as his mouth continued to ravage her, and wave after wave of orgasm roared through her being.

"Please," she gasped, not knowing what she was asking. "Please."

He pulled away, and she whimpered with mingled relief and sorrow. Her breath came in heaving gasps as she struggled to regain her awareness. She paid little attention to the noise of rustling fabric until she heard the unmistakable sound of a zipper. Jayden's eyes snapped open, and she was treated to the glorious sight of his naked body before he gripped her thighs and entered her in one smooth slow thrust.

The aftershock of the orgasm was still upon her, and she could feel herself pulsating around him. From the awed look on his face, he could feel it too. His hands slid up her hips, across her stomach, and up her torso before he gripped her and pulled her up towards him.

"Wrap your legs around me," he whispered.

Though her limbs were weak and trembling, she managed to comply. He held her in his arms tenderly as he thrust inside her hard. The contrast drove her insane with lust, and her hips bucked against his, matching the furious rhythm.

Jayden leaned in to kiss him, and her eyes widened as she saw his bared fangs and the feral look in his eyes.

"Do it," she cried, tossing her hair back.

His fangs plunged into her throat the same moment another climax hit. She screamed and clung to him for dear life, afraid the intense pleasure would send her hurtling from her body never to return. Razvan continued to feed as she felt him spasm inside her, drawing the shock waves out until she collapsed in his arms.

"Are you all right?" he asked softly.

"Mmm-hmm," she managed.

Razvan chuckled and lay down, not releasing her from his embrace. He stroked her hair and back until the tremors ceased.

Never before had she had a more attentive lover…or one that she knew almost nothing about. She thought about his sexy accent. That was as good a place to start as any.

"Razvan?" she began.

His eyes slowly opened. "Yes?"

"Where are you from?" She hoped the question wasn't too forward.

He released her and propped up on his elbow. "You will laugh."

She frowned, confused at his response and indelibly curious. "No, I won't. I promise!"

He sighed. "I was born and brought up in a village in a land that was once considered part of the Hungarian empire, but is now part of Romania." At her blank expression, he added, "Transylvania."

She took a deep breath to hold back a startled giggle. "You're kidding. Transylvania? That's where all the vampire stories come from."

"There have always been vampires everywhere." His stern frown seemed to dare her to contradict him.

"Hey, I didn't laugh." Still, she couldn't keep from smiling at the irony. "I wonder why so many vampire legends came from there."

His frown deepened in irritation with the subject. "One can only imagine."

"Akasha said you have a brother…" she ventured again, hoping she wasn't toeing the line of propriety.

Naked pain slashed across his sinister features. Jayden swallowed in fear that she had angered him.

Razvan took a deep breath and released it in a long sigh before he replied, "Yes. His name is Radu. We are twins. I haven't seen him since our mother and father were killed."

"I'm sorry for the loss," she placed her hand tentatively on his. "How did they die?"

"The villagers set our castle aflame one morning. I do not know if the flames or the sun got to them first." He closed his eyes as if in remembrance. "I wasn't there. Radu and I had fought."

She longed to ask about the fight, but the shame and sorrow on his face made her hesitant to prod. But she doubted she could hold back her questions for long. His story was more intriguing than she imagined. Twin vampires living in an ancient Romanian castle, vampire parents slain by angry villagers…A thought struck her. If his parents had been vampires, then… "Wait a minute, vampires can reproduce?"

He shook his head, "No, we were adopted. Do not worry, Jayden, I cannot impregnate you."

"Why would a vampire want to adopt children?" This conversation was growing more fascinating by the second.

"Our father, Alexandru Nicolae, was *Voivode*, the lord of our *ţări,* or what you would call a village." Razvan's gaze grew distant in remembrance over unfathomable centuries. "The people knew what he was and often provided him with sacrifices. If the humans they offered were indeed terrible criminals, he would kill them, but often the crimes were either small or imagined. In that case, he would feed and then release them with riches, except for my mother. Crina was sacrificed to Alexandru by her own husband. She had suffered a fourth miscarriage, and the bastard accused her of witchcraft." His lip curled in derision. "She wanted children very much.

Admiration shone in his eyes. "She wanted to be a mother so much, in fact, that when the *Voivode* fell in love with her gentle beauty, she refused to become his consort because he couldn't give her children. Father was not a man to allow anything to keep him from his desires, so he scoured the village in search of a child for his lady."

Jayden leaned forward, absorbed in his tale.

"One night," the vampire continued, "Alexandru came across a peasant hut in which a woman was giving birth to twins. The couple was very poor and had five children already, so they did what many in that situation used to do. While the firstborn fed at his mother's breast, the husband took the second born out of the hut and into the woods to abandon it to the elements. I would have died if the *Voivode* had not taken me." Before Jayden could form her astonished reply, Razvan added, "Alexandru then decided to take Radu as well. He left a fortune in gold in the empty cradle. When our new father brought us to the castle, cradled in each arm and with a wet nurse trailing behind, Crina was overjoyed, and she agreed to let him Change her."

"Wow," Jayden said, flinching at the lame response, but unable to do better at the moment. "What was it like, being raised by vampires?"

Razvan smiled, "Besides being on a predominately nocturnal schedule so that our mother was able to dote on us, I would say that our upbringing was the same as that of any child in the nobility. We had the best of everything, fine clothes, skilled tutors, and anything we could ever desire. In fact, I believe that we were luckier than many noble children in that we had each other for companionship while they were often raised in solitude."

He yawned. The gleaming fangs in his gaping mouth gave her a jolt, hitting home the reminder that she was sharing a bed with a predator, not a normal man. "I believe you must rest now. You have your training tomorrow, and I have business in my city to attend to."

He rolled over and turned off the lamp without so much as a kiss Goodnight.

Jayden lay in the bed and stared up at the darkness, marveling at the enigma that slept next to her. She had learned so much about him this night. He was Romanian, his brother's name was Radu, and their last name was Nicolae. She suppressed a bitter chuckle that she'd slept with a man without knowing his last name. There was a country song about that out there, she thought sleepily.

The bedside clock read six A.M in a soft green glow. It was past dawn yet Razvan's soft breathing was still audible. Now she also knew that vampires did not turn into corpses during the day. Jayden sighed. Still, there was so much she did not know about him. One minute he was generous and tender, the next he was sinister and secretive. And what about his brother?

Akasha said that he used psychics to try to find him, but he still hadn't asked her to try, even when she brought it up.

What would happen if I did find him? Jayden closed her eyes and imagined Razvan's sardonic features soften into joyous gratitude…perhaps even love. Yes, love, she admitted to herself. This mysterious man who had turned her world upside-down while simultaneously offering her shelter and pleasure had woven his spell around her. She was helpless to resist. Now in the cool hush of the morning, she recognized that her earlier outburst had resulted in a panic that he'd leave her once Silas had finished her training. But if she succeeded where all others had failed, if *she* found Radu, then surely Razvan would not give her up.

She imagined his cold, cynical visage softening into joy. She imagined two brothers embracing for the first time in centuries.

I will do it, she decided. Her mind raced as she pondered the risks and possibilities of using her powers intentionally for the first time.

Chapter Eight

After an hour of futility in their practice sessions, Silas could tell that Jayden was preoccupied. "What is the matter, lass?" he asked carefully.

She sighed before beginning. "Silas?"

"Yes, Jayden?" Silas hid a smile of amusement at the woman's hesitant tone.

"When Razvan um, requested your help in finding Radu, how exactly did you go about it?" She looked down at her toes.

"Ah, so he's enlisting your aid now, is he?" He raised a brow. "I thought he'd given up."

"He hasn't asked me," she said quickly, blushing strawberries and cream. "I just wanted to…that is, I thought I could…"

"Help him?" he prodded gently. It was obvious the poor lass was infatuated with his maker. A wave of pity engulfed him. Though she was taller than his wife, Jayden was a timid little mouse compared to Akasha. He was not at all certain if she would be able to stand up to Razvan's bouts of cruelty or withstand his mind games.

Jayden nodded. Her green eyes flicked up to his and darted away. She toyed with the ashtray on the table, spinning it with a trembling finger. The cat padded up to her and, as if sensing her agitation, rubbed against her legs. Jayden reached down with her other hand and petted Isuzu absently, still spinning the ashtray.

Silas took a deep breath before presenting her with an unpleasant truth. "When I tried to find Radu, I came close a few times, but every time I ran up against a block. The block was so powerful there was no way it was not put there on purpose."

When Jayden gave no sign of kenning his meaning, he sighed and continued. "I believe that Razvan's twin does not want to be found."

Her eyes widened. "Did you tell Razvan?" The ashtray was a spinning blur on the table.

Silas suppressed a bitter chuckle at her accusing tone. "Indeed I did, lass. And he nearly tore me from navel to nose for it. He can have quite the temper when things don't go his way." He shook his head. "That probably comes from being spoilt as a lad."

"Razvan told me he and Radu fought before he disappeared," Jayden said. "Do you think that—"

The doorbell chimed. The ashtray flew off the table and shattered on the cherry wood floor. Silas was glad that he had the foresight to empty it earlier. Otherwise, there would be ashes and cigarette butts all over the place.

She tried to apologize, but Silas waved his hand dismissively and went to answer the door.

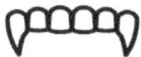

Jayden wondered if it was one of Silas's subordinates or if Akasha had ordered a pizza in advance as she sometimes did when she and Max were on their way home from the bar.

She turned to look and frowned as she saw that no one was there. Silas was bending over to pick something up from the front stoop.

"What is—" she began, getting up from her chair.

"Stay back!" Silas ordered. His eyes glowed neon green, and his fangs bared as he scanned the area for whoever left the missive. He turned back to her, and she bit back a gasp at his feral expression.

"Lock the door behind me," he hissed before walking out into the darkness.

Jayden scrambled across the room to obey. Her heart pounded in her throat as she flipped the deadbolt into place. She'd never seen Akasha's husband act this way before. Something had to be very wrong. She leaned back against the wall and closed her eyes as a multitude of horrible possibilities assaulted her imagination. What if something happened to Akasha? Or Max? Or, oh God, it didn't bear pondering, Razvan?

It seemed to be an eternity before she heard Silas's keys jangling the knob. She still held her breath, ready to bolt if it wasn't him. The door opened, and she sighed in relief as she saw that it was. She also heard Akasha and Max coming up the walkway behind him.

"Silas, what's wrong, honey?" Akasha asked.

"Yeah, what's going on?" Max asked. "You're pale as hell. And that's a hell of an accomplishment, considering."

"We've been invaded," Silas growled.

"Invaded?" Jayden's heart crawled up into her throat at his obvious rage.

The vampire ignored her and proceeded to explain. "One of Selena's underlings left us a message."

"Which one?" Akasha demanded. "'Cuz if it was that prick, Michael, I'll…"

"I didn't see who it was. The bastard took off before I got to the door."

Akasha's mouth dropped open before she burst into laughter. "The guy pulled a 'ding-dong-ditch?' Are you serious? What a pussy!"

Silas gave his wife an adoring half-smile. His eyes stopped their eerie glow, and he looked like himself once more. Jayden silently said a prayer of relief.

"Well, what does the note say?" Max asked, bringing all attention back to the sinister missive.

"I haven't read it yet," Silas said. The envelope was crumpled in his grasp. "But I'm getting a bad feeling about it."

"Do you see anything?" Jayden asked.

The vampire shook his head. "Nothing clear."

"Do you want me to try?" she offered hesitantly.

Silas gave her a long assessing look. "Only if you feel up to it after I read it." He sliced the envelope open with his thumbnail, frowning at the writing scrawled on the front.

"You're not going to wait for Razvan, are you?" Akasha asked.

Silas laughed, "Why? He likely would not wait for me if our positions were reversed." He pulled out the letter, frowning again as he unfolded it. The vampire cleared his throat and read:

"Dear Lord McNaught:

"It has come to my attention that Lord Nicolae passed through my territory without requesting my permission. I am also aware that he had in his possession a human female of considerable psychic ability.

"That stated, I will be lenient to Lord Nicolae and forgive his grievous insult of trespassing on my lands if he will entrust the psychic to my care. She could be a great asset to my order.

"I have had visions of her, and I fear greatly for her safety, as any woman with more than a passing acquaintance with Razvan would. I implore you, Silas to persuade our maker to see reason.

"Ever yours,

"Selena Vespucci, Lord of Post Falls, High Priestess of the Order of Eternal Night."

Akasha chuckled. "Is she fucking kidding? She's crazy if she thinks we're just going to hand Jayden over to her and her cult like she's a lost puppy or something."

Silas raised a brow. "She *is* crazy, Akasha. Don't you remember? You've met her."

"Oh yeah," she laughed drunkenly. "Bat-shit crazy!" Her voice was louder than normal as she wandered into the kitchen and came out with another beer. "Wait a minute, did she say that Razvan *Changed* her? I had no idea."

The vampire looked back at the letter with wide eyes. "This is the first I'm hearing about it as well. However, she could be lying."

Akasha nodded. "Or it could be another of her delusions." She took another long swallow of beer and hiccupped.

Jayden thought that more alcohol was the last thing Akasha needed, but an intervention wasn't her top priority, not when a crazy vampire lady wanted her for her cult. "Who is Selena, and what does she want with me?" She hated the quaver in her voice.

The compassion in Silas's eyes was almost too much to bear. "Selena has always been addicted to power and your abilities make you especially desirable." He headed over to the sideboard and removed a decanter of what looked like whiskey. He uncapped it and took a big swig straight from the bottle.

"Yeah, but I don't think that's her main point," Max spoke suddenly. "From the run-in y'all had from her the last time, she's been waiting for any excuse to make her move." He scratched his beard thoughtfully. "Come to think of it, in light of current and past events, it makes sense that Razvan's the one who turned her into a vampire. First, she tried to play him against you, Silas, and now she's seeing if she can play you against him."

Before Jayden could speak, Akasha interrupted. "Wait, so you both banged her? Ewww!"

Silas sighed. "A vampire doesn't have to 'bang' every mortal he Changes, Akasha. After all, Razvan Changed me, and you can bet that there was nothing sexual in that incident."

"Yeah, but it's still looking like Razvan has a thing for redheads," Max said with a salacious wink

"Hey!" Jayden cried. "I still have no idea what's going on, and I'm sick of being left in the dark. Will you *please* tell me who this woman is? And why is she so pissed at you and Razvan?"

They all quieted and looked at her.

"I'm sorry, Jayden," Akasha said. "I didn't think about how fucked up all this has to be for you."

"I apologize as well." Silas inclined his head. "It must be like walking in on the third act of a play."

"Yeah, kinda," Jayden said, forcing a smile.

Max patted her shoulder awkwardly. "Don't feel too bad, girl. I came in at the end of their last adventure and was lost in the beginning." He guided her to the table and pulled out a chair. "Ya' better sit down and have a cold one. It's quite a long story."

He handed her his beer, but she pushed it back. "No, thank you…On second thought, is there any wine?" A crazy vampire cult leader being thrown into her already surreal situation did call for a drink. She just didn't care for beer most of the time.

"I'll get it!" Akasha sang and shambled off to the kitchen.

Silas pulled up a chair next to her and took another minuscule sip of his whiskey before he began. "Four years ago, the eldest vampire in the world informed me that I was to guard five mortals whose fate was indelibly linked to that of our kind. Those five were Akasha and the musicians you know as Rage of Angels."

Jayden sucked in a breath at the mention of her favorite band.

Akasha came in with a bottle of wine and a glass. "This is Xochitl's favorite Riesling. I bought some because they're coming to visit after their concert next Friday."

"That's right! They'll be here next week," Max said. "I wonder if Selena knows..."

"Hey!" Jayden said, "You guys are doing it again."

"Sorry," they mumbled and went back to nursing their beers.

Silas returned to his explanation as Jayden sipped her wine. "I was able to secure Akasha when I became her legal guardian," Silas began and the shock on Jayden's face must have been obvious because Akasha interrupted, "Don't look at him like he was playing *Lolita* with me! I was really nineteen, but the fucking state rigged my I.D. Besides that, we fell in love."

"Sorry," she mumbled, embarrassed.

Silas nodded in understanding. "Anyway, once she was with me, I soon met Xochitl, Sylvis, Aurora, and Beau. I allowed them to drink their beer, smoke their cigarettes, and most important of all, practice their music. So naturally, since I was so 'cool,'" he smiled at the memory, "my home became a haven for them. Circumstances led me to Mark them all as my property in the eyes of other vampires, and that's when disaster struck. Selena had been spying on me ever since I left her and her cult, the Order of Eternal Night."

"What's her cult about?" Jayden asked.

Silas sighed. It was apparent that Selena had been an irritation to them for a while. "It started up when Selena stole some scrolls from Delgarias. He is the eldest of our kind. One of them was the legend of the creator of vampires, and the other referred to a prophecy telling of another world in which the sun will die and then a savior would bring it back. Somehow she twisted this into a religion dedicated to worshipping Mephistopheles, the creator of vampires, and finding the prophesied savior so she can stop her and colonize the other world. That's where Xochitl comes in. Not only is she the prophesied savior of the other world, but she is also the daughter of Mephistopheles."

"Wow." Jayden breathed. "That's messed up."

"What I don't understand," Akasha said suddenly, "is why she doesn't go after Delgarias instead of screwing with us."

"Because," Silas said patiently, "Delgarias would crush her like an insect. I only wonder why he has not done so yet. She has been enough of a nuisance."

"Sorry I got the conversation off track," Jayden said. "So you Marked Akasha and Rage of Angels and Selena's spies informed her..."

"Yes," Silas said. "Well, she saw that as the perfect opportunity to get revenge on me for leaving her, and she wrote a report to the Elders, our governing body. She made it out to look like I either marked so many mortals because I was building up my power base to go rogue or that I was some sort of pedophile. She made Akasha's friends seem like they were twelve instead of nearly eighteen." He snorted. "The Elders sent Razvan to investigate, and things would have ended there if Akasha didn't possess super-human strength and Xochitl wasn't so, ah, unique. So, there was a trial, but in the end, it didn't go well for Selena. She is now angrier with us than ever, and just last month, she moved to Post Falls, right between Razvan's and my territories. We've been waiting for her to make a move against us ever since."

Jayden was too stunned to speak. It was like she'd been transported into a preternatural soap opera.

"So, now you know," Akasha said. "And now we need to figure out what to do about the situation."

"What situation?" Razvan's dark chocolate voice filled the room, making Jayden quiver.

Silas sighed and held out Selena's message. "This situation."

Razvan snatched the paper from Silas's hand. His brows drew together as he read the contents. Then he burst into the most sinister laughter Jayden had ever heard.

"*This* is her move?" He shook his head. "The woman must have grown dafter over the years."

"Yes, we all know she's doolally. But you never told me that you made her," Silas said with a raised brow, leaning his elbow on the table.

"Would you think I'd admit to something that foolish?" Razvan replied coolly.

"He's got a point there, buddy," Max said.

Akasha groaned. "Please don't tell me you slept with her as well. It's bad enough that Silas did."

His stony silence was answer enough. Jayden clenched her teeth as jealousy raged within her. To her humiliation, Razvan looked at her and seemed to read it in her face. He smirked before turning to Silas. "At least I did not join her cult."

Silas flushed in embarrassment. "Aye, and I paid for that dearly. The bitch poisoning me was only the least of it." He shook his head. "But that's all in the past. Now she wants Jayden, and I don't think a simple 'no' will dissuade her."

"Well, that is too bad for her, is it not?" Razvan said and pulled out his phone.

Jayden watched nervously as the room fell silent as the vampire pushed buttons on the phone with the rapid efficiency of a gossiping teenager.

"Holy shit," Akasha breathed. "Did you just *text* her?"

Razvan gave her a wicked grin. "I would never be so uncouth. I sent her an email. I cannot very well 'invade her lands' again to deliver her message in person, can I? Even though she had no qualms with invading yours, McNaught."

"What did you say to her?" Jayden asked.

He regarded her with a smug grin. "I wrote, in the most professional manner possible, 'fuck you.'"

Max laughed until his face was an alarming shade of red, and he was clutching his large belly. To Jayden, he looked like a redneck version of Santa Claus. "I don't think the 'High Priestess' is gonna like that very much."

"No, she will not," Silas said, looking far more serious. "Though I agree that a personal reply would have been more dangerous, I believe this will be trouble."

"It was trouble that was due anyway." Razvan countered. "And I *don't like* her thinking she can take what is mine." He placed a possessive hand on Jayden's shoulder. "It is getting late. We shall discuss this further tomorrow. Good night."

"Thank you," Jayden said when they were downstairs.

"For what?" Razvan asked with a frown.

"For not giving me up to that crazy woman," she replied. "I mean, you hardly know me and—"

"You are mine," he said simply and cut off her reply with his kiss. From then until dawn, he went about proving to her how true that was.

Chapter Nine

Selena gaped in stunned disbelief as she read the email from Razvan. With every scathing word on the screen, her temples throbbed with unbearable pressure. How dare he? Not only was Lord Nicolae completely unrepentant for his invasion of her lands, but his refusal to relinquish the girl and his insults to her and the Order of Eternal Night went beyond the pale. And his mode of reply, an email! *Email!* As if they were mere mortals discussing a luncheon!

Her fingers crept up to grasp a lock of her hair. Her teeth clenched as she tugged on the strands, feeling the satisfying pain in her scalp. Such rudeness was not to be borne.

Her eyes darted back to the computer screen, unable to stop rereading the offensive words. An inhuman shriek of fury escaped her lips as her fist flew out in a blur to shatter the offending piece of technology.

"Jessica!" she screamed, oblivious to the blood dripping from her hand onto the white carpet.

A moment later, a scrawny vampire with short brunette hair peeked through the doorway. "Yes, my lord?"

Still tugging on her hair with one hand while the other oozed blood and broken glass from the touch screen, Selena hissed. "You have failed me."

Jessica's eyes widened in terror as she stammered, "No, my lord, I delivered the message as you asked, I promise!"

"Then why have they refused to give me the woman? Why didn't you persuade them?"

"I left your note on Lord McNaught's doorstep because I couldn't speak to them. They have immunity, remember? They would have killed me!" The vampire stepped back as Selena advanced towards her. Her mouth went dry as she struggled to speak, then she remembered the one thing that may persuade the high priestess to spare her. "Lord Nicolae Marked the clairvoyant!"

Selena stopped as if a switch was thrown in her brain. She remained still for an interminable moment. Jessica shivered. Her lord resembled a coiled snake ready to strike. Finally, she blinked.

"He *Marked* her? But he's never Marked any of his other psychics, not even me." For a moment, she pouted, looking like a child with a broken toy, then her features shifted to a mask of unadulterated malice. She looked down at her bloody hand, still full of broken glass, noticing it for the first time. Her lips curved into a smile that would have been winsome if not for the coldness in her gray eyes.

"We must have a meeting, but first, attend my wound."

Jessica approached her cautiously. The sight of the blood made her stomach churn in hunger. It had been so long since she'd fed. Selena was a firm believer in fasting. But something about the high priestess's generosity gave her pause.

"First, I must get something to remove the glass, my lord," she said.

"No," Selena said. "You will be rewarded for delivering the message and for the information, but you will have your punishment as well."

"B-but, my lord…" Jessica stumbled back.

"I can think of other punishments."

Jessica dropped like a stone to her knees. She had seen Selena tear a vampire's heart out once and suck out the blood until it became a dry husk. The scene still gave her nightmares.

Reverently, she took her master's hand in hers and lowered her trembling lips to the wound. A moan escaped her lips as the powerful blood touched her tongue.

But the pleasure soon dissipated as she encountered her first shard of glass. Her tongue screamed in pain as she used her teeth to pull it out. Gently she nudged it inside her cheek, cutting her tongue further. If she could put it all in one place, maybe it wouldn't be so bad.

"Swallow it," Selena commanded as if reading her mind. For all she knew, she probably had.

Tears streamed down the vampire's face as the glass cut her throat, her belly. Her insides were on fire. She had made the wrong choice. Having her heart torn out would have been so much quicker and perhaps would have hurt less.

"There is still more," the high priestess whispered.

A pathetic animal whine escaped her lips as she returned her attention to Selena's wound. The blood was no incentive anymore. She couldn't taste it over her own.

By the time it was finished, Jessica collapsed onto the floor, curled into a shrieking ball of agony.

"Michael! Lionel!" Selena shrieked.

Almost immediately, her two favorite apostles filled the doorway.

"Yes, my lord?" they chorused obediently.

"Take her to her room." She pointed at Jessica's sobbing form. Then she gestured at her shattered monitor. "And see that I get a new one of those."

Jessica screamed as Lionel threw her over his shoulder like a sack of potatoes. "Yes, my lord."

"Michael, please schedule a meeting after the first hunt tomorrow. We must discuss our enemies as well as the upcoming Rage of Angels concert."

Chapter Ten

Her body tense with anticipation, Jayden waited until Razvan's breathing settled into the even rhythm of deep sleep.

I'm ready, I think. Another voice countered, *but what if it doesn't work?* She shoved the doubting voice aside. *So what if it doesn't? He won't know either way.*

She placed a tentative hand on Razvan's shoulder, momentarily luxuriating in the silken feel of his skin. Then she took a deep, shuddering breath and let down her shields. At first, nothing happened.

Jayden bit her lower lip, and for the first time, she closed her eyes and intentionally reached into that wayward part of her mind that nearly drove her insane and flipped on the switch…actually, it was more like turning a dial.

As she was swept from her body and into another place, another time, another world, she had a split second to think that perhaps she had turned the dial too far.

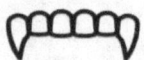

Two identical boys on the brink of manhood lounged indolently in velvet-covered chairs. The stone walls lined with torches, and the embroidered tapestries on the walls indicated that they were in a medieval castle. They were speaking in another language, but for some reason, Jayden could understand them. One boy had a mischievous twinkle in his eyes that was achingly familiar. This was a very young, more carefree Razvan.

"I'm bored," the other boy complained. He had to be Radu.

Jayden felt Razvan's lips curve into a smile of fondness for his twin. Suddenly it was as if she were one with him, hearing his thoughts, feeling his emotions, and experiencing his senses. She could even smell the rushes on the floor and the burning tallow candles nearby.

"Let's go into the village," Razvan suggested.

Radu's eyes widened. "But Father says that we are forbidden until we are older."

"Father will not awaken until dusk. How is he to know?" he asked his twin with an impish challenge.

"He has his ways."

Razvan tried another tack. "Come now, Radu. Someday we are to be *Voivodes* of this *ţări.* Surely it would please Father if we proved to him that we are ready, and what better way to become ready than to become familiar with the people we shall one day rule?" When his twin still appeared reluctant, he added, "I am sure there will be many pretty girls."

Radu's gaze turned speculative, "Well, perhaps we wouldn't get into too much trouble…"

At seventeen, Radu's weakness for the opposite sex was an object of great amusement for his twin. As many serving wenches dreaded being caught alone with him as the ones who sought him out. Razvan appreciated the pleasure that a comely woman could offer. Indeed he'd enjoyed wenches of his own, but he could not fathom why they would merit such obsession.

The twins crept through the corridors of the castle, ever wary that the head housekeeper, or worse, their aging nursemaid, would spot them and question their destination. They made it outside without detection and breathed in the fresh spring air. The sun sparkled merrily on the fishing pond to the west.

"I wonder why Mother and Father can't go out during the day," Radu said sadly, gazing at the pond. "They are missing such beauty."

"You have the sentiments of a poet," Razvan chuckled as he hitched the horses to the steward's wagon. "Whatever the reason, it must be important. Father said he would tell us when we are old enough."

Radu sighed impatiently. "He's been saying that for years. I wish he'd get on with it." He climbed up to the wagon seat and sat down with a huff.

The mystery was forgotten the moment the wagon began its trundling path to the village. When the first cottages came into view, Radu nearly fell off his seat as he twisted and turned in all directions trying to see everything at once. Razvan smiled and held his dignified posture as he flicked the reins softly to urge the horses to a canter. However, he was just as excited as his brother.

The twins had been isolated from the world, with only their parents and the servants for company. The occasional visitor to the castle was a cause for extreme celebration and gossip that would last for months.

To their disappointment, the cottages were mostly empty. The inhabitants were still out working in the fields, their forms barely visible in the distance. Radu slumped in his seat, his displeasure evident in every line of his body.

Razvan patted his shoulder. "Don't worry, brother, I am certain the market will be full of interesting sights."

His words were confirmed moments later. The market was a bustle of activity with an endless array of things to look at.

"Look, Radu." Razvan pointed. A man was standing on an overturned bucket and somehow making four balls spin in a circle through the air. "How does he do that? Why is he not dropping them?"

Radu was not paying attention to the juggler. He was watching a woman with a garishly painted face who was lifting her skirts to show passing men the charms that lay beneath as she called out her price.

"I've got that much!" he said, digging through his pockets.

Razvan grabbed his brother by the collar before he leapt from the wagon. "She's a harlot. I've read about them. They have a sickness that'll shrivel your prick if you fuck them."

Radu's face turned the color of rancid cheese. "Do you think that's true?" His gaze narrowed as a man handed the harlot a coin and followed her into an inn. "Then why is that man going with her?"

"Because most commoners can't read," Razvan explained patiently.

"Oh." Radu's face filled with disappointment.

As the wagon made its way through the market, many people stared openly at the twins in awe of their fine clothes and identical looks. The twins stared back in equal fascination at their first taste of civilization.

Their initial impression was the utter noise of it. Shouts of vendors hawking their wares blended with customers rattling off orders among the endless hum of bleating sheep and clucking chickens.

"I want to get down and look around!" Radu said, nearly squirming with excitement.

It was just as well since they reached a point where the market was impassable by wagon. Razvan held out a coin and called loudly for assistance. In moments, he paid a boy to take the wagon to a stable and feed the horses. He was feeling quite sophisticated.

The boys walked now, nearly tripping over heaps of refuse on the road because they were too busy craning their necks to see everything. Booths, pavilions, and tables were all around, covered in trinkets, fabrics, and tools. It seemed anything a man desired could be purchased here. There were even crates and pens full of chickens, hogs, geese, and dogs. The stench of animal excrement hung heavy in the air.

But soon, another scent overpowered the unpleasant odors: food! The twins eagerly reached into their pockets. There were stalls selling meat pies, cheeses, breads, stews, and even tarts. For once, their formidable appetites were satisfied.

Razvan was wiping berry juice from his mouth when he noticed a woman staring at them. Only this stare was unlike the others they had received. It was as if she knew them. Her black eyes met his, and his heart skipped a beat.

Radu had noticed her too. "Look at that woman. There's something odd about her. Her eyes look like ours."

Before he could ponder that statement, the woman rushed forward. "My boys!" she cried, "God's mercy, I never thought to see you again. How you've grown!"

"Madam?" Razvan asked.

Tears brimmed in the woman's eyes. "And you have your father's voice!" Finally, she seemed to notice their confusion. "Come join me for supper. I shall explain everything. And there are some people you will like to meet."

The twins followed her down narrow twisting roads. They exchanged questioning glances that deepened with worry the further they went. Razvan didn't know if they'd be able to find the place where their wagon was kept.

They were now in a nicer part of the village. The streets were cleaner, and the houses were larger and made of wood instead of the small wattle and daub cottages they'd first seen. The woman led them into one of the biggest houses, and Razvan and Radu both froze in place when they saw a man who looked like an older version of themselves, only taller and broader of shoulder. The man stared back at them with mirrored astonishment.

The woman smiled, "Boys, this is Dorin, your older brother. And I am Ihrin, but you may call me Mother."

"You're not our mother!" Radu said, brimming with outrage. "Crina Nicolae is our mother."

Ihrin smiled and shook her head. "Crina was sent to the Voivode nearly eighteen years ago because she couldn't bear children."

"She has to be telling the truth." Razvan seized his brother's arm. "Look at her, look at *him*!" He pointed at Dorin. "Only blood could be the reason for such a resemblance." He turned back to Ihrin. "Please, explain this to us."

She nodded. "Come into the kitchen. Talking is thirsty work."

Once they were settled at the table with mugs of cold cider, Ihrin began her story.

"I was not as well off as I used to be. My husband and I were serfs. Poor ones at that, for our crops did not always perform well, and we had many children to feed. I already had five when I delivered twins." She regarded them both solemnly. "It was a difficult pregnancy, and we did not have the means to care for two babies. I feared I would be unable to provide enough milk for even one in my weakened state. A difficult, painful decision was made.

"My husband took one of you outside to be exposed to the elements or carried off by the wolves. I don't know which of you it was; you look so similar."

Radu and Razvan sucked in startled breaths at the news.

"You tell us that you are our mother in one breath," Radu said with an accusing glare, "and then in the next, you tell us that you cast one of us out to die?"

"It was our only choice!" Ihrin cried. "We had to give up one in hopes that the other would survive." When they did not answer, she took a shuddering breath and continued. "But the fates must have smiled upon you both. When I awoke in the morning, there was no baby at my breast, and the cradle was full of gold. My husband went to the place where he'd left the other, but there was no dead baby, nor any blood that would have given a sign that it had been carried off by a wolf. And when the news was heard that the Voivode took Crina to wife and they now had beautiful twin baby boys, I had my suspicions. From that day on, I kept my eyes sharp when at the market, hoping for a glimpse of you. But after all these years, I had given up." She burst into tears then.

Dorin took her into his arms and looked at them with a slight smile. "I am glad to finally meet my little brothers. What are your names?"

After introductions were made, Ihrin sent Dorin to fetch their other brothers and sisters. Their mother insisted that they stay for supper.

Razvan couldn't bear to refuse her. "But we must be home before dark," he admonished.

While Dorin was gone, Ihrin insisted on hearing every detail of their lives with the Voivode. Radu and Razvan took turns indulging her and were thrilled with her interest.

"I am so happy that you are treated well," she said. "It seems they love you very much."

Dorin returned then, accompanied by two beautiful dark-haired women and an older man with red hair.

The women rushed the twins, covering their faces with kisses and embracing them fervently. Razvan's mind spun with affection. These were his older sisters. He couldn't believe that he had sisters.

Dorin frowned as he addressed their mother. "Stela couldn't make it. Her back is aching dreadfully. I think the baby will come soon."

"Did you hear that, brother?" Radu said, "We're soon to have a niece or nephew."

The youngest of the sisters laughed. "You already have several!"

More excited introductions were made until their birth mother interrupted, "To the table with you all before the food gets cold!"

The meal with their long-lost family was a revelation to the twins. Never before had they experienced such warmth and cheer. Their adopted parents never ate with them, and until now, Razvan believed that was the way things were done. He didn't want this time to end.

Unfortunately, just as they were about to dig into a heavenly smelling pie, the sun began to dip toward the horizon. If they didn't hurry, they would be too late.

Radu looked out the window with alarm and leapt from his seat as if it were on fire. "We must go now."

"What is the hurry?" Anica, the youngest of their sisters, asked with a teasing smile.

"Our father has forbidden us to go to the village. We must get home before he discovers us gone," Razvan explained.

Anica giggled. "You naughty boys. You will come back and visit again?"

Razvan bowed and kissed her hand. "I swear it!"

The vision faded into gossamer threads no matter how hard Jayden tried to grasp it. As her eyes fluttered open, her mind raced with all she'd seen. Razvan had been so young then! So full of life and optimism which the centuries must have eroded, leaving behind the cold, cynical man she now knew.

And Radu…Jayden sighed, feeling the bond between the twins. No wonder Razvan continued to search for him. What had happened to separate them? She closed her eyes once more and focused on Radu. Maybe she could find him now.

But nothing happened, except Jayden was beginning to get a headache. With a huge yawn, she rolled over and hugged Razvan tight, burying her face in his hair and inhaling his sinful spicy scent. Tomorrow she would hopefully learn more about this captivating man.

Chapter Eleven

Jayden was unable to get inside Razvan's memories again for nearly a week.

"I don't know what I'm doing wrong," she complained to Silas for the umpteenth time. "It was so easy the first time."

Silas sighed, drumming his fingers on the dining room table. "I've told you over and over, lass, your powers are unstable, and things won't always work consistently. After all, you often fail to read Max, though he is incapable of shielding…and you never get anything from Akasha unless you touch her."

"I know," she began, "but—"

"Not to mention," he interrupted. "You're not only attempting to do something far beyond the scope of your training. You're also attempting something I have never heard of a psychic doing on quite the scale you're daring to try…if that makes sense." Silas's finger crept up to his mouth in an age-old musing gesture. "In fact, it almost borders on a new kind of power. Those do tend to manifest as one gains control of their abilities. I would not be surprised if you end up pulling more tricks from your proverbial hat."

Jayden shuddered. "God, I hope not. What I have is frightening enough."

The vampire smiled. "You seemed to enjoy using them for Razvan's sake."

Her cheeks heated, and she opened her mouth to respond when a deep rumble of thunder stopped her. A quick peek out the window at the clear starry night made her skin prickle. It was coming from inside her head, the aftershocks still throbbing in her skull. Silas heard it too. The vampire's eyes were wide, and he jumped as the thunder sounded again.

A shadow appeared in the chair between them, swirling ominously as it gathered substance. Silas leapt to his feet, but Jayden remained frozen as her heart tried to beat itself out of her throat.

"Hello, Jayden," the thing said in a melodic voice laden with authority before turning to the vampire. "Silas, how are you?"

"Delgarias," Silas whispered and sank to his knees.

Now that the creature was identified, Jayden should have felt better, but she didn't. As she looked at the first vampire ever created, her flesh wanted to crawl from her bones and flee. It wasn't that he was horrifying in appearance. On the contrary, he was ethereally beautiful, but so alien as to unnerve her base human instincts. His waist-length hair was enough to hold her in disquieting rapture. The strands were thicker than normal and clear as glass on the outside and contained jet black cores within. From the light of the chandelier above, the mass looked like a living night sky, framing an angular face that would make artists weep.

Pale sapphire eyes peered out under sharply arched brows. Full, sensuous lips curved in a knowing smile. It felt like he could see inside her soul. He throbbed with power, so much that his presence nearly made her teeth ache. He had to be at least twice as old as Razvan. For the longest time, Delgarias sat and smiled at Jayden before he finally turned to Silas and gestured for him to rise. There was something about his hands…

"You honor me with your presence, my lord," Silas said with only the slightest bit of inquiry creeping into his tone as he stood up. "Ah, would you like something to drink?"

Jayden's pulse sped up. Surely he didn't mean...?

Delgarias grinned at her, flashing fangs before nodding. "I would like a glass of water if you don't mind."

She sagged in her seat, unable to hide her relief—until Silas left her alone with the strange vampire.

"Be at ease, Jayden Leigh," Delgarias said in a voice that would have been more soothing if not for his vast power ramming down her throat. "I am not here to hurt you."

"I…" she tried to speak, but the reverberations in her skull made words impossible.

Delgarias's eyes shone in understanding. "I am overwhelming you, aren't I?"

Jayden nodded, and the creature closed his eyes. The intensity ebbed away, and the tension drained from her body as if she'd slipped into a pool of cool water.

"Thanks," she said, now noticing what was wrong with his hands. The fingers were at least an inch longer than those of a human.

"I am sorry about that," he said. "You are far more powerful than I anticipated. This is good."

Silas returned with a glass of water and a piece of paper. Handing both to Delgarias, he said, "We are having problems with Selena, my lord."

Delgarias sipped his water and read Selena's letter with a chuckle. "Yes, Akasha told me about this when I paid her a visit earlier. Selena is more insane than ever, it seems. Poor thing."

Silas grimaced. "My sympathy for her mental instability evaporated centuries ago. I don't suppose you could speak to her?"

"I could," Delgarias replied disinterestedly, "but at this point, I'm certain it would have no effect. Only killing her will make her stop her nonsense and that I cannot do."

"Why not?" Silas and Jayden chorused.

"I have other things to attend to," he said vaguely. "I only stopped by to see how you are getting on, and now I must be off."

The vampire stood, towering over Silas by at least five inches. He bent down and placed a long-fingered hand on top of Jayden's head. "It was a pleasure to finally meet you. Take care of Razvan. He has endured much loneliness."

He gave Silas a slight nod and vanished. The rush of air barreling into the spot he vacated turned Jayden's stomach.

"Ye mean ye dinna think her threat is serious enough to merit yer almighty attention," Silas growled to the now empty chair.

"I'm not certain that's what he meant," Jayden said, scooting back slightly in case her statement upset him.

The vampire raised a brow. He opened his mouth, shut it, and sighed. "Yes, I know. He was just being his usual enigmatic self."

"What did he mean by checking to see how we were?" Jayden asked. "He didn't even ask how anyone was doing."

Silas smiled. "He didn't have to, not with his power." He turned and nodded as the front door opened. "What concerns me most is that he made an appearance at all."

Razvan strode into the room trailed by Max and Akasha. As usual, Jayden's heart clenched at his dark beauty.

"Ah, so he came here too." His Romanian accent was thicker than usual. "I expected as much."

Akasha darted around him to place a possessive hand on Silas's arm. "How did he get here so fast? He was just at the shop five minutes ago."

Max cut in, "Don't answer her, I don't want to know. That guy shivers my skin as it is."

Razvan stalked behind Jayden, sliding his hands down to cup her shoulders, holding her frozen in her chair as he addressed Silas. "I presume he came to reiterate his instructions to me?" He laughed, low and dangerous. "As if you could stop me."

Silas leaned back in his seat, undaunted but for a silky undertone in his voice. "And what instructions would those be?"

"I am not to Change Jayden without Delgarias's permission."

"Ah," Silas replied with a slight smile. "He didn't tell me anything of the sort. He really didn't say much of anything."

"Wait!" Jayden interrupted as their words became clear. "You mean, change me into a vampire? I'm not sure I—"

Razvan squeezed her shoulder painfully, then absently rubbed it as if in apology. "Yes, I was told not to…yet. Not that I intended to do so at this point in time."

Jayden felt a pang of disappointment, even as her mind screamed at her. *What's the matter with you? You don't want to drink blood!*

Max went to the kitchen and scooped three bowls of chili from the crockpot as Akasha heated the cornbread. During dinner, Silas and Razvan speculated as to the significance of Delgarias's visit.

"I think it's starting," Silas said. "The events of the prophecy."

Razvan scoffed. "I think the old bastard just wants to keep us on our toes."

Jayden shivered as the memory of the ancient vampire's power washed over her. She hoped he wouldn't drop by again.

Forcing her thoughts from the terrifying creature, she focused instead on getting back into Razvan's memories. Maybe this time, it would work again.

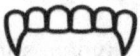

As dawn broke and the vampire's breathing delved into a deep slumber, Jayden focused her will on Razvan, concentrating with all her might. Nothing happened, and she heaved a sigh of disappointment before trying again. Her consciousness began to float away, and her heart surged in triumph. It was working!

Jayden left her body behind and drifted into a dark chamber, poorly illuminated by banked coals in a warm fireplace. A figure sat in a chair, facing away from her. Was it Razvan, or Radu? Just as she reached forward with invisible fingers, the chair swiveled to reveal Delgarias's ethereal countenance. His brow rose in amusement as he looked right at her.

Slowly, Delgarias shook his head and pointed an abnormally long finger to the right. His other hand rose, waving her off in that direction. Jayden was catapulted away from Delgarias and back into Razvan's memories....

The twins hurried out the door of their birth mother's home and down the winding streets. Nothing looked familiar in the waning light. After an hour of searching for the square and doubling back, the twins sighed in defeat.

"Father is going to strap us raw for certain," Radu said glumly.

"He's not really our father," Razvan countered. "And I intend to confront him about that fact before he can say a word about his stupid command to stay away from the village. It's because he didn't want us to know the truth. You know that, right?"

Before Radu could answer, a voice behind them said, "That is not the reason, not entirely, anyway."

Alexandru Nicolae stepped out of the shadows and surveyed them with a stern frown. Razvan shivered despite his earlier bravado.

"I wanted to wait another year or two to tell you the truth, but now that you have learned some of it, I suppose I'll have to tell you the rest tonight." He let that cryptic statement hang in the air before he asked suddenly, "Where is the wagon?"

Razvan cleared his throat, his ears burning with embarrassment. "We paid a boy to tether it while we explored, but we got lost and cannot find the place where he put it."

"Did you offer him more coin upon its return?"

"No."

Alexandru frowned. "Then it has probably been stolen."

Humiliation poured through Razvan in waves. His face felt like a hot coal.

"I should have taught you better," the Voivode said.

Radu spoke up in defense of his brother. "Razvan protected me from a harlot today!"

Alexandru's eyes bulged in surprise, then he burst out laughing. Neither had heard him laugh that hard before. It seemed to echo through the village. There was an eerie quality to it that made goosebumps rise all over his flesh.

Finally, the laughter faded, and Razvan couldn't help his relief.

"Well, that is probably fortunate. Diseased things, they are," Alexandru said. "Never mind about the wagon. I will deal with it tomorrow. A long walk will teach you boys a lesson, I think. And it will give me time to explain a great many things."

They walked with Alexandru in the darkened village. The moonlight reflected in his eyes, making him look otherworldly.

He told them the tale of how he met Crina and how her longing for motherhood persuaded him to take the twins.

"But why was she 'sacrificed' to you in the first place?" Razvan asked.

"Ah, now here is the most important part of my tale," Alexandru said. "I and, thanks to me, your adopted mother are no longer human beings. We are something far greater and far more powerful."

"What do you mean?" Razvan asked.

Alexandru answered him with another question. "Would you care to hazard a guess as to how old I am?"

Radu answered, "You look to be no more than five and thirty. But then you've always looked the same."

Razvan sucked in a breath at his brother's observation. Radu was right. The Voivode seemed not to have aged in all these years…it was the same with their adopted mother. Now that he thought of it, Crina only looked to be a few years older than themselves! The oldest of his newfound sisters seemed to be older than her. How could that be?

The Voivode looked at them gravely before answering, "I am six hundred years old and I have been Voivode of this *țări* for nearly five centuries. For you see, my sons, I am immortal." He smiled at them, and the moonlight fell full upon his face, revealing gleaming fangs where his canines should have been.

The twins gasped and took an involuntary step back. Razvan shuddered. Crina must have such teeth as well.

Just then, the door to a nearby inn was flung open, and a man stumbled out, singing loudly to himself as he shambled down the road.

Alexandru put a finger to his lips. "Watch and see how I maintain eternal life."

One moment, he was standing before them. The next, he was gone. Razvan felt a phantom wind brush his cheek.

"Look!" Radu said, pointing.

Alexandru held the drunkard in his arms. The man's eyes were glazed over as they stared back at the Voivode. Slowly, Alexandru tilted the man's head to the side. He looked up at the twins and smiled before plunging his fangs into the drunkard's neck.

The twins were rooted to the spot as he drank. Razvan couldn't decide if he was fascinated or repulsed. Radu's jaw was slack, and his eyes looked ready to topple out of his face. After an interminable amount of time, Alexandru released the man to gently slump against the wall of a smithy. At first, Razvan thought the man was dead. Then he saw the gentle rise and fall of the man's chest, revealing that he was in a deep sleep. Alexandru bit his index finger and allowed his blood to drip on the man's wound. The puncture marks slowly disappeared.

"*Strigoi*!" Razvan whispered.

Alexandru shook his head. "No, my son. A *Strigoi* is a walking corpse. I am quite alive." He showed them his finger. The wound had healed. "I know not what we are. Only that we must drink blood to survive, and that the light of the sun or fire is death to us. Some of us can see the thoughts of mortals and some of us can fly."

Before they could digest that information, Alexandru rose in the air as if pulled by invisible ropes. He flew up until the darkness nearly obscured him from view, did a somersault in the air, then he came to a graceful land in front of the twins.

Radu gasped and stepped back.

"Do not fear me, my sons. I have raised you both since you were babes suckling from your nurse's breasts. It is my intention to give you the choice to become as I am. When your beards have grown this long," he held his fingers around two inches below his shaved chin, "I will hear your decisions."

For the rest of the walk home, Alexandru explained more about the nature of his powers. "When the time comes, I will drink nearly all the blood in your bodies. Then I will cut my wrist and feed it back to you. That is how the magic is passed on."

Later that night, when the brothers were alone in their bedchamber, Radu asked, "What do you make of this, brother? The man we thought was our father is not our sire, and he is also an immortal creature that drinks the blood of humans." His mouth twisted in revulsion.

"He doesn't kill them," Razvan said defensively. "He even healed that man's wounds when he was finished." He got up to stoke the fire burning in their chamber. "Just imagine, Radu, being able to fly like that!" He couldn't suppress a rapturous sigh as he imagined such powers. "To live forever!"

"I don't know if it is worth it," Radu said. "I don't know if I could drink blood, and to never see the sun again… or to never again spend a day fishing? I couldn't bear it!"

"Do not worry," Razvan said calmly. "We have at least ten years to think about it, maybe more." He stroked the minute fuzz on his chin. "I wonder that our beards will ever get that long!"

"And what of our real family?"

Razvan smiled. A wave of tenderness for his brother engulfed him. "Why, of course we shall continue to visit them. I do not see why that should change."

As the boys became men, their closeness to their birth family grew. Ihrin behaved as if they had always been family, and Razvan soon found himself seeking her approval. Still, as was the case with Crina, Ihrin seemed to prefer Radu with his openness and fervent joy with life. Shortly after they had discovered the truth of their birth, Razvan learned why.

Radu, it seemed, had gotten the whole story from the Voivode. Razvan had been the one that Ihrin had given up. Radu was paid for. He was the one that was wanted. The knowledge was like a spear through Razvan's heart, but he would die before letting anyone know how badly it hurt him. As his beard grew, he increased his efforts to distance himself from his emotions. It didn't take long for him to conclude that there was nothing for him in the mortal world, and he anticipated the night when he would be Changed into a powerful being that could thwart death. Unfortunately, his whiskers didn't share his urgency and continued to grow at a snail's pace.

Finally, in the twins' thirty-third year, their beards grew to the requisite two inches. Radu scratched and grumbled about his beard daily. Razvan rather liked his, although he would like it to be better groomed.

"I cannot wait to shave this infernal thing. I am sick of discovering weeks-old bits of food trapped in this mess!" Radu said.

Razvan's breath caught at the statement. "Have you made your decision yet?"

"No, I've tried not to think about it. Have you?"

He nodded. "I think I've wanted it since the night we first saw father take to the air in flight."

Radu was silent for a long while before he abruptly changed the subject. "We should leave for the village now. Ihrin is expecting us, and we don't want to be late."

During their visit with their family, Razvan was struck by two things. The first was that Radu was avoiding speaking of their upcoming transformation into immortality. The second was how old their birth mother looked. Ihrin's hair was now almost completely gray, and her cheeks were beginning to sink into her face. Her aging looks disturbed and frightened him, but not as much as the sight of Dorin's balding pate. He didn't want to grow old. He looked at Radu and noticed that he was studying the changes in their family as well. Razvan craved immortality, but he didn't want to leave his brother behind.

The wagon ride back to the castle was silent and pensive. Razvan tried to converse with his brother, but he remained hunched in his seat, staring at the sunset, deep in thought. After a while, he gave up and prepared himself to announce his decision to let the Voivode Change him.

As the vision faded, Jayden tried once more to link her mind to Radu. At first, she felt a flicker of…something, but then she was once more forced back into consciousness with nothing but a throbbing headache as a reward for her efforts. Sighing, she let sleep close over her. *Maybe next time….*

Chapter Twelve

A loud knock on the door pulled Jayden into wakefulness.

"Jayden, wake up!" Akasha's voice sounded from the hallway outside. "The concert starts in two hours! We need to get ready!"

Razvan yawned and stretched before getting out of bed. He crossed the room to his dresser and grabbed a pair of pants. "I am starving," he said. "Would you care to feed me, my pet?"

Jayden groaned and resisted the urge to pull the covers over her head. She doubted that she got any rest with her foray into Razvan's memories, and now he wanted her to volunteer to be his breakfast. She looked up at him, searching his face for signs of the tousle-haired boy he used to be. It seemed that the centuries had swept him away, leaving a sardonic stranger in his place.

"On second thought, I will seek my meal elsewhere," Razvan said, studying her. "You look like you did not rest well."

"Why thank you," Jayden said sarcastically. "You'll turn a girl's head with such flattery."

She did her best to tamp down jealousy at the thought of him drinking from another woman. She couldn't be his blood donor every night, and besides, Akasha assured her that a vampire's feeding usually wasn't sexual.

He chuckled. "Perhaps you should go back to sleep until your mood improves."

"Forget it," she said, getting out of bed and heading for her dresser. "I am going to this concert."

By the time Jayden and Akasha were loading up in the car, Razvan returned to slide in beside her. As they set off, she stared at his handsome profile, wondering if he sensed that she had been in his mind. She doubted it. He would have said something. Excitement and trepidation of the upcoming concert warred within as she stared out the backseat window of Silas's '68 Barracuda.

"Are you certain you want to do this?" Razvan asked again.

She nodded. "It's not like I'll get another chance to see my favorite band in concert, much less with backstage passes." She managed a wry smile. "Besides, it's too late to go back. Akasha will freak if there's another delay."

"Damn straight," Akasha said from the passenger seat. "It's bad enough that we have to take Highway 54 and go through Hauser instead of a straight shot down 1-90."

Silas moved his hand from the stick-shift and patted his wife's thigh. "You know that if we go through Post Falls, Selena will find some way to make things ugly for us."

Akasha sighed. "I still think it's bullshit. I miss that seafood and smokes store on Spokane Street. They have damn good chowder."

Jayden continued to watch the waxing moon hovering over the tall pine trees. Soon the trees gave way to the vast prairie. The giant sprinklers in the hay fields cast sinister shadows, or maybe that was just her mood. Tonight was the first time she would be in a public situation since she lost her job. The visions almost always magnified when she was among crowds.

Would the shielding techniques Silas taught her be enough? Or would all of her hard-won control shatter before the music started? She flicked a glance at the car's other occupants. If she lost it in front of Razvan and her new friends, the humiliation would kill her.

They got back on I-90 shortly after they crossed the state line into Washington. The car seemed to hurtle closer to the Spokane Arena, and Jayden's mind raced over all of Silas's lessons. It seemed they reached their destination in seconds.

"Well," Akasha said as they locked up the car, "at least the traffic wasn't too bad."

Jayden's legs felt wooden as they crossed the parking lot and got in line. Silas, Razvan, and Akasha surrounded her like an honor guard, and her heart swelled with gratitude.

"Breathe, Jayden," Akasha said as they made their way to their seats. She reached out, maybe to pat her shoulder, then snatched her hand back.

Jayden managed a wan smile and took a deep breath as she struggled to keep her mental shield in place. With a crowd this size, it was hard. As with every Rage of Angels concert, the Spokane Arena was packed. Random visions of dirty secrets flicked through her mind like a television weaving in and out of reception.

A guy a few seats to her left worried about the results of his HIV test. A woman to her right had an argument with her husband earlier today. The husband told her that if she didn't get off the meth he would leave her and take the kids. She knew he was right, but the addiction had her enslaved. She also worried about what her friends and family would say if she checked herself into rehab.

But it was the girl directly three rows in front of Jayden that was the loudest. She was fifteen years old, pregnant, and contemplating an abortion. The girl was certain that if her pregnancy was discovered, her eighteen-year-old boyfriend would go to jail, and her mother would lose custody of her and her little brothers.

"To tell you the truth, I don't like crowds much either," Akasha whispered from the seat next to her, interrupting the psychic onslaught. "I mean, I'm not getting any visions from it, but things like this always make me a little claustrophobic. It'll get better once the show starts. And if doesn't, I promise I'll take you backstage."

"Thanks," Jayden murmured weakly. Her nerve endings felt like they were being prodded with a Taser. Razvan placed a hand on her shoulder, and she felt a small measure of comfort.

I never should have come. Max had stayed behind, declaring himself to be "too old for that shit." His gruff company was more desirable than ever right now. But Silas and Akasha had worked their charm on her. Silas said her training had gone well enough that she should test her abilities out in a public place. Akasha had spent the week regaling her with stories about the times she had spent with Rage of Angels.

"They were the first friends I ever had," she'd said with a far-off glimmer in her eyes and a soft smile. "I can't wait until you meet them." The adoration in her voice was impossible to resist. As was the moment when Akasha turned toward her with a speculative look and said, "You know what? I like you, Jayden. You're easy to talk to."

The way she said, it as well as what she knew of Akasha's cynical demeanor, told Jayden that Akasha didn't like many people, but she would hold undying loyalty to those who earned her regard.

The opening band came on, and it was all she could do not to scream from the noise and the vortex of energy assaulting her senses. She clung to Razvan's hand and bathed in his strength. The lead singer was pretty good. From the octaves he was able to hit, it was apparent that he was a trained opera singer. Still, he was no match for Xochitl's powerful vocals, and she couldn't help but feel impatient for the act to finish. When at last the band left the stage, Jayden applauded along with the audience and fought back guilt for her relief that they'd finished.

The lights dimmed, and the crowd roared as four figures emerged on stage through a mist of manufactured fog. As Aurora Lee began a primal and impossibly fast drum beat, Jayden forgot about her surroundings as she was transported into the awe of the performance. Aurora Lee was the fastest drummer in the world, made even more impressive since she was the most famous Black woman drummer in the world of heavy metal. Still, until she saw the incredible blur of Aurora's hands on the drumsticks, Jayden had thought the percussion had been digitally altered.

Beau's bass thrummed a compelling rhythm soon punctuated with Sylvis's and Xochitl's guitars.

Jayden blinked. It seemed that she could see the faint lines of force linking the band members together. Was it a stage effect or a vision?

Xochitl opened her mouth and sang in a powerful soprano rivaling those of the greatest hair bands of the eighties. Goosebumps rose on Jayden's arms, and she fell under the spell of the music until the song ended.

Xochitl yelled out her greetings to the audience. Her black and purple hair waved around her like a live thing as she bathed in the crowd's cheers. The next song began, transporting all into a place of blissful energy. Jayden had always felt better after listening to their music, but that was nothing compared to this live performance. All her troubles seemed to drift away as the melodies carried her into symphonic ecstasy.

Razvan took Jayden's hand as the song ended, and the crowd around them surged with applause. Her skin was clammy and trembling in his grip. Silas was wrong. She wasn't ready to be out among the public just yet. Her mind was still too fragile to withstand the energy of such a seething mass of humanity. But he was unable to leave her behind. Not only did he not trust Max to make sure that she stayed put, but Akasha had also whipped up Jayden's enthusiasm so much that she wouldn't hear of not attending this concert.

His gaze flicked to the stage and the singer's inhuman power seemed to lift every hair on his skin with her voice. He was usually pleased to see Xochitl and her companions, as he'd had a hand in the development of their success, but not this time. The situation with Jayden made their visit unwelcome. They would stay with Silas and Akasha for a week, and Razvan was worried that Jayden's mind would be unable to withstand Xochitl's power.

Jayden squeezed his hand as another raucous shout from the audience pierced his eardrums. He looked at her and noticed that though she was pale and trembling from the psychic onslaught, her lips were curved in a genuine smile of enjoyment of the show. His heart surged at her bravery. He struggled to tamp it down. It wouldn't do to get too attached to this woman. Not with his luck with females. His last long-term lover had been Selena…before she lost her mind. And Jayden was far more powerful than Selena had been…and more beautiful.

His eyes took in her glorious hair. It was a far deeper red than his former lover's, whose hair faded to a dull orange without henna treatments. Her legs were long, her lips more generous and soft, her breasts more…his cock stirred with arousal, and he fixed his attention back to the stage. He would enjoy her while he could and do his best to keep her safe from Selena's cult and ensure that she didn't go mad. But he must keep his emotions under control and remember that this magic between them could not last forever. The best he could hope for was that once she regained her sanity and had control of her powers, her infatuation with him would fade, and she would leave him peacefully to make her own life.

Throughout the remainder of the performance, Razvan kept a close watch on Jayden for signs of distress even as he fought his attachment to her. When the show neared its conclusion, he realized that someone else was watching her as well. Surreptitiously, he scanned the mass of heads turned to the stage to see which were not. All were captivated by the show. He pretended to yawn and turned to observe those meandering in the area behind the seats. There they were. Two vampires bearing Selena's Mark stood by the exit. Their heads were bent towards each other, no longer looking at Jayden as they spoke in hushed voices. Though vampires from other territories were welcome in his city to attend public events such as concerts, the Post Falls vampires were banned as long as Selena reigned.

Those two were disobeying his decree. He bared his fangs for a moment at their insolence, then suppressed a chuckle. They must believe they were safe as long as they remained in view of mortals. Well, they would learn. He sought out a few of his Spokane vampires and issued silent commands. Silas caught his eye.

What is going on, Razvan?

Razvan telepathically explained before they escorted their women backstage.

The backstage area was crowded and noisy, but it was still an oasis of peace compared to the arena. Jayden stepped back from the rush of people heading towards the refreshment tables and took the air in deep, easeful gulps. Razvan placed a possessive hand on her shoulder, and she leaned into him, grateful for the secure stability of his presence.

Suddenly, the incessant buzz of conversation bled away. The door opened and the hairs on the back of Jayden's neck stood up. The four band members entered the room, energy thrumming from them like an electrical storm. She shivered and pressed closer to the vampire, momentarily overwhelmed. Perhaps coming here had been a mistake.

"'Kash!" Xochitl Leonine cried and ran towards them, black and purple hair flying.

As the singer hurled herself into Akasha's embrace, Jayden flinched. Most of the energy was coming from her. She was like a walking livewire. Xochitl was not human. She wasn't a vampire either. Whatever she was, she vibrated with enough power to level mountains, despite being even smaller than Akasha.

"And this is Jayden," Razvan was saying as the creature hugged him.

Xochitl turned to face her. As honey-colored eyes met hers and perfect lips curved into a smile that could beckon the dawn, Jayden took an involuntary step back.

Oh God, please don't let her touch me! If she touches me, that power will surge through my brain and make it explode! Oh God, if she touches me, I'll either go insane or die!

"I'm h-honored to f-finally meet you," Jayden stammered, struggling to smile and keep her shield in place. She hoped she just sounded star-struck instead of revealing her terror.

"So Razvan finally got a girlfriend?" Xochitl said. Was it her imagination, or had the smile dimmed a bit?

"In a manner of speaking," Razvan put his arm around Jayden and drew her close. She leaned into him, grateful for his protective presence.

Xochitl blinked at him in confusion. "Well, you'll have to tell me the whole story later."

"How long will you be staying with us?" Silas asked, changing the subject.

"Only a week. We gotta be back in Seattle in time for the Halloween concert at The Mortuary." She glanced at the line of people forming behind her. "I gotta go sign autographs and stuff. Talk to ya later."

Jayden's mouth went dry. *A week?* How the hell would she be able to stand an entire week with her around?

Something cold touched her hand, and she jumped. Akasha was handing her a bottle of water.

"Here, you look a little pale." Her amethyst eyes were wide with concern.

Jayden took the bottle gratefully. After she uncapped it and took a big swig, she gasped, "Oh my God, Akasha, she's not human!"

Akasha and Razvan nodded. "We know."

That knowledge gave her a semblance of relief. "But what *is* she?"

Silas answered, "That, lass, is something we're not quite sure of." He had his own bottle of water and sipped it pensively. He kept glancing at Razvan as if he were trying to send him a message.

"But she's *good*, Jayden," Akasha said fervently. "I promise. It'll get easier once you get to know her better. Now, remember, Xochitl and the others can't know about vampires. Delgarias forbids it."

Jayden nodded, only half hearing her as she focused on the vampires. Razvan seemed to get Silas's signal, and they both headed away. They probably needed to feed. Akasha didn't seem bothered, so Jayden decided everything was okay.

"Come on, let's go meet the others."

Jayden realized that the other band members had been swarmed by fans before they could reach Akasha. Xochitl was the only one who wasn't. She noticed now that the singer's line of autograph seekers was smaller than those of the rest of the band. Each person looked almost scared of her, and they were being extra careful not to touch her.

Whatever it is, they sense it too. They know somehow that she is different. Xochitl's eyes had darkened to a puppy-brown. She seemed hurt by their trepidation. Jayden felt a wave of sympathy for her. She must be very lonely. As if sensing her scrutiny, Xochitl's eyes met hers. Jayden smiled. Xochitl smiled back.

"Akasha, look," Jayden said. "They act like they're almost scared of her."

"Yeah," she agreed. "At first, I thought it was because somehow they know she's not human. But now I'm pretty sure it's not that. If they really knew her, they'd want to fall to the ground and worship her." Akasha shook her head. "No, I don't think it has anything to do with her genetic difference. It's more that she's one of those people who are truly great. I'm damn sure plenty of people were scared of Da Vinci, Ben Franklin, Tesla, and Einstein."

"Wow," Jayden gasped, overcome with the depth and insight of Akasha's statement. "That's…."

"Hey, 'Kash!" a voice interrupted.

Aurora Lee left her group of fans and enveloped Akasha with muscular brown arms. "I've missed you like hell, girl! How've you been?"

"Pretty good," Akasha answered. "Shop's making money. This is Jayden, Razvan's… er, girlfriend."

Before Jayden could pull back, Aurora's warm hand gripped hers and shook it. "Pleased to meet you. Jayden's a pretty name."

Jayden got a glimmer of information from the drummer before her shields went back down. *She had a fight with her mother today. She hates Aurora's music.*

"Beau, Sylvis! Come here," Aurora called. "Akasha wants you to meet someone."

A pretty young man with spiky burgundy hair and a tall woman with a blue bob-cut came forward.

"Hey, baby," Beau said as he kissed Akasha on both cheeks. "Long time no see."

Sylvis grinned and shook Jayden's hand as Aurora introduced them. No visions came, to Jayden's profound relief. Sylvis was the comedian of the group. She'd hosted Saturday Night Live last week, and Jayden had nearly peed herself laughing. Akasha swore up and down that her performance was a hundred percent improvisation.

"Razvan's girlfriend, huh," Beau said. "And here I was hoping he'd swing my way. Oh well, I guess I'll have to move on." His gaze swept over her. "Has anyone ever told you that you kinda look like Tori Amos?"

Jayden flushed at the compliment. Akasha was right. Beau was a sweetie.

The bassist grinned. "Speaking of Razvan, where is he? And where's your sexy husband, 'Kash?"

"Oh, they're around somewhere," Akasha said with a shrug. "Are you coming to the Powder River with us after this?"

A look of boyish shame came over his face, "No, I already invited Eric out for drinks. We're going to stay in Spokane for the night."

"Who's Eric?"

He pointed. "That roadie over there. Isn't he cute? Anyway, the Powder's not really our style and…"

Jayden didn't hear the rest of the conversation. She sensed she was being watched. Sure enough, there were two vampires, not ten feet from her. She reached out to tap Akasha's shoulder, but one of the vampires, a large male that somehow resembled a cowboy, shook his head and spoke in her mind.

"Don't be afraid. Razvan sent us to guard you ladies while he and Silas take care of some business."

"What business?" she asked silently.

He flinched in mingled surprise and pain at her response. *"Jesus, woman, you don't have to yell. Tone it down! They didn't say. I just take orders. Now go back to your friends before Silas's woman notices."*

Slowly, Jayden turned back to Akasha and Beau. Sylvis and Aurora had gone back to sign autographs. Xochitl had more people surrounding her than earlier, and not so many looked scared. *"It'll be easier once you get to know her,"* Akasha had said.

"So this is what has been occupying the master lately." Jayden heard the voice in her head. Out of the corner of her eye,

she saw the second vampire guard, a tall, but voluptuous blonde woman. *"She looks pretty scrawny to me."*

"Yeah, but she's damn powerful," the other vampire answered.

Jayden realized she was somehow eavesdropping on their conversation. She took another drink from her water bottle and studiously focused on Beau's chatter. Her hackles rose at the blonde's possessive tone when she'd said "the master."

"It doesn't matter. He'll be done with her eventually, as he is with all of them." The blonde seemed to sneer. *"And then I'll be waiting."*

Jayden seemed to hear the male snort. *"Waiting for what, Hilda? He's done with you too. He never comes back for seconds, you know that."*

They stepped away, and she couldn't hear them anymore. She shivered. Was Razvan some sort of man-whore? She lifted her chin and glared at the blonde's back. *He won't throw me away if I find his brother.* She checked to see if either had heard the thought. There was no reaction as they faced each other, still involved in their silent argument. Some guards they were. She was tempted to yell "help!" as loud as she could just to see what they'd do, but decided against it. It would be hard explaining that to Razvan. She giggled at the thought.

"What's so funny?" Akasha asked.

Jayden smiled. "I was just wondering if Razvan knew Beau has a crush on him."

They both laughed, but Jayden didn't hear Akasha's reply. Something caught her eye—and her mind. The pregnant fifteen-year-old had just come in. The girl's frantic worry was still amplified like a loudspeaker, but that wasn't what made Jayden's stomach churn. A hazy reddish vision was overlaying her view of the girl as if Jayden was viewing her through 3-D glasses.

Without thinking, she focused harder. The red haze solidified into ropes and blobs pulsating in a familiar rhythm. They blurred, then solidified, and Jayden's heart skipped a beat as she realized what she was looking at. Everything was insanely clear and yet somehow tangible. There were the uterus, the ovaries, and the Fallopian tubes. Jayden had a strange feeling that she could somehow touch them. She frowned. There was nothing in the uterus. The girl wasn't pregnant after all! She would be fine and hopefully would be more careful in the future. She began to focus her will to bring her shields back in place, but she was stopped by a force that was like a thunderclap in her skull. There was something in the girl's left Fallopian tube. It glowed with a malignant light.

Oh God, it's a tubal pregnancy! Jayden's throat tightened in fear for the girl. If she didn't get to a doctor, she would die.

She returned her concentration to her vision of the girl's insides to see how long she had left. The embryo was not yet straining against the tube, but…Jayden focused harder…it would in about three weeks. The feeling that she could somehow touch it multiplied to the point that she had to brace her hand on the wall to keep her balance.

I could destroy it. The thought came suddenly, but she didn't doubt its conviction. Some hidden, almost cruel part of her reveled in the thought of reaching out with those hot invisible fingers and crushing the embryo. *It would save the girl's life,* it whispered. But it wouldn't be good if the kid had a miscarriage backstage at a heavy metal concert. Her mother's reaction would be the least of her problems.

Breathing became the hardest task in the world. It felt like the first time she smoked pot. Her thoughts were racing, but the forces of the universe were doing their best to slow her down. At that time, Jayden had curled up in a ball on her friend's couch and waited for the so-called "high" to wear off. Now she wondered if this thing would ever go away.

What do I do? She closed her mouth before the shriek escaped her lips. Her heart went out to the girl and her predicament; that alien part of her wanted to do something about it, and her mind longed to help her but didn't want to do further damage.

Her eyes darted randomly across her surroundings as if imploring for aid amongst the sweating, music-shirt-garbed masses. But she could still see the girl's insides and the microscopic potential for death that threatened insidiously.

Jayden's gaze skimmed across the male vampire guarding her. He was watching her, but doing a stellar job of not making it obvious. She remembered his shout in her mind: *Jesus, woman, you don't have to yell...* The idea was like a plug in a socket. But would it work on a normal human? She turned her full attention back to the girl and focused her thoughts before forcefully, but silently saying, *go see a doctor.*

Nothing happened. Jayden focused harder on the girl and elevated her mental voice to a shout. *Go see a doctor! Something is wrong.*

The girl blinked and looked around. Jayden took a swig from her water bottle and turned to the person on her right as if occupied in deep conversation. She counted to ten and glanced back to see that the teenager was looking in the opposite direction.

Go see a doctor tomorrow! She thought louder…or she hoped it was louder.

The girl flinched as if struck, then her eyes widened, and her shoulders straightened. She looked up and gave the ceiling a nearly imperceptible nod. She would go to the women's clinic, at least just to weigh her options…and as soon as possible.

Jayden sighed in relief and her shields clanged into place with minimal effort. It seemed that this direction of her powers took effort.

But once the red haze vanished and she was relatively herself again, the realization of the past few moments struck her with such force that she had to brace her weight against the wall.

Oh God, what's happening to me? She screamed silently.

Chapter Thirteen

Just as Silas and Razvan left the backstage area, they spotted their quarry. The two Post Falls vampires were circling the area, looking for another way in. And they had conveniently slipped out of sight to mortals.

The Lord of Spokane exchanged a glance with the Lord of Coeur d'Alene before they were on the invaders in a flash of preternatural speed. Razvan's captive was a fledgling vampire resembling a boy in his mid-twenties, though he was about fifty years old. His Adam's apple jerked and bobbed above the collar of his Rage of Angels tee shirt as if it had a mind of its own. The vampire Silas held was older, but so frozen in terror a strong breeze would likely topple him.

"And what brings you here this evening, flouting my decree, youngling?" Razvan asked silkily.

"W-we just wanted to see the show," the vampire lied.

"You may as well tell him," Silas's hostage said. "They'll find out anyway."

Silas grinned. "Wise words, lad."

"Yes," Razvan said. "You should heed them."

The vampire swallowed audibly. “Our Lord commanded us to bring her the psychic… and the creature Xochitl, if possible.”

Both Silas and Razvan laughed. “There’s no chance in hell you could have taken Xochitl,” Razvan said.

“And if you did,” Silas added, “There’s no way you could have kept her. She’s under the protection of every Lord vampire in the world as well as the entire Elder’s council.”

The vampire Silas held sighed. “We know, but the commands of our lord and high priestess are impossible to refuse.”

Razvan’s sinister laugh made both captives shiver. “But if you had refused, you may have lived. It is a shame you have to pay for your mistress’s foolishness.”

He tightened his grip on the vampire, reveling in his victim’s cry of pain.

“No, please! You don’t understand. Selena is crazy. We had to obey!” the vampire cried desperately as Razvan bared his fangs.

“Selena’s madness has been obvious for many years. You are a fool if you were not aware of that,” Razvan replied in a bored voice.

“Besides,” Silas added. “You could have applied to be transferred to another lord’s territory.

From the vapid expression on his face, it was apparent that Razvan’s captive hadn’t thought of it. Silas’s prisoner, however, slumped his shoulders in defeat. “A few have tried. When Selena found out, the punishments were unspeakable.”

Silas frowned. “Forced loyalty is no loyalty at all.”

Before Silas’s compassion could get them in trouble, Razvan spoke up, “No matter. The fact is, you both have disobeyed my decree banning all Post Falls vampires from my territory and now you must suffer the consequences.”

With that, he plunged his fangs into the youngling's throat. Razvan drank the young one down, absorbing all the vampire's meager powers as thoughts and images of his relatively short lifetime flashed before Razvan's eyes. Normally he closed his mind to such dull visions, but this time he allowed his victim's experiences to wash through him in case there was important information to be gleaned.

Visions of Selena's twisted "worship" sessions danced through his mind, making his stomach churn in revulsion. Indeed, her punishments were harsh. She frequently starved her followers, tortured them, and sometimes executed them by tearing out their hearts. Razvan frowned, realizing it was a trick she'd learned from Silas centuries ago.

Amongst all the chaos and carnage, Razvan learned one thing that was worthwhile. There was a spy in his territory. Unfortunately, his victim, who he now knew was called Daniel, didn't know the vampire's identity, since he'd only eavesdropped on the end of Selena's conversation with her "apostles."

The last images of Daniel's life drained away with the final drops of his blood. Razvan dropped the drained husk on the floor with a growl.

"It seems I have a spy in my territory," he told Silas.

"Well, well, that *is* interesting," Silas said, locking his gaze on his hostage. "Perhaps if *you* have any edifying information on this matter, you may live to feed another night."

"But we can just kill him and learn all we need," Razvan argued. "After all, I am still hungry. A starved vampire is hardly nourishing."

If the captive was a mortal man, he would have wet himself by then. "Please, let me live! I swear I'll tell you all I know."

Razvan toyed with his beard. "Your lord would show you no such mercy. Why should you expect it from us?"

The vampire had no reply for that, but Silas answered, "Because we are better than she is."

"I suppose so," Razvan sighed with exaggerated regret.

The other vampire slumped in relief. "Thank you, lords!"

Silas shoved him against the wall. "We have not yet decided, Laddie. Tell us what you know, and we'll judge whether the information is worth your life."

The captive tried unsuccessfully to lick the beads of sweat from his upper lip before the words poured out in a frantic rush. "I don't know who the spy is, Selena only shares that sort of information with her apostles, but from what the rest of us have overheard I do know that the spy was installed sometime after construction of our lair in Post Falls was completed. That is all I know, I swear!"

Razvan and Silas exchanged a look. "What sort of construction?" they both inquired.

The vampire swallowed again and squared his shoulders in resignation. "We dug an underground fortress beneath a cul de sac of suburban houses."

Razvan chuckled. "That is clever. What say you, Silas? Is that worthy information?"

"Perhaps," Silas replied. "I do not think this creature looks remotely appetizing, anyhow."

"Very well," Razvan said before turning to the captive. "Take your worthless life and run. But know this, if you enter my lands again, *my* punishment will rival that of your former mistress."

The vampire needed no further urging and was off in a flash of preternatural speed.

"As a rogue, it is doubtful he will get far," Razvan commented as he sent out a mental call to the nearest of his subordinates.

"Indeed," Silas replied.

A blond vampire who looked more like a corporate intern approached and bowed. "You sent for me, my lord?"

Razvan pointed at the body at his feet. "I want this disposed of in a place that the sun will find. But first, James, give me your wrist."

James cringed but complied. Razvan sank his fangs into the sensitive flesh. A quick sip revealed that this vampire was loyal.

"Do you think you can handle this task, James?" he asked with deceptive casualness.

James looked down at the body and paled in disgust. "Yes, my lord."

Once the body was out of sight, Silas asked, "What are you going to do about this spy predicament?"

Razvan sighed. "It shouldn't take too long to flush out the traitor. In the meantime, I shall keep Jayden away from Spokane until I deem it safe for her."

Jayden and Razvan followed Akasha and Xochitl out to the parking lot and to the most interesting Datsun she'd ever seen. The car was a pale sparkling blue with flames on the fenders and skulls and crossbones on the hubcaps.

"What's up, Little Beast," Akasha said. An almost maternal smile crossed her lips. Jayden would bet money that the mechanic beside her was responsible for this vehicle's restoration.

Xochitl dug the keys out of her pocket, which was quite a feat since she held a Siamese cat in her arms. This one was much slimmer than Akasha's cat, Isuzu, and had paler markings. It could be none other than the infamous Isis, the only cat known to go on concert tours. Isis squawked a protest at her owner's shifting grip.

The rock star chided, "No, Isis, you can't sit on my shoulder. You'd hit your head when we get in the car."

Akasha called shotgun once the car was unlocked.

Razvan smiled. "It seems we shall always be relegated to the backseat."

"Wait a minute," Jayden said. The first time Razvan had taken her somewhere, he had flown, the second time they took a cab and all other times were riding in someone else's car. "You can't drive, can you?"

For a second, he looked embarrassed. It was an adorable expression on him. Then his features settled into his typical arrogant smirk and he leaned over to whisper in her ear. "Why drive when I can fly?"

Once they all loaded up into the car—Isis climbed under the driver's seat with only her tail remaining visible—Akasha asked Xochitl to go around Post Falls.

The three of them held their breath in fear that the rock star would protest, but instead, she shrugged her shoulders. "Good point. The traffic always sucks there after a show."

The ride was uneventful as Xochitl chattered away to Akasha and attempted to draw Razvan and Jayden into the conversation. Jayden tried to contribute, but Razvan remained silent. An ominous frown turned his features malevolent. She wondered what he was thinking about even as she cursed her luck that he was in a bad mood when she wanted to talk to him about her nightmarish experience with the pregnant girl backstage. On second thought, maybe that was a bad idea. Maybe he'd be disgusted with her.

She wished they would have ridden with Silas. Even though there was no way she could talk to him with the band members in the car, the presence of someone who understood what she was going through would be soothing. Instead, she was stuck with a grumpy vampire, a hard-ass mechanic, an inhuman chatterbox…and a cat.

They arrived at the house at the same time as Silas. Isis was dropped off to keep Isuzu company and Xochitl lectured them both on getting along. Max had left a note saying he would meet them at the bar. It was a short drive, only four blocks from Akasha's shop.

Stepping into the Powder River Saloon was like going back in time a few decades. The tavern was dim and smoky like an old Western movie. Pictures of John Wayne lined the walls along with countless dart trophies. The bar was made from hand-carved, polished wood, worn and scarred. Johnny Cash played on the jukebox instead of the blistering loud heavy metal she'd expected with Akasha's taste.

"Well, look who Akasha dragged in!" the bartender, a balding man with a white beard and bushy eyebrows called out.

"Hi, George!" Xochitl exclaimed and practically leaped over the bar to give him a hug.

"We better watch out," another man said with a smile as he lifted his beer in a toast. "The rock stars have arrived."

Xochitl made her way around the bar, hugging the patrons one by one. The crowd was predominately older blue-collar men, many still in their work clothes. The few women there were either sassy middle-aged women or silver-haired smiling matrons who looked like one's ideal grandmother.

To Jayden's astronomical relief she was not bombarded with thoughts, visions, or emotions. For once it was like she was a normal person…though what she had done tonight was leagues away from normal. She forced the thought away, determined to enjoy an evening free of psychic assault.

As they sat down at the bar, Silas signaled George. "I'm paying for everyone tonight."

George nodded as if he expected nothing less. "Does that include Max?"

Silas smiled as if they shared a private joke. "Indeed."

George chuckled. "He's not going to like that."

The vampire smiled. "I know."

The bartender turned his attention to Jayden. "Who is this pretty young lady and does she have I.D.?"

"This is Jayden," Razvan said while she fished in her purse for her wallet.

"What have you been up to, Razvan?"

He managed a laugh far more cheerful than his usual sinister modus operandi. "You know how it is, nothing but work."

Jayden ordered a glass of White Zinfandel and admired the mason jars hanging from little hooks on the support beams. Johnny Cash gave way to the Rolling Stones on the jukebox.

"This is not at all the kind of place I pictured Akasha and her friends liking," Jayden said to Razvan. "I mean, look at that." She pointed at a sign which read: "*You say F**K, you pay.*" A picture of a quarter was below the caption. "How does Akasha's shop mouth survive here?"

Silas laughed. "She does better some nights than others. They use the money to fund a summer camping trip for all the regulars."

"The charm of the place is in the conversations," Razvan said. A shadow of his bad mood remained in his eyes, but it appeared that he was trying to force it away.

Sure enough, his words were proven a moment later.

As Xochitl, Akasha, and Max began a dart game, an animated and educational discussion of guns and hunting followed. To Jayden's surprise, both Xochitl and Sylvis hunted. It shouldn't have been a shock since they both grew up in the area, but it was hard to conjure up an image of the two girls with their crazy colored hair wearing bright orange vests and toting rifles. In a blink of an eye, the conversation bled away to debates on classic literature. Of all people, Xochitl and a man resembling an aging cowboy dominated the argument, quoting Voltaire and Mark Twain breezily between drinks.

Sylvis challenged Razvan to a game of pool and Jayden darted a glance at Silas. She needed to talk to him, needed to figure out the horror that happened.

He gave her a slight nod and headed to the seat Razvan vacated. Underneath the loud laughter and constant music, Jayden told Silas what happened with the pregnant girl at the concert. To her undying relief, he didn't look at her like she was a monster.

"That is very intriguing," he said finally, eyes narrowed against the constant smoke. "It almost sounds like Jonathon's power."

"Max's doctor?"

Silas nodded. "And you say you aren't getting any visions or impressions of anyone here?"

Jayden shook her head.

"Interesting," Silas mused aloud, taking a minuscule sip of beer. "It seems this power borrows strength from your usual abilities. But why, or how, I do not know."

"Do you know why it happened in the first place?" Jayden asked, darting nervous glances around the bar in fear they were being overheard.

The vampire shook his head. "No. Psychic powers are usually not like in the movies, where it's one thing only. I can get images from touching people or personal property. I can sometimes predict the future, usually the weather. And, once or twice I've been able to move small objects with my mind, though it exhausted me." He sighed. "My best advice is not to invite this new power directly until you can manage your shields better. Only then can you come to understand it."

Jayden nodded as a small measure of relief washed over her. "Thank you, Silas. Now may I ask a small favor? Could you maybe not mention this to Razvan?"

She didn't want him to be disgusted with her.

An unreadable expression hardened Silas's features before he gave her a brisk nod. "Very well, as long as you understand the matter will have to come out eventually."

Razvan returned the cue ball to the bartender and regarded Silas with a savage glare. "Have you been monopolizing my woman, McNaught?"

Before Silas could reply, Sylvis burst out, "I am not a lesbian!"

The bar roared with laughter at that and the guy next to her said, "Jesus, woman, I didn't say you were, I only wanted to know if you were seeing anyone." He gave her a rakish wink.

Sylvis blushed. "Sorry, the stupid tabloids are hinting at it. Just because I want to find the right guy, and I don't sleep around like other celebrities doesn't mean I swing the other way. What I don't get is why they don't say the same thing about Xochitl or Aurora."

Aurora had an answer for that. "Xochitl's too flirtatious for anyone to question her sexuality. As for me, some members of the Black community are too busy accusing me of 'trying to be white' to bother caring who I sleep with. It's bullshit! Our people invented rock and roll! White people only embraced it when some rhinestone-covered redneck from Memphis started doing it."

Xochitl burst out laughing.

Aurora laughed and raised her beer glass in a toast. It seemed that Jayden was the only one that detected the bitterness in her voice. She remembered her vision of Aurora's fight with her mother. It wasn't just 'some' of the black community who were unsupportive of Aurora's career.

Jayden glanced over at Xochitl, who rocked on her barstool and sang along to The Doors. "She almost seems human here," she commented, hoping to keep the distraction going.

"But she is not," Razvan said. "And if people paid more attention, they would see that she reveals that fact in a thousand ways every day."

"Like how?" she asked.

He favored her with a sinister smile. "She is incapable of fear, for one thing. Watch this."

Slowly, he stalked towards the girl. The other customers noticed and quickly hid their smiles with sips of beer. Xochitl remained oblivious, in thrall to the music.

The vampire clapped his hands on her shoulders and shouted, "Boo!"

Xochitl bounced up at least a foot off her barstool and shrieked. Then she burst into delighted laughter and swiveled around to face Razvan. "That was awesome!" she squealed. "Do it again!"

There were a few stunned, quizzical looks at her odd reaction, but most just laughed. "Girl, you are a strange one," George said as he made another round with the bar rag. "But it's nice having you around. We like your spunk."

Spunk was an understatement, Jayden thought as she remembered Xochitl's overpowering aura. Perhaps the people here were energized by it instead of intimidated. Still, she had no idea how she would handle an entire week in her company.

Chapter Fourteen

Jayden fell asleep the moment her head hit the pillow. But she awoke at two in the afternoon. The sun would be up for at least another three hours. Razvan lay next to her in a deep sleep. She rolled over to bury her face in his soft hair and timed her breathing to match his, focusing her mind to blend with his. This time it didn't take so much agonizing effort. In seconds, she was back in the vampire's memories.

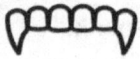

"I am ready, Father," Razvan regarded the Voivode, stroking his beard. "I want to become as you are."

Crina looked up from her sewing. Pride and approval shone in her eyes, making him feel warm all over.

Alexandru smiled, "I knew you would be." He turned to face Radu. "And what of you, my son? Will you join your brother?"

Radu stepped forward. "I will, but under one condition: I wish my mortal family to be given this gift."

The Voivode's eyes widened in horror, but something else glimmered in his expression: pity. "I cannot do that, Radu."

"Why not?" Radu demanded, "They are my blood, my brother's and mine. I cannot bear to watch them die."

Alexandru shook his head sadly. "I fear that you must. It is part of what we are. That is why I forbade you to go to the village in the first place. It grieves me deeply that you both have disobeyed me and must learn this hard lesson so soon."

Razvan understood his father's words, but he could see that his twin did not, at least not yet. His heart surged in sympathy for him even as his stomach roiled in guilt. If he had not been so curious about his birth family, Radu would not have gotten attached to them and now be suffering the painful consequences.

"Damn you!" Radu shouted. "How can you be so heartless about this?"

Crina stood up. "Don't speak to him so. Your father is right."

Her words inflamed him further. "Damn it, he is not my father!"

The fight went on for over an hour before Radu stormed out of the castle. Razvan went to follow him, but Alexandru stopped him with a hand on his shoulder.

"Your brother needs time to think," he said. "Leave him in solitude for a little while. In the meantime, I advise you to witness your last sunrise and sunset. If your decision still stands, I will Change you tomorrow night."

Razvan nodded and set out for the castle parapet. Crina kissed him on the cheek on the way out.

Radu did not return until the next night. Razvan paced back and forth through the solar, darting nervous glances at the door. He did not want to be alone during his transformation.

"We can wait no longer," Alexandru said, beckoning him to come forward.

Razvan stepped closer, and the Voivode embraced him. “Welcome to the family,” Alexandru whispered before sinking his fangs into Razvan’s neck.

The pain was sharp and sudden, and he couldn’t hold back a weak cry. The pain faded into a warm tingling which gave way to euphoria. His vision went black, and soon he was weightless.

Then something wet and hot touched his tongue and his body jolted as if prodded by a thousand tiny needles. He couldn’t stop drinking the elixir, guzzling the sweet fluid as if he would die without it, and perhaps he would. Suddenly, he was jerked away from the source.

Razvan let out a roar of rage, even as he curled up in a ball on the floor, shivering and bereft. A warm hand touched his. He opened his eyes. Radu knelt beside him. His eyes regarded Razvan solemnly as if he were imparting his strength to his brother. The shivering subsided, though the world seemed to explode with color and sound. And his mouth ached like the fires of hell.

“It will be all right,” Alexandru said, and his voice felt like a lash against his skin. “You will get used to it.”

For hours he lay on the stone floor, willing his mind to adjust to the assault on his senses, to separate the fusillade of odors and sounds. Radu stayed with him the whole time, the only solid tether to sanity.

Eventually, the sensations blended and dimmed to a tolerable level, and he was able to sit up. But another sense arose. Razvan could see the pulse beating in his twin’s throat. He stared, hypnotized. Saliva built in his mouth, and he discovered that he was starving. A low, alien growl trickled from him.

“Ah, it is time,” Alexandru said. “You had better step back, Radu.”

Crina rang the bell to summon a maid. When she arrived, Alexandru bespelled her with his eyes and led her to Razvan's side. Razvan was on the maid in a flash, nearly weeping with ecstasy when his new fangs punctured her flesh, and the hot blood poured into his mouth. It was over too quickly, and Alexandru had to wrestle her from his grasp.

"We must not kill them," he said as he healed the girl's wounds. "Such an act would bring peasants to our door bearing torches in no time."

Razvan barely heard him. The world swayed in his vision. He felt wonderful, but incredibly tired, and his mouth still ached from his newly-grown fangs. Crina supported him with an arm at his waist and led him down a hidden passage to a luxurious bed-chamber below the castle. There was an identical door beside it, presumably meant for Radu.

His adopted mother tucked him into the mammoth bed, and he knew no more.

When he awoke the next night, the blood hunger was upon him so fiercely that he nearly whimpered in desperation for sustenance. Alexandru was ready for him. He led him out on the parapet, took him in his arms, and rose up in the air, carrying Razvan to the village. There he showed him how to capture the mind of a mortal long enough to take his meal and erase his victim's memory of the feeding.

"When shall I be able to fly?" Razvan asked.

Alexandru laughed. "So eager, you are. Your powers won't really manifest until your second or third century."

"That long?"

The Voivode chuckled. "It is not nearly the eternity you think it is. We have all the time in the world. Besides, you have other skills to occupy you for now."

"Like what?"

Alexandru's answer was a mysterious smile. "Run," he said.

Razvan obeyed and whooped with joy as his feet devoured the ground at an impossible speed. Now he knew how wolves felt when they ran with the moon.

When they arrived back at the castle, Radu was waiting. He looked deep into his twin's eyes and said simply, "I cannot let you take this journey alone."

Razvan fought back tears and embraced his brother. "I will always be your family," he vowed.

Alexandru changed Radu the next night. From then on, the twins returned to their inseparable state. And for the very first time, they did not look identical. Radu shaved off the beard and mustache at his first opportunity, sighing with relief as he stroked his now-bared chin. Razvan kept the mustache, but trimmed his beard until it was a small point at the end of his chin.

"You look like a devil," Radu teased.

Razvan grinned and bared his fangs. "Perhaps I am."

The twins continued to look in on their birth family, but did not visit them any longer, fearing that their Change would be detected. Instead, they kept to each other and their new shared experiences and powers. Their bond with their adopted family grew every night as they spent many a delightful evening listening to endless stories of Alexandru's immortal adventures.

When Ihrin died, Radu and Razvan wept over her grave and made certain the site was always adorned with flowers. When the simple marker decayed over the years, they replaced it. Razvan remained desolate over the death of their birth mother, but Radu reminded him of the existence of continuing generations. Eventually, he found peace in looking after them.

Chapter Fifteen

Jayden wasn't able to access any more of Razvan's memories for over a week. She was too exhausted. Silas's normally quiet house became a noisy world of chaos for the time that the members of Rage of Angels were guests. Jayden worked on her psychic training as often as she could, often going to the shop with Max and practicing on him as he worked on cars because it was too loud in the house.

Still, she'd never had a more exciting time. Every evening was full of laughter, music, and those eerie meowing conversations that Xochitl had with her cat.

The band really did live and breathe music. When they weren't practicing or putting on impromptu concerts for their hosts, they monopolized Silas's stereo—and his collection of 80's mix CDs—and sang and danced for hours.

They didn't maintain a consistent schedule. Sometimes they stayed up all night watching the most awful B horror movies Jayden had ever seen. Other times they whiled away afternoons reading, shopping, and conversing on every imaginable topic. Jayden had never met anyone like them or seen Akasha so happy.

Everyone went to bed early the evening before *Rage of Angels* had to depart… except for Xochitl. Jayden got up to get a glass of water and found the singer pacing frantically in the living room, hugging her arms as if she were cold. Her energy ricocheted through the room, making Jayden feel as if she were surrounded by lightning.

"Xochitl," Jayden said quietly, cautiously making her way to the living room. "Are you okay?"

Their eyes met, and that alien energy pelted Jayden, making her hair stand on end.

"I'm okay," Xochitl said, every tremble of her body revealing the lie. She pulled an electronic cigarette out of her pocket and took a puff, breathing out a cloud of blue vapor.

Although every instinct screamed at her to run, Jayden held her ground. "No, you're not." In a gentler tone, she continued, "Want to talk about it?"

Xochitl didn't answer. She picked up an empty glass from the coffee table and walked past Jayden into the kitchen, pulling out a can of Red Bull and a bottle of Stolichnaya from the fridge with brisk efficiency. The vodka was half gone, and since no one else in the house drank vodka, Jayden was willing to bet the rock star was already three sheets to the wind.

After mixing another drink, Xochitl went back to the living room. Jayden followed her. For the longest time, Xochitl stood still, staring at the waxing moon through the picture window.

"He's coming for me," she whispered. "Just like he said he would."

"Who?" Jayden whispered even more softly.

"The dark man. I've dreamt of him for years, and now he's finally coming. I don't know what he wants." She took another swig of her drink and swayed. "I think he's following me."

Chills broke out on Jayden's skin as she remembered dreaming of Razvan before they met. But what sort of creature could cause Xochitl to sound almost afraid? Razvan had said she was incapable of fear and her cheerful ease amongst the company of vampires seemed to prove the point.

"I don't know what he wants from me!" Xochitl said as if Jayden wasn't there.

"Maybe—" Jayden began, but was cut off by a shrill meow that sent her heart careening into her throat.

Xochitl whirled around, blinking at Jayden in surprise before looking down at the Siamese cat perched by her feet, glaring at her with turquoise eyes.

"Yes, Isis, you're right," she told the cat before meeting Jayden's eyes. "Good night, Jayden. It was nice meeting you."

Jayden watched her walk away with catlike grace despite her obvious drunkenness. Whatever Xochitl was involved in, it likely went deeper than even Silas could guess.

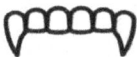

When Rage of Angels left, the silence was almost overwhelming. Akasha's cheer was gone, and she returned to being the coarse beer-swilling mechanic that Jayden had met. It was obvious she missed her friends. The weekends were worse. Akasha was like a sullen ghost haunting the house with a book in one hand, a beer in the other, occasionally breaking the silence with a pensive sigh. On Halloween, she shut herself up in the library.

"She's always like this for a while after they leave," Silas explained as he filled large bowls with candy for the trick-or-treaters. He sighed. "It's a little worse because of the season, I believe, because she first met them this time of year." Something in his voice didn't ring true, however.

"You sense something," Jayden said with conviction.

"Aye." He met her eyes solemnly. "And I'll bet you do as well."

She hugged herself as if she were cold. "It's like I swallowed a rock. The feeling that something bad is going to happen, it just never leaves. And with Akasha being so distant..." *And Razvan as well.*

"Perhaps it's because you've been shut up in this house too long," he said with forced calm. "Max is going to try to get Akasha to go to the Halloween party at the Powder River. There's to be a dart tournament, and she hasn't missed one yet. It may do some good if you joined them."

"I don't know," Jayden said, "I'm not really in the mood to go out drinking, and I should probably wait for Razvan."

"Razvan will not be back until after the bars close," Silas countered smoothly. "And I meant that it would be good for Akasha. She needs a friend."

Jayden flushed with guilt. "Oh. You're probably right." She was quiet for a moment. "Akasha told me that Xochitl and the others were her first and only friends, but Aurora told me they didn't meet until their senior year in high school. Why didn't she have friends before? I've tried to ask her, but she is so evasive."

The genuine empathy and desire to help in Jayden's eyes almost undid him. "I could tell you, but it would be better if you asked Max."

She raised a brow. "Why can't you tell me?"

"Because, she would never forgive me, but she would forgive Max anything. Also," he added with a wink, "the man's tongue gets awfully loose after a few pints."

"Well, in that case, I better get my costume ready. Speaking of, yours is nice. It looks authentic."

Silas looked down at his kilt, and his plaid draped over his shoulder, fastened by the McNaught crest. "It'll be even more so when I wear my sword. Now would you hold this bowl for a moment?"

Jayden smiled with wry amusement when he filled the bowl with full-size candy bars. "I'll bet your house is a favorite stop."

He grinned, showing a hint of fang. "Aye, it is. I don't know why."

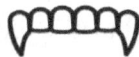

Silas sighed in relief when Max and Jayden, with a reluctant Akasha, headed out the door a few minutes later. The moment they were out of sight, he pulled out his phone and called a few of his strongest vampires to keep watch over them. Caution was imperative these days.

Razvan had received another message from Selena. This one threatened "dire consequences" if they failed to give her Jayden within a month. They had agreed to keep this information from the ladies for now. Razvan believed that Jayden's mind was still too fragile to handle too much undue stress. And Silas worried that Akasha would lose her temper and try to confront Selena herself.

To make matters worse, Razvan still had a spy among his Spokane vampires. While he worked on weeding out the traitor, Silas tried to track down Delgarias. He'd already sent a letter to the Elders informing them of Selena's actions, but he had little hope they'd do anything. After his trumped-up trial in Amsterdam, he had few allies among them. There was only one he could call a friend amongst the Elder's council. But Ian

Ashton, Lord of London, had the typical stiffness and lack of imagination that was the stock of the British aristocracy, so it was hard to tell how seriously he would respond to the threat.

Delgarias was his only hope of sorting out this situation. But so far, the ancient vampire was nowhere to be found. It was a regular occurrence with the Thirteenth Elder, but lately, it drove Silas mad. The son of a bitch had a knack for disappearing when he was needed the most. In fact, if Delgarias had been around four years ago, Selena wouldn't have been able to cause as much trouble as she did the first time.

Silas admired Akasha's sexy pirate costume as they walked down the driveway, pleased that Jayden persuaded her to wear it by threatening to call Xochitl and tell her if she didn't. Her bottom looked luscious in the tight-fitting trousers. Silas struggled to tamp down the lust. It wouldn't do if his kilt stood up before the eyes of the approaching trick-or-treaters

The Halloween party at the Powder River Saloon turned out to be a lot of fun. Besides the dart tournament—which Akasha won—George's wife had organized party games and "trick or treat walks," in which she had everyone line up to pull out paper bags from a huge garbage sack behind the jukebox. The bags contained treats like candy, chips, disposable lighters, and pepperoni sticks. But there were also tricks like dog biscuits, toilet paper rolls, and George's old socks. Before Jayden could toss away an old ace bandage, Max informed her that there were over a hundred dollars hidden amongst the tricks. Sure enough, she found a buck rolled up in the bandage.

When the festivities wound down around midnight and Akasha was occupied with another dart game, Jayden decided it was time to seek her information.

"Max?" She tried to speak softly yet still be heard over the din. "What happened to Akasha?"

He blinked at her suspiciously before darting a paternal glance at his business partner. "What do you mean?"

She took a deep breath and began. "When I first met her, I shook her hand, and I saw people being shot. I think they were her parents. And then I saw her in a home where she was abused by a crazy lady, then she was on the streets, and well, a whole bunch of stuff. I was wondering if you could maybe explain it."

Max scratched his beard. "Have you asked her?"

She blushed. "Yeah, and she doesn't want to talk about it. But even though I haven't known her long, I really care about her," she said quickly before he could respond. "I know she's suffered a lot, and that's probably why she drinks so much, but if she keeps drinking like that, it's going to ruin her life."

He gave her a long, steady look. "With all the shit that girl's been through, it's a wonder that all she does is drink. If it had been me, I'd either have killed myself or been out of my mind." He gulped down the rest of his beer and signaled for a refill before he leaned closer to her and lowered his voice further. "Fine, I'll tell you, but if she finds out, she'll kick my ass. During the Gulf War, there were a bunch of top-secret government experiments in attempt to create the perfect soldier. Akasha's father was one of the soldiers experimented on. Somehow his genes were mutated, and he and his fellow lab rats ended up with superhuman strength, extreme endurance, and a few other goodies. But for some reason, the higher-ups were unsatisfied with the results. They ordered the experiment to be terminated, meaning the soldiers."

Max lit a cigarette. "Akasha's dad managed to escape. He met her mother, married, and passed his mutation along to his daughter. Eight years later, the government goons found them, and they shot down her parents right in front of her. The only reason Akasha knew how old she was then was because she had finished blowing out eight birthday candles only minutes before it happened."

"Oh my God," Jayden breathed, horrified by such a tragedy. "I couldn't imagine."

The bartender came to collect his empty glass, and Max requested a large pitcher before he continued, "Somehow, she ended up in an orphanage, and then later in a foster home. The foster lady was one of them religious nuts. You ever seen the movie, *Carrie*?"

Jayden nodded, dreading to hear the rest of the story.

"Well, this bitch was ten times worse than Carrie's mom. They shut her down after she starved a three-year-old boy to death. She said he was 'fasting.'" He grimaced and lit a cigarette. "And there wasn't a kid in that place that didn't have a bruise, burn, or damaged knees from hours of kneeling. But Akasha ran away long before the lady's abuse was found out." He swept another look around the bar to make sure no one was listening.

"Anyway, she spent over two years on the streets, sleeping in cardboard boxes and sharing canned beans with the other bums. One of the bums was a crack whore, and she sent Akasha away because her pimp noticed her and had 'Johns' that would love a little girl."

Jayden took a small sip of wine and pushed the glass aside, her stomach roiling with revulsion.

The bartender came with a new pitcher of beer and a fresh frosty glass. Max paid and waited until he was out of earshot. "When I met Akasha, she was taking food out of my garbage can.

She'd been living in my shed. This was in Montana in the early winter. If I hadn't caught her then, she would've gotten frostbite or hypothermia. It damn near broke my heart." His voice cracked, and he coughed. "Anyway, I made a deal with her. I wouldn't turn her in to the system if she'd stay with me and help out around the house and in my garage, just with the legit stuff, mind you, she didn't know about the chop shop thing I had on the side. She became like a daughter to me, of course, I wasn't a very good dad since I'm the one who taught her to drink and smoke and cuss and all that.

"We had some good times, that was for sure." He grinned in remembrance. "Girl handled a wrench like she was born with one in her hand. I discovered her strength when the jack stand slipped out from a car I was working on. Akasha grabbed the El Camino, which probably weighed over a ton, and held it up long enough for me to get out from under it. That's when she told me about how her parents died. But she didn't know about the government's involvement at the time. Still, we suspected people looking for her. So when the cops showed up to arrest me, I told her to run. God, I wish I hadn't." He wiped a tear from his eye, and Jayden shivered in dread of his next words.

"She was raped at gunpoint on the side of the road that very night. That's another reason she's scared of guns. First, her parents got shot, then that."

Jayden could only manage a sympathetic murmur. Her throat locked up with tears. She knew Akasha had a bad childhood, it was etched into her eyes, but this was more horrific than she imagined.

Max ground his cigarette into a pulp in the brass ashtray. "She got the bastard though. Knocked the gun out of his hand and beat him to death with her bare hands."

"Good," Jayden said, meaning it with all her heart.

He nodded in solemn agreement. "Then she took his car and drove until it ran out of gas. She ended up here in Coeur d'Alene and was immediately picked up by the cops and placed in a group home.

She refused to tell them where she came from, and it really griped their asses, so since she didn't have any I.D. they somehow convinced the state to make one for her. They made her two years younger than she actually was, thinking she'd get pissed and give up her background."

"Oh," Jayden said. "So that's what Akasha was talking about when she said that Silas wasn't 'playing Lolita' with her."

Max muttered a curse under his breath. "Yeah, and even if that weren't the case, they didn't become romantically involved until after she was legally eighteen. Still, there was some ugly talk around town when they got married, but most people understood. It wasn't like he raised her from a baby or anything."

"So, he became her legal guardian when she was seventeen, but really nineteen?" Jayden prodded, urging him back to the story. It looked like Akasha's dart game was nearly finished.

"Yeah, and it was the best thing that ever happened to her. Of course, at the time, she didn't see it that way." He grinned. "Here she was, swept away by Prince Charming, taken to live in a castle, offered anything she could ask for. But by then, she was so full of fear and pain that she felt nothing but suspicion."

"I can understand that," she said, her heart aching with sympathy. "It likely seemed too good to be true."

"Eventually, Silas broke through her defenses and taught her to love and trust again." Max's voice rang with pride and gratitude. "Xochitl and her posse helped with that. As that ancient bloodsucker, Delgarias, had predicted, Akasha finally made friends. Silas nurtured that friendship inadvertently since he was instructed to guard them. Since he pretty much let them all run wild when they were visiting, his house became the official hangout. Hell, from what I hear, those kids practically lived with Akasha."

"When did she find out that he was a vampire?" she asked.

Before Max could answer, the dartboard blared, and Akasha dashed over to the bar.

"I smoked 'em," she said and beckoned the bartender for a refill.

Jayden averted her face and took another sip of wine, afraid that Akasha would discern the naked sympathy on her face. She knew there was more to the story, but after all that she'd already heard, anything else was hard to fathom.

Max was never able to tell her the rest.

Chapter Sixteen

On the walk back home, Jayden mulled over Max's story. It was almost inconceivable that a person could have been through so much and yet be functional. No wonder Akasha drank so heavily. She glanced at the woman walking beside her. She was so tiny and delicate, yet so strong. Jayden's heart went out to her, and she hoped she could be a worthy friend.

When they arrived home, she watched Akasha step into Silas's arms and felt a twinge of envy at the love they shared. So far, Razvan had never displayed more than a passing affection for her, only lust, and lately, there had been little of that. Was it because of the excitement with Selena's drama? Or had Hilda, that blonde vampire at the concert, been right after all? Was he finished with her?

Silas bent down to whisper in Akasha's ear, and her husky laugh made Jayden feel like an interloper. Without bothering to say goodnight, she left them in their own little world and headed downstairs. She needed a shower. She reeked of cigarette smoke from the bar.

When she entered the room she and Razvan shared, Jayden heard the shower already running, and her heart skipped a beat. He was back. *He was naked.*

With a trembling hand, she opened the bathroom door. The sight of Razvan stole Jayden's breath and awakened things low in her body. Through the glass shower door, beaded with moisture and just beginning to fog with steam, she could see rivulets of water running down his lithe, muscular form. He looked like an aquatic god.

"Hello, Jayden." His deep voice echoed in the small room. "Would you care to join me?"

He still wants me! An inner voice cried out in triumph. *For now,* another said dryly.

It took her a moment to find her voice amidst the clamor of hope and doubt coupled with the delectable sight of his nakedness.

"Sure." She hoped she sounded nonchalant. "I needed a shower anyway."

She took pains to remove her costume slowly so as not to reveal her eagerness. The cool air on her skin made her nipples harden instantly. Jayden slid the shower door open and stepped into the steamy cocoon to meet the apotheosis of her desires.

Razvan's eyes met hers as he reached for the bar of soap. As he worked it into a sudsy lather, his gaze promised dark pleasure.

"I bathed you the night I found you," he said. "Do you remember?"

She shivered as she remembered waking up in a deliciously warm bath with him poised over her like a dark angel. His touch had been gentle then but full of heat. Before she could reply, his soapy hands were working their magic on her again. Every inch of her body was treated to his sensual ministrations, and he spent as much time on one area as he did in the last. By the time he was finished, she felt like she was going to melt into a puddle.

"You had better get your face," he said, breaking the spell. "I don't want to get soap in your eyes.

As she washed her face, she marveled at the intense pleasure that he was able to give her. She wanted to return the favor. When she was finished, her gaze slid down his body to rest on his hardness below.

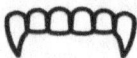

Razvan watched with astonishment as Jayden sank to her knees. He sucked in a breath as her fingers wrapped around his shaft and nearly came out of his skin when her tongue darted out to flick across its tip. Her lips encircled him, and she began to make love to him with her mouth. He groaned and braced his hand on the tiled wall, overcome with the sensation of the warm water pelting his shoulders and Jayden's hot mouth around his cock.

When the pleasure nearly became too much to bear, he grasped her under her arms and pulled her to her feet. He covered her neck with kisses and nipped her earlobe before whispering, "Wrap your legs around me."

With a low moan that threatened to bring him to his knees, Jayden obeyed him. As he lifted her, cupping her delectable rear, her heated core writhed against his cock, but he held her back. That wasn't yet what he had in mind. Razvan turned her so that the shower spray was drenching her hair, making her look like a water nymph.

"Hold on to me," he commanded.

Her eyes narrowed in confusion as he let go of her and reached for the shampoo. As she clung to him, he proceeded to wash her hair. The mixed sensations of him massaging her scalp as his shaft ground against her clit made her whimper most delightfully. As he tilted her back to rinse her crimson tresses, Razvan licked and sucked her breasts until she was squirming in desperation. Her slippery wetness drove him mad.

"Do you want me to fuck you, Jayden?" he asked.

"Yes!" she cried.

He turned his back to the spray and set his woman down. Before she could say another word, he forced her around and gave her a split second to brace her hands against the wall before he thrust into her from behind.

Jayden's throaty cry fanned the flames of his lust, and he pounded into her like something crazed. Her hips bucked against him, straining to match the frantic rhythm. When her sheath tightened and convulsed around him, he nearly roared in ecstasy as he exploded inside her.

When he took her into his arms and lowered his head to kiss her, the adoration in her dark emerald gaze was like a spear through his heart. If she would look at him like that forever, he would keep her for all eternity. But he knew better. Jayden was only infatuated with him because he was her rescuer. Once she gained control over her powers and her mind healed…and most of all when she was free from Selena's threat—a threat which was his fault—she'd want to be free of him. He wasn't a fool. He knew he had nothing to offer her besides money and skilled lovemaking. Jayden wasn't greedy. And the lust would fade. It always did.

He tilted her chin up, noticing with a guilty pang that she had dark circles under her eyes. She had been through so much. And he made it worse by putting her in Selena's path.

Razvan kissed her, savoring the delicious softness of her lips against his. "You should get some rest now."

When they were tucked into the large bed, he cradled her in his arms and silently vowed to enjoy her for as long as he could.

Chapter Seventeen

Jayden watched the glowing numbers on the digital alarm clock on the bedside table and listened to Razvan's breathing even out into the rhythm of sleep. Finally, the clock blinked: 6:30 AM. The sun would be coming up now.

She took a deep breath, dropped her shields, and willed her mind to link with Razvan's. In moments, she plunged into his memories.

In the spring of the twins' third century, in the year 1437, Radu fell in love. Her name was Uta, and she was the rich widow of one of their numerous great-grandnephews. Uta was a vision of loveliness with her silvery-blonde curls and wide, gray eyes. But every time Razvan looked at her, a bitter taste filled his mouth. When Radu kissed her, Razvan wanted to vomit. He couldn't explain his hostile feelings for the wench, nor could he completely hide them.

"Why are you growing your beard back?" he'd asked his brother, unable to hide his look of disgust. "You hated it."

Radu stroked his scraggly whiskers and shrugged. "Uta thinks it makes me look more fearsome."

"Your fangs should suffice," Razvan countered. "Not only are you a fool to change yourself to please a wench, but you look like one with that unkempt mass upon your chin."

"Why do you hate her so?" Radu asked with deceptive casualness.

His twin frowned. "I do not hate her…I just have a feeling that she is not all she seems. And you are different as well. Your conquests with women used to be a legend. I cannot fathom why you would now settle for only one."

"Perhaps I've changed. After all, it's been three centuries."

Razvan shook his head and quoted their father: "Time does not change a man. It only makes him more what he is."

Radu glared back at him. "I believe you are merely jealous, brother!" With that, he stomped from the room and left the castle.

The brothers did not speak to each other for over a month. Radu spent every night with Uta, to their parents' growing worry.

"It's as if she has him bespelled," Crina said one evening over her embroidery. "Do you suppose she is a witch?"

Razvan looked up from the sword he was polishing. "I don't know, Mother, but I do not like her."

Alexandru tapped out the bowl of his pipe and snorted. "Witches do not exist anymore, no matter what the mortal church declares. Radu is going through a phase. It will be painful for him, but it shall pass, and he will learn. It is a rite for our kind."

The matter came to head a few nights later.

Radu entered the family solarium and bowed before Alexandru. "I implore you, Voivode of this *țări* and Lord vampire of this territory, to allow me to take my fair Uta to wife and make her one of us."

Alexandru sighed. "I hear your plea, but I cannot grant your request, my son. I know this will cause you pain, and I can only hope someday you will understand my refusal."

"But why can't I Change her?" Radu protested. "You have your *Bride.* Why can't I have mine?"

His eyes swam with unshed tears, and Razvan felt his twin's pain as if it was his own. However, Razvan doubted that the fair Uta felt the same deep affection for his brother.

"You are not ready, my son," Alexandru said.

"Who are you to say when I am ready? Were you 'ready' when you met Mother? Who is ready for love? For the love of God, I am three hundred years old! A mortal man weds at thirty!" Radu's fist shattered a stone protruding from the wall.

Crina rushed into the chamber, nearly tripping over her elaborate skirts. "Radu! There is no call for you to destroy our home. Your father only wants what is best for you, my son." She reached forward to cradle him to her breast as she always did when he was upset.

Radu pushed her away and strode out of the room, tears falling unchecked to drench his beard. His black eyes glittered with fierce resolve. Crina's face fell in hurt astonishment. Razvan stepped forward and gathered her in his arms, expecting to feel victorious, but a hard lump rose in his throat at his mother's sorrow.

Alexandru pulled Crina from Razvan's embrace, leaving him bereft of affection as usual. She went willingly, sobbing against her husband's chest.

"Go and find your brother, Razvan," the Voivode commanded. "Try and talk some sense into his thick head."

Razvan grabbed a torch from a wall sconce and headed down the corridor in pursuit. But Radu was not in his chambers. He cursed Uta under his breath and headed for the village. Uta's home was also empty. He remembered the look of determination on his brother's tear-stained face and was filled with foreboding. Was Radu planning something foolish?

His pulse raced as he searched the village for his twin. It was an hour before dawn when he was forced to give up.

To his relief, when Razvan returned to the castle, he heard Radu moving around in his bedchamber. He opened the door, and his greeting died on his lips at the sight before him. A traveling satchel lay on the bed, and Radu was furiously stuffing clothing and sentimental objects into it.

Razvan closed the door carefully and leaned against the wall, closing his eyes. Radu planned to disobey their father and flee with Uta. Father would have no choice but to report such a transgression to the Elders, who would then hunt him down and punish his offense…possibly by death. Razvan couldn't let his brother die. His mind raced as he weighed his options. Radu would never listen to him in such a state, and they were so evenly matched in combat it was doubtful Radu could be subdued. Razvan sighed. There was no choice but to approach Uta and try to reason with her. And he had to do it now, for he would bet his inheritance that Radu planned to take her at dusk.

Cursing the sun for working against him, Razvan thrust open the door to the parapet and leaped out into the waning night, flying faster than ever before. The sky was changing from black to gray when he arrived at Uta's doorstep. He didn't bother knocking and jerked the door open.

"Radu!" Uta leapt up from her seat. Her embroidery tumbled to the floor. An expression that resembled guilt too much to be anything else swam in her large eyes.

"It is Razvan," he said and strode to her, grasping her shoulders. "Uta, you must not let Radu carry out his plan with you. If he does, you will both die."

To his astonishment, Uta laughed, her eyes narrowed in flinty malice. "No, it is he that shall die. He and your accursed family. I know what you all are. I will not become a demon, and this *ţări* will be safe."

"What are you saying?" Razvan demanded, gripping her tighter.

Uta's laughter returned, high and girlish and bubbling with madness. "You are too late! He has told me your secrets. I know how to bring God's wrath upon you abominations, and my soul has been cleaned in confession and penance."

"You don't love my brother at all!" He shook her. "Tell me what you have done, woman!"

She continued to laugh. "You're too late! Too late!"

Uta's laughter kindled Razvan's rage to a furious peak. He shook her harder, screaming at her to explain her betrayal. He didn't see the figure approaching the open doorway until he heard the snap of Uta's neck breaking.

"You bastard!" Radu shrieked and charged at him.

"Listen, Radu, let me explain!" But his words had no effect. He was silenced as a fist connected with his jaw. The corpse of Radu's lover slid to the floor.

The twins fought and grappled until Uta's richly furnished home was in shambles. Razvan's face began to burn as a feeble ray of the approaching sun fell on his profile. Radu stopped his assault and grabbed at his own face, groaning in agony.

"We finish this tonight," he hissed. Unadulterated hatred flared from his red-rimmed eyes before he fled to seek a resting place from the killing dawn.

Razvan sighed and dashed off to find his own haven. The morning sapped his strength to fly. He only hoped Radu would be calm enough by evening to hear his explanation. It was too late to reach the castle, so he bedded down in a cave where he and Radu had taken refuge in their early days when they prowled too late.

Nightmares of fire and screams tormented him until the sun went down. As he awoke, it seemed he could still smell the smoke. In fact, the odor was so strong he could taste it. Razvan's eyes snapped open. This was no dream.

The acrid smell of smoke seared his sensitive nostrils when he stepped out of the cave. The air was hazy, and the moon obscured. The fire had been big, and it had been close. He quickened his pace, wishing he had the strength to fly, which would not come until he fed. He came to Uta's home and stopped. Not only was there a pervasive odor of a recent fire, but the unmistakable scent of fresh blood rode the air nearby. The house was not burned. He stepped inside and saw the abode had been ransacked and stripped of everything of value. A moment later, he discovered the source of the second smell. The place on the floor where Razvan had dropped Uta's body was covered in blood. A deep groove was hacked into the wood. Someone had chopped off her head.

A smear of crimson trailed across the floor where the body had been dragged out the rear entrance. Razvan followed it. The scent of charred wood and flesh grew stronger with every step. Outside he found the smoldering remains of a funeral pyre. The vampire sucked in a breath. There was only one reason for someone to cut the head off a corpse and burn it: fear that it would rise again.

Uta's last words echoed in his head. *"You are too late! He has told me your secrets. I know how to bring God's wrath upon you abominations, and my soul has been cleansed in confession and penance."*

Razvan ran for his family's castle. If the villagers had feared Uta's corpse enough to desecrate and burn it, and she had told them the secret of the Nicolae family's immortality... He ran faster, but each step and pump of his heart seemed to scream, *too late...too late!*

The village was unnaturally still and silent as he passed through. The inns were dark, and though a few candles burned in the windows of the houses, not a whimper of humanity was heard. Each and every door was adorned with some sort of symbol or talisman to ward off evil.

The closer he drew to his home, the stronger the stench of smoke became until he was choking on it. Even though he anticipated the worst, Razvan still fell to his knees with an agonized cry when he saw the scorched ruin of Castle Nicolae.

It looked as if it had been under siege for months. Large sections of the stone walls had crumbled and collapsed. A human arm protruded from one pile of rubble, a chisel still gripped in the white fist. The mystery became clear as Razvan pictured in his mind's eye an army of stonemasons hacking at the walls with their tools, using their skills to attack the weak points. And all the while, he had been asleep in the cave, helpless to come to his parents' aid.

The wooden door was gone, the stone archway scorched to mark where it had been. With a sinking feeling, Razvan entered the ruin of his home. Over the years, the Nicolae family had been replacing the wooden ceilings with stone, but the progress was fatally slow. The stars shone through gaping spaces above him. His skin burned with the realization that the sun's deadly rays had pierced these chambers only hours ago.

Black chunks of charcoal littered the floor, making it hard to walk. It seemed hunks of burning wood had been thrown in to add to the conflagration. But there was still hope. The family's sleeping chambers were below the castle.

"Mother?" Razvan called, wincing at the hollow echo of his voice against the blackened stone. "Father?"

There was no reply besides the muted whisper of the wind. He let out a breath he didn't know he'd held. His meager hope ebbed away when he reached the passage to the sleeping quarters. The narrow corridor was nearly impassable, clogged with burned wood. Razvan pushed the obstructions away, shrieking in agony as a few remaining embers struck his hands and face.

His parents' once luxurious chamber was a horror of scorched walls and charred rubble. He stepped forward and heard a sickening crunch. A blackened rib cage engulfed his boot. Razvan jumped back with a small cry and clapped a hand over his mouth. Another skeleton, this one smaller, lay nearby. Its bony fingers reached out as if seeking the hand of the other.

For an eternity, his eyes stared into the gaping eye sockets of the skulls before him. They seemed to stare at him in furious accusation. He bit into the thick flesh of his hand until it bled, until the scream could be held in no longer.

It seemed he screamed for hours, screamed until his lungs burned and white stars danced in his vision. Razvan collapsed, oblivious to the pain as his knees struck the floor. He sobbed and gibbered like a madman, hitching in an occasional breath to call out for his mother and father. He longed for the comfort of his family; he longed for Radu…*Radu!*

He leaped to his feet and rushed to his brother's chambers. Had the villagers gotten his brother as well? Razvan didn't think so. They were twins. Surely, he would feel it if Radu was dead. The chamber was empty, and not nearly as damaged from the fire as their parents' bower. There were no bones. Razvan breathed deep and murmured thanks to the fates. It appeared his brother was safe. But where was he?

Frantically, he kicked aside the burnt obstructions in his path as he made his way back up the stairs. Once outside, he sucked in eager gulps of fresh air before calling out his brother's name. His voice reverberated for miles. He had no doubt that the whole village could hear him, but he didn't care. Let them come. His fangs bared in anticipation of making them pay for murdering his family. When he found Radu, they would avenge Alexandru and Crina together.

As he returned to the village, it became apparent that Radu had been there as well…and that he knew what had happened. Countless bodies littered the streets. All had their throats torn out. He heard a shout behind him and turned to see a man charging at his back, wielding an ax. With lightning speed, Razvan disarmed the man and sank his teeth in his throat. He drank until his belly could hold no more, then seized his attacker's head and squeezed, gratified when he heard the crunch of the skull crushing.

Now that he had nourishment, he could fly. Razvan rose up in the air, calling for Radu. He flew until his muscles ached, and with a heavy sigh, he landed to search for another meal. The scent of terrified prey came to him from a hut nearby. He kicked open the flimsy door with a growl, eager to punish another murderer. A small sound crept out of a narrow cupboard. Razvan opened it and seized a little girl by the scruff of her neck.

She couldn't have been much older than eight. Her blue eyes were so wide with fear they nearly overtook her face. Razvan sighed in disappointment. He couldn't kill an innocent child.

He forced his features into a gentle countenance and said softly, "It is all right, little girl. I will not hurt you."

Those enormous eyes with fan-like lashes blinked up at him for a moment before the child hurled herself into his arms.

"Monsters," she sobbed. "*Strigoi*!"

She didn't recognize him, he realized. It made sense, being that she was lower caste, and he looked human. When her sobs died away, he tilted her chin up and asked, "What happened, child?"

Her tears streaked into the dirt on her cheeks which she rubbed with a grubby fist. "There were *strigoi* in the castle. Mama and Papa helped burn them up in the castle today because the priest said we had to, but one got away. Papa was k-killed when part of the castle fell down on him. Mama told me to hide when the monster came. It was flying."

Razvan wondered if it was him or his brother she saw. Before he had a chance to ask, the door was thrown open, and a blood-curdling scream rent the small space. The child's mother had returned. He forced his will upon her, hoping that hers wasn't strong enough to fight him. Luckily, she seemed desperate for any reassurance, and he felt the pull of his mind upon hers.

"I mean you no harm, but you are in danger here. You must take the child and leave this place." He detached his purse from his money belt and handed it to the astonished woman.

"But my husband!" Her mind struggled against him. "He needs to be laid to rest!"

"I will attend to that for you, madam," he said. "But first, you must pack your things."

While mother and daughter obeyed Razvan's command, he fetched a container of ale from a shelf and two crude wooden cups. He filled them and turned from view to pierce his finger with a fang. He allowed a few drops of his blood to fall into the cups. It wouldn't Mark them permanently, but the protection would hopefully last until they were safe in another *ţări*.

After he helped them load their meager possessions on a horse-drawn wagon, he asked the mother, "Have you seen a man that looks like me, only with less of a beard?"

The woman nodded. "Yes. That is why you frightened me so. I thought you were he." She shuddered. "He was *mad*."

"Where did you see him?" he demanded.

"By the ruins of the castle." She grabbed his arm. "But do not go there! It is dangerous."

Razvan laughed bitterly, "I will be safe. If you see him again, tell him his brother is looking for him."

He slapped the horse's flank and sent them galloping off before she could reply.

Razvan returned to the ruins. Radu was not to be found. He searched until dawn. He searched the next day and the next, never guessing that he wouldn't see his twin for nearly seven hundred years.

Jayden came back to herself. Her pillow was soaked with tears for Razvan's suffering. It seemed she could still smell the smoke from the fire that burned his parents to death. If she had a time machine, she would have gone back in time and killed that bitch Uta herself. The woman had caused the deaths of a family and split two brothers apart.

But Jayden was going to try to bring them back together. Through Razvan's memories, she'd seen Radu and heard his voice. Through those memories, she knew him. Now she was going to try to find him with her mind.

She took another deep breath, let it out slowly, and focused on Radu Nicolae. The sound of his voice, his face, identical to Razvan's except that his eyes held more laughter. In and out, she breathed, focusing her energy to a pinpoint. Her skull began to throb, and she realized she was clenching her teeth. Jayden forced herself to relax a little. She tried something else. Keeping her focus on Radu, she flexed her powers, then willed them to cast outwards as if she were fishing. In a way, she was.

Her metaphysical seeker drifted out for what felt like a thousand miles. It seemed like she could touch people across the globe. Her inner vision blurred, and again she was propelled towards something or someone. As her sight cleared, Jayden heaved a sigh of disappointment.

Again, she found herself with the vampire Delgarias. Again, he looked up at her and smiled. And again he shook his head and pointed, this time to the left, and she was blown away under the currents of a phantom wind.

Then it happened. There was a tug on Jayden's psychic line, a feeling that it had grabbed something. It was so sudden that she nearly dropped the connection in her surprise. Slowly, shades and colors crept into her vision.

Radu lay on a stone slab in a cavernous chamber deep underground. The room was full of cobwebs and ancient debris, chunks of rotting wood, crumbled bits of rock. A thick layer of dust lay like a blanket over everything. The stone walls were spotted with a patina of scorch marks, chillingly familiar.

Jayden drew her power closer to Radu's still form. Her mind brushed against his. She slipped under the very surface of his thoughts.

Radu had been sleeping for six-hundred and seventy-three years...but now he was preparing to wake, to face the world again...and to seek—

Jayden gasped as she suddenly realized where Radu was. He had been resting under the ruins of Castle Nicolae this entire time!

Radu's eyes opened, and narrowed. It was like he could see her! His mind clenched onto hers like a vice. In a way, he had. His force built up like rumbling thunder, and he shoved her out. She slammed back into herself with such force that it was like being thrown against a wall. Black spots danced across her vision, and her inner sight faded like a dying sun.

Seconds later, her eyelids fluttered open, and she placed a shaking hand over her pounding heart. She had found Radu!

Chapter Eighteen

When Jayden awoke, Razvan's side of the bed was empty. She hoped he'd only gone hunting rather than having left again for Spokane. It would be agony to wait that long to tell him her revelation. She practically leaped out of bed to open the closet door. She wanted to look her best when she told him what he had been longing for centuries to hear.

After an eternity of deliberation, she settled on a dark green velvet dress. The matching shoes were uncomfortable, but it was a gorgeous outfit. Her hands shook as she buttoned up the dress and imagined various scenarios of Razvan's responses to the news that she had found Radu.

She longed to see him smile and give a sign of the enthusiastic boy he used to be. Maybe he would sweep her up in his arms and say, *"Jayden, I knew you could do what all others have failed. I am glad I chose you. Will you stay with me forever?"*

Jayden paused and made a face. No, that was a little melodramatic. He would likely be a little more formal, maybe kiss her hand and bow before saying, *"Jayden, you have done me a great service. How may I repay you?"*

No, too polite for him. The most likely case would be that he would incline his head slightly and favor her with his sinister smile and a pat on the head. Still, she knew he'd be overjoyed. Jayden frowned in self-disgust at her naked desperation for the slightest scrap of affection from him. She didn't dare allow the fantasy of the three words she ached to hear: *"I love you."*

After what felt like the longest hour of her life, Razvan returned home from his hunt.

"So, what is this momentous news you have for me?" Razvan asked once they were alone in their room.

He smiled down at her. He was so handsome it nearly made her heart stop.

"I've found Radu!" she said, unable to conceal the pride from her voice. Now he would feel something for her. She looked up at him in happy anticipation for his reaction.

The vampire's face paled. All semblance of expression vanished. For a moment, he resembled the corpse he was fabled to be.

"What?" he whispered.

"He's still in Romania, sleeping beneath the ruins of your family's castle." Jayden smiled, pleased at his surprise. She must have succeeded far beyond her expectations. "Oh, Razvan, he's going to wake soon!"

He moved forward in a flash and grabbed her arms. "How do you know about my family's castle? How do you know any of this?" His grip was like a vise.

Jayden was suddenly nervous. She knew he would be surprised, but he seemed almost angry. Still, she took a deep breath and plunged on, hoping he wouldn't break her arms. "I used my power to see into your memories when you slept. Eventually, through your visions of Radu, I was able to make enough of a connection with him to sense his location. He's been under those ruins all this time. You both have suffered so much and—" She moved to embrace him, and he thrust her away. She looked up at him in hurt confusion.

As his eyes narrowed and turned to that eerie glittering black, her throat went dry. Yeah, he was pissed.

"*You invaded my mind?*" Razvan growled.

Jayden took a trembling step back. She didn't expect him to see it *that* way. "Y-yes, but…but I only wanted to help."

"I didn't ask for your help," he snarled. "And if I had, I certainly wouldn't want you to go about it in such a sneaking, invasive manner!"

"I'm sorry!" She fought back tears. "I didn't mean to…to…" Jayden stumbled over her words. She *did* mean to invade his mind. She just didn't mean to make him mad about it.

Razvan didn't seem to care either way. He turned away from her and strode to the door.

"We will discuss this later," he said over his shoulder before the door slammed with a crash that nearly shook the house.

What the hell just happened? Jayden sank to her knees and gave in to her burgeoning tears.

Razvan strode up the stairs, fists clenched so tight his nails drew blood. He passed Silas in the living room. Silas opened his mouth to ask what was wrong, but Razvan held up a hand to ward off his questions and continued out of the house.

She knows, his mind repeated in time with his rapid steps down the frosty road. *She knows everything!* Never in all of his centuries of existence had he allowed anyone to know of his past. To know the pain he'd suffered, his foolishness in killing the woman that Radu loved rather than exposing her as the woman who'd betrayed him. His mistake had caused the deaths of their parents and, until now, no one had ever known that Razvan had been the one to set in motion the events of their destruction.

Even after nine hundred years, he heard his own voice: *"Let's go to the village, Radu."* If they hadn't met their birth-family and formed a centuries-long bond, his parents would likely still be alive, and his twin wouldn't be in a coma of grief.

His breath made transparent clouds before him as he walked down the steep hill. Razvan shivered and wished he'd brought a coat. The cold wouldn't kill him, but it was damn uncomfortable. When he reached 15th Street, he looked north, then south, having no idea where to go, only that he needed to be alone, that he needed to think. His feet continued to carry him south and then west until he found himself in front of the Powder River Saloon.

Razvan grasped the smooth elk antler handle and the door opened with its signature groan. The bartender, a pretty older woman he didn't recognize, greeted him and was quick to bring a cup of coffee. Though the bar was practically abandoned, she seemed to sense that he wanted solitude and returned her attention to a football game on TV after he paid, giving him a small chiding remark over his lack of a coat.

He wrapped his hands around the hot mug, grateful for its warmth. He still couldn't believe Jayden's audacity in invading his mind, in doing what all others feared to attempt. With Selena, Silas, and countless other psychics, he'd fed them his blood and revealed to them only his happiest memories with his twin, never letting on to the truth that it was his fault that Radu was missing.

But Jayden knew. Jayden, the half-mad waif he picked up in a stinking alley and committed to the dangers of his world. Jayden, a woman who was so powerful that she had been able to connect to a vampire's mind through another's. His lips curved in a rueful smile. Despite his anger at her violation, he was impressed.

He sighed and reached into his pocket for his pipe and tobacco, and unwittingly, his mind crept back to her revelation. Jayden's eyes had been so open and shining with adoration as she told him what she'd done.

As he loaded and lit the pipe, a low, throbbing pain began to pulse in his gut. Razvan frowned and shifted uncomfortably on his bar stool.

He'd been a little harsh with her, he admitted, taking a deep draw on his pipe. She had truly been trying to help him. Jayden didn't know that four hundred years ago, Silas had made enough of a connection to Radu to determine that he wanted nothing to do with his twin. Or that after another three hundred years, Razvan finally reconciled himself to that fact.

Yet now, Jayden had discovered his brother's exact location. It was hard to believe that Radu had been under the ruins of their old home all this time. Though in retrospect, it made sense.

When his coffee had cooled a moment, he sipped the acrid beverage to warm his lips. Yes, he had been overly harsh with Jayden. In truth, another emotion had overridden his anger at her intrusion: fear. A low growl built in his throat at the debilitating emotion, but it would not leave. The facts continued to haunt him.

It was possible that Radu was still furious at him for killing the woman he loved. If his twin knew that there was a woman Razvan cared about…. He shook his head in a futile attempt to ward off fear's icy fingers. Suddenly he wasn't so eager for Radu to awaken. Jayden was already in enough danger from Selena…yet another folly of his past.

He would have to apologize to Jayden… but not too much. After all, perhaps his behavior towards her would be useful in dampening her dangerous infatuation with him. And as much as her adoration pleased him, he would have to resist succumbing to her charms. Razvan sighed and took another draw from the pipe, mentally tracing the curves and hollows of Jayden's body. Such a thing would be easier said than done.

The bar door emitted its gravelly groan, and Razvan was mildly surprised to see Max stroll in. He hid a smirk from the aging mechanic. Had Akasha been carrying tales?

"Hey, I didn't expect to see you here!" Max said jovially as he plunked down on the barstool next to him.

It seemed his presence was a happy accident. The man's cheeks were flushed from the cold, but his heavy breathing was somewhat alarming. The vampire decided to stay with him for a while.

As he listened to Max's tirade about the inefficiencies of the local parts store, Razvan tapped out his pipe and formulated his apology. It was difficult, for apologies were not something he was accustomed to.

Jayden's heart leapt in surprise when Razvan came into the library. She'd been hanging out with Akasha and struggling to read in a vain attempt to shut out the pain of Razvan's angry reaction to her confession. And now was the moment. He was going to send her away. She knew it. It was time to go back to the streets and cold sleepless nights in her car.

He dipped his head and shoulders in a stiff bow. This time she could detect no sarcasm in the gesture, but there was something else.

"I apologize for my currish behavior earlier. I overreacted." His words were as rigid as his stance and gave the impression of a rehearsed speech. "I would also like to thank you for locating my brother. I am certain the information will prove useful in time. You have my gratitude."

He favored her with another overly formal half-bow and left the room before she could form a response.

Akasha's mouth hung open, and the book she held looked in danger of falling off her lap. "What the fuck was *that*?"

Jayden forced a weak laugh. "I don't exactly know."

Her friend blinked at her with amethyst eyes that were so penetrating that Jayden confessed the story of how she entered Razvan's mind and found Radu. When she finished, she shook her head. "And after all that time being in his head, I still can't figure him out."

Akasha gave an indifferent shrug. "He's always been a mystery. I think he prefers it that way. But I know he likes you, so don't worry, he may be pissy for a while, but he'll come around."

As it turned out, Akasha was wrong. Razvan avoided her for the next two weeks. The vampire spent most evenings in Spokane. The few times he was around, he treated her with deferential courtesy when she spoke to him and otherwise ignored her. Max and Akasha observed Jayden's futile attempts to mask her hurt with growing outrage, whereas Silas seemed to grow more cheerful every evening. If his kindness to her had not remained during their training sessions, Jayden would have suspected that the Lord of Coeur d'Alene didn't like her. But his regard seemed to have grown, which made his joviality in the face of her pain all the more confusing.

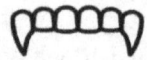

After the evening worship session, Selena summoned Lionel and Michael, her two most trusted apostles. She allowed them to remain on their knees a moment longer than necessary, reveling in their loyalty and adoration. At last, she bade them rise and held up her arms for one of them to remove her ceremonial robe.

As Michael gently untied the sash, she shrugged out of the garment and spoke, idly tugging on a lock of hair. "The deadline has arrived, and our enemies have failed to deliver what we have demanded. They must be punished. Who will go forth and deliver our wrath?"

"I will, my lord," they both chorused and fell to their knees.

Such devotion was music to her ears, but she had already chosen her emissary.

"Rise, dear Lionel," she said and stroked his short blond hair, enjoying the sight of such a powerful male bowing to her.

Michael's lower lip jutted out petulantly, and Selena suppressed her amusement. He would be placated when she related the details of her commands to Lionel.

As her chosen apostle departed to fulfill his mission, Selena turned to Michael, placing a gentle hand on his cheek. "You see now? I have much greater plans for you."

Michael rose and took her hand, bringing it to his lips. "Indeed, my lord, and I shall be overjoyed to obey."

Chapter Nineteen

Razvan's fingers dug into his palms deep enough to draw blood. He had found the spy. A mirthless laugh escaped his lips as he flew over his city towards his prey. He was a fool. Doubly so, since not only had he not considered that particular vampire, but also because it had taken him so long to figure it out. Snowflakes blew into his eyes, but they didn't burn half as much as his rage to think of the danger Jayden had been in.

He drifted closer to his quarry, fangs bared in predatory anticipation. Flesh would tear, and blood would flow. The traitor would be nothing more than a butcher's leavings before he would be satisfied…if ever.

Razvan reared up, ready to dive upon his victim when his heart suddenly seized up in his chest, and searing pain exploded behind his eyes. The Mark between him and Jayden flared up, shrieking in urgency. Something was happening to Jayden.

He swerved east so abruptly that a gust of wind sent him twisting through the air in a sickly spiral. For a moment, Razvan didn't know what was up or down. Clawing madly at the wind, he regained equilibrium. With a deep breath, he concentrated on the Mark. Nothing indicated that Jayden was hurt or in danger but the sense of urgency hammered at his psyche with an ever-increasing tempo.

Casting a regretful look over his shoulder at the spy, Razvan resumed his flight back to Coeur d'Alene. The matter would have to be dealt with later. For now, Jayden needed him. Unfortunately, the December wind was against him, and he had to fight for every inch of distance. Teeth gritted against the biting cold, Razvan only hoped he could get to her in time.

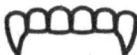

Monday evening, Jayden was surprised to see Akasha wander past the dining room and into the kitchen to grab a beer. Silas was hunting, and Razvan was gone—again. She thought she'd been alone.

"What are you doing home?" Jayden asked, putting down a book on Romanian history. "I thought you had to work."

Akasha opened her beer and slumped into the chair across from her. "I had a splitting headache earlier, so Max is covering for me. The winterization rush is almost over, so we've been pretty dead," she added defensively. "Is Razvan in Spokane again?"

Jayden couldn't hold back a sigh. "Yeah."

Akasha gave her a sympathetic look that nearly brought a lump to her throat. "Well, he is the Lord of Spokane, and that's a way bigger city than Coeur d'Alene, so I imagine he's twice as busy as Silas."

"Yeah, but why doesn't he take me with him?" Jayden hated the frustration in her voice. "I mean, I've never even seen his home. What if he's got someone else there?"

"I don't think that's it," Akasha said quickly. "Actually, I'm starting to wonder if there isn't something else going on. Razvan's always been an evasive bastard, but lately, Silas seems to be taking a page from his book…"

Jayden didn't hear the rest of it. Images were superimposed upon her sight, and she closed her eyes and was sucked into a vision.

She saw inside the shop area of Resurrection Wrenches. Max's back was turned to her. He was bent over the engine compartment of a little Honda, grunting and cursing as he worked. Something crept up behind him. He turned and dropped his wrench. His scream echoed against the cinderblock walls.

The vision faded, and she opened her eyes to see her friend staring at her with a perplexed frown.

"Akasha!" Jayden cried. "We have to get to your shop now!" She bolted up out of her chair so fast that it crashed to the floor.

"What?" Akasha asked, looking at Jayden like she lost her mind.

"Something's happening! I heard Max screaming. We have to go *now*!" She ran out of the dining room without looking back.

Akasha needed no further urging and beat Jayden to the garage door. She grabbed her keys as Jayden got in the passenger side of the Roadrunner and pushed the garage door opener. Akasha got in, and the engine roared to life. She had barely closed the door before she gunned it into reverse. Metal squealed as the Roadrunner shot out of the garage, scraping its roof on the slowly opening door.

As the car catapulted down Cherry Hill, Jayden wondered fleetingly if Akasha would kill them both before they made it to Resurrection Wrenches. When they reached 15th Street, and the speedometer climbed to sixty in the 25 mph residential zone, cops were added to her worries. By the time they reached Sherman

Avenue, and Akasha ran the red light as she turned right and swerved, narrowly missing a Dodge Ram, Jayden hardly noticed. She was overcome with a sinking dread that they were too late.

The shop was quiet when the Roadrunner screeched to a stop in the parking lot.

Too quiet.

Akasha flew out of the car, leaving the door hanging open. Jayden followed, but closed her door. Her new friend could be touchy about her cars. The women ran to the shop. Akasha threw the door open and bolted through the small customer area into the service bays.

Akasha's blood-curdling scream signaled the worst and stopped Jayden's heart. She closed her eyes, not wanting to see what happened, but traitorously, they opened.

"Max!" Akasha shrieked and ran to her mentor.

Max lay slumped against his toolbox. His skin was a chalky gray.

Akasha seized him by the shoulders and shook him. "Max, wake up! Please wake up!" The desperation in her voice was gut-wrenching.

"Akasha!" Jayden cried. "Check his pulse!"

Akasha didn't listen and continued to shake him as his head rolled around his shoulders as if his neck were broken.

"Stop! You might hurt him." That got through to her, and she stopped, though Jayden was quickly suspecting that the man was beyond hurting.

Slowly she walked to Max's unconscious form and placed trembling fingers against his neck to feel for a pulse. His flesh was cool and rubbery-feeling. There was no indication of a heartbeat underneath her touch. She noticed a faint mark on his ashen neck that was quickly fading. As her fingers grazed it, a vision assailed her, and this time she didn't fight it.

A tall, emaciated vampire approached Max. A fanatical fire roared from his dead gray eyes.

"I have a message for your master," he said.

Before Max could reply, the vampire was upon him in an inhuman burst of speed. His fangs plunged deep in the mechanic's throat.

Before the vision faded, Jayden caught his name. "His name is Lionel," she muttered.

"What?"

Jayden didn't answer. There was a piece of paper in Max's right hand. She pulled it from his stiff fingers. It was a note.

"*We warned you,*" it said simply.

"Oh, God," she whispered, her throat almost too tight to speak. "I think he's dead. I think they killed him."

"Nooooooo!" Akasha screamed, nearly drowning out the sound of another car pulling into the parking lot.

Jayden pulled her phone from her coat and dialed 9-11. Akasha grabbed a pry-bar and turned to face the door, crouched into a feral fighting stance. If the person coming wasn't a friend, they were in for a world of hurt.

Silas's welcome form filled the doorway just as the 9-11 operator answered. Jayden wasted no time explaining the situation, despite the unfriendly look Akasha threw her before rushing into her husband's arms.

"I'm at Resurrection Wrenches on the corner of 15th and Sherman. There's a man unconscious, probably dead. Please, hurry!" She hung up before the operator could ask her name.

"What the fuck are you doing?" Akasha demanded.

"We can't just deal with a dead body ourselves," Jayden said. "Besides, maybe he's not dead, maybe they can help."

"She's right, my love," Silas said. "Also, we need to come up with an explanation as to why we are here. I highly doubt that you ladies decided to randomly drop by." He looked at Jayden. "I presume you had a vision as well?"

She nodded. "Yes, it must have come from our practice sessions. This was in his hand." Jayden handed him the note.

Silas scanned the message, and then his eyes fluttered closed. Jayden had no doubt that he was seeing the same scene that she had when she'd touched Max's body. When his eyes opened again, he looked at her, silently pleading for cooperation.

"Call my phone, Jayden," the vampire commanded. "That way, it's on record that you called me afterward."

Quickly, she obeyed, grateful for his stabilizing calm and logic. His ringtone was "Dead Man's Party" by Oingo Boingo. Both she and Silas flinched at the morbid incongruity of the tune. He shut off the call in mid-ring and turned to Akasha. She'd gone frightfully pale and was muttering under her breath.

"But he didn't get his tattoo finished," she said. "It was a bitchin' nautical star, and the color stills needs filling in. And we need him on our team for the dart league this spring. And we were supposed to—" Her words cut off, and she dropped the pry-bar and ran to Max. She threw her arms around the body and cried in thick, hitching sobs.

The metallic clang of the dropped tool faded and gave way to the sound of approaching sirens.

Why did they do this? Jayden sent the thought to Silas.

Later, was his curt answer.

The firemen arrived first with the police at their heels. At first, Jayden didn't know the purpose of the firemen until she realized that they were trained paramedics. They were the ones to declare Max dead. The police questioned the three of them. While Akasha stood there in a grieved stupor, Jayden explained that she and Akasha came to the shop to bring a tool he needed. and she called Silas when they found the body.

"And what tool did you bring him?" one of the officers asked, voice laden with suspicion.

Jayden's fist clenched, and she had to bite her tongue to keep from voicing an outraged retort.

To her surprise, Akasha spoke up. "He needed this pry bar." She picked the tool up from the floor. "I had it at home when I was changing the C.V. axles on Jayden's Camry." Her voice was monotone and rusty as if she hadn't spoken in ages.

The discovery of a dead body was not like on T.V. and in movies. There was no media circus, and since the officials seemed to believe that Max had died of natural causes, nobody put up any police tape. They were, however, made to stand outside in the cold for over an hour before a plainclothes detective arrived to do a cursory examination. Then they were questioned for another hour before the coroner finally showed up with his bland white van and gurney.

Jayden was worried about Akasha. The woman was visibly alternating between cold shock and white-hot anger. Her tenuous hold on her rage became apparent when the cops asked her for the second time with patronizing disbelief to verify that she was the owner of the shop.

"What, you don't think a woman can turn a wrench, much less run a business?" Her eyes seemed to shoot amethyst sparks. "My best friend, my business partner, practically my surrogate father is dead, and you're being all petty and sexist? Who the fuck do you think—"

Silas put a hand on her shoulder and pulled her close. To the detectives, he calmly asked, "Will there be an autopsy?"

The detective glanced at Akasha and coughed in embarrassment. "Yes, as this was an unattended death, that's standard policy. Do you have any reason to believe that Mr. Gunderson didn't die of natural causes?"

Before Akasha could speak, Silas squeezed her shoulder and replied, "We just want to be sure that nothing…out of the ordinary happened."

The coroner and the paramedics came out then, wheeling the sheet-covered gurney. Jayden cursed them for their lack of tact in neglecting to give a warning. The sight of Max's still shape underneath the white cloth was guaranteed to bring nightmares for many days to come. It had to be much worse for Silas and Akasha, who had known him for so much longer.

The stress eventually became too much for Jayden. Her shields dissolved with a tangible tremor, and slowly but with increasing intensity, the visions began to encroach upon her consciousness. From the EMT's secret porn addiction to the coroner's Vietnam flashbacks, she was assaulted with psychic vibes. She nearly wept with gratitude when Silas took her elbow and led her away.

Chapter Twenty

Jayden and Akasha climbed into Silas's Barracuda and left the Roadrunner at the shop after locking up. Akasha was in no shape to drive. She seemed almost catatonic with shock and grief. It killed Jayden to see the contrast from the tough, no-nonsense woman she'd grown to admire.

Razvan was waiting for them on the front porch when they arrived home. Jayden's heart leapt at the sight of his beloved form, illuminated in the darkness by the embers of his pipe.

She got out of the car and nearly stumbled on the driveway. Her legs turned weak and rubbery, and she braced herself with a hand on the car's roof before he arrived to steady her with a firm grip on her hips. She felt like a shell-shocked victim of a nuclear war.

A wordless cry escaped her lips as she flung herself into his arms. The support of his warm hard body and the strength of his arms around her felt like a healing elixir. He could ignore her all he wanted later if only he would continue to hold her now.

"What has happened?" he asked, his eyes taking in their grave expressions.

"Max is dead," Silas said. "One of Selena's servants killed him. The bastard was smooth enough to make it look like a heart attack, so I am uncertain if there is an opportunity for possible redress with the Elders." He went over to the passenger side of the car, opened the door, and lifted Akasha out of her seat.

She whimpered and struggled for a moment before relaxing in her husband's arms. Jayden and Razvan followed them into the house. Once they were settled in their usual seats around the dining room table, Silas filled Razvan in on the details while continually darting worried glances at his wife.

Akasha slumped in her seat. Her face was a chalky white, and her eyes looked glazed and feverish. Jayden had just turned to tell Silas that perhaps his wife should go to the hospital when a piercing scream rent the air, followed by a crash.

"We have to go after her. Selena must die. I'll kill the bitch myself!" Akasha had jumped out of her seat and tossed her chair aside. She spoke with rapid-fire demands. "Come on, I'll drive."

"I'm sorry, lass," Silas said softly. "But we can't do things that way. It's exactly what she expects, and no doubt she has a trap waiting for us. I will contact the Elders and inform them what she has done. We will do things by the book for now, and if that fails, we will come up with a plan." His eyes held hers, despite her fury. "I swear to you, my love, Selena will answer for this tragedy, just not right now."

Akasha's shoulders rose and fell with her rapid breaths. She closed her eyes and threw back her head. An agonized, animalistic howl escaped her lips.

Then chaos struck.

With a roar of rage, Akasha's fist struck the mahogany table. It cracked with a nightmarish sound that promised to reverberate in one's skull for near eternity.

Jayden and Razvan had a second to get up and move out of the way before she flipped it over like a piece of cardboard. Then she grabbed a chair and slammed it against the wall, heedless of the flying splinters. One cut a gash in her forehead, but Akasha didn't seem to notice.

She screamed, and before the agonized sound faded, she took a hitching breath and screamed again until it was one endless, blood-chilling siren.

Razvan pulled Jayden further away, his arms wrapped protectively around her.

Akasha grabbed one chair after another, throwing them, smashing them into the wall, into the floor.

Silas called her name, but she didn't hear him. Silas's wife was gone and in her place was a juggernaut of demonic destruction.

Her husband had to dart out of the way when the chandelier came crashing down, narrowly missing his head.

When all the chairs were decimated, Akasha began to punch the wall. She pounded hole after hole into the sheetrock. Blood ran down in her eyes and coated her hands. Drywall dust caked her face until she was an unrecognizable monster. Still, she screamed, the audible razors of rage and pain piercing the psyches of her helpless spectators.

Jayden could only stand there slack-jawed at the insanity and destruction before her. Her heart went out to Silas, who stood impotent before his wife's grief and rage.

After what felt like hours, Akasha's screams died down, and she collapsed. Silas sighed in pained relief and carried her to the couch before he called the doctor.

"Is she going to be okay?" Jayden asked worriedly as she looked at Akasha's mangled hands. They were a swollen bloody mess, resembling something to be thrown away at a butcher shop.

Silas looked up at her as he bathed his wife's face with a damp washcloth. "Her body will heal fast, but her mind... It will take time. She is strong, but she's suffered a terrible blow. Max was like a father to her."

Jayden frowned. "But her hands! It looks like she'll never be able to hold a wrench again."

Razvan touched her shoulder. "Don't worry. Her hands will be fine. You'll see when the doctor gets here."

Dr. Greenbriar arrived soon afterward. His brows rose for a split second at the sight of the decimated dining room and Akasha's ravaged hands before composing his features into bland professionalism. He opened his classic black medical bag and laid out three syringes on the coffee table. Jayden looked away when he administered the first shot.

Akasha jerked up with a cry of pain, then lapsed back into unconsciousness. She barely stirred when the doctor administered the other shots, one in each hand, presumably to numb them. Silas offered Greenbriar a vague explanation of what happened as Akasha's hands were cleaned with brisk efficiency. The tale was hardly necessary, since the wreckage of the dining room loomed in plain sight.

Jayden wondered how the doctor would be able to tell where the bones were broken without an X-ray, but it seemed that Jonathon Greenbriar had powers of his own.

He grasped one hand at a time and closed his eyes. His pupils darted under the lids as if he was in REM sleep, but Jayden knew what he was doing. She could almost feel it. Jonathon was *seeing* the breaks. Just as she'd seen that girl's tubal pregnancy at the Rage of Angel's concert. Silas met her eyes with a silent question, and she nodded.

We will have to discuss this with Jonathon at a later time, his mind whispered to her. *I didn't forget.*

After Dr. Greenbriar completed his examination, he went about bandaging the minor cuts and stitching the worst ones. Carefully, he wrapped Akasha's hands in a complex network of splints and bindings.

Jayden thought he was finished, but then the doctor pulled out two more syringes and asked Silas to roll up his sleeve. She watched with astonishment as he drew the vampire's blood into the syringe and then injected it into each of Akasha's hands.

"Our blood has incredible healing powers," Razvan whispered in her ear.

Despite the terrible events of the evening, her traitorous body stirred at his voice. She averted her heated face from his gaze and focused on Silas, who was writing a check for Jonathon.

"She should be healed in about three days. I'll give you some syringes so you can give her an injection every evening after you feed." Yet again, the doctor reached into his black bag of prescription tricks. "Here are some pain killers with a sedative effect. With her metabolism, I'd say she could have one every four hours."

Jayden's brows rose in curiosity as to what he'd prescribed, but Silas pocketed the pills before she could glimpse the label. The doctor turned to her, and before she could say a word, he had his stethoscope and blood pressure cuff out.

"Now let's see how the other mortal is faring."

Jonathon examined her for what felt like forever. The way one of his fangs peeked out from under his upper lip as he inspected her pupils was unnerving. She couldn't stop shaking.

Finally, he was finished. "She's in shock, but it's a fairly mild case. I recommend a hot bath, fluids, and at least twelve hours of rest." The black bag opened once more, and again he handed Silas a bottle of pills. "Give her one of these. She may have another if symptoms persist. And *don't*, for God's sake, mix these up with

the ones I've prescribed Akasha," he admonished. "I have a stomach pump at my clinic, but I would rather not use it."

Silas smiled. "I don't think we have to worry about that." He tossed the pills to Razvan. "She's his charge, after all."

Jonathon looked immediately flustered at that remark. "I knew that, my lord. I sensed his Mark on her. It's just that—"

"Don't worry, Jonathon, you followed the correct protocol." Silas gave him a reassuring grin.

Protocol? Jayden wondered.

Razvan sensed her confusion. "Since Silas is the Lord of this City and we are in his home, he is, in an official sense, in charge of us. If we were in my home, the good doctor would have spoken to me regarding Akasha's and your treatment."

"What's your home like?" she asked, unable to hide her curiosity.

He smiled grimly and replied, "Empty." The vampire fell silent and did not indulge her further.

The doctor bowed to all three of them and said his goodnights. Immediately Razvan brought her a glass of water and a very familiar blue pill.

"Valium? Seriously?" Her voice was a squeak of outrage. "He thinks I need Valium?"

"Doctor's orders, Jayden," Razvan said with a forceful edge in his tone.

"Please, lass," Silas added. "I've been blocking your mind from outside influence for over an hour. It has taken some effort. The pill will help."

Jayden immediately felt like an ass. She hadn't noticed how exhausted Silas looked. It had to have taken a ton of work to block her mind from Akasha's rage. "I'm sorry." She took the pill with no further argument and guzzled down the water, realizing she

was incredibly thirsty. There was an acrid, coppery taste in her mouth, and it was a relief to wash it away.

When she set the glass down, Razvan scooped her up in his arms. Her heart fluttered at his gesture, and she hoped in vain that she wasn't blushing. From Silas's slight, amused smile, it appeared that the hoping was no good.

The vampire carried her down the stairs in a smooth, gentle gait, and once again, she marveled at his incredible strength. But Akasha was strong too. Jayden had no idea how strong her friend truly was, until tonight. She shivered at the memory.

"We'll get you warmed up soon." Razvan's voice rumbled against her ear, and she was too tired to protest.

He had her stripped down and lowered into a steaming bubble bath in record time. Her teeth chattered as the warm water closed over her. She was cold, after all. The pill began to kick in, and she closed her eyes and gave herself up to Razvan's ministrations, reveling in the feel of his touch. It was too bad it was because of the night's terrible events.

Too soon, her bath was over. He dried her off briskly and threw a billowy nightgown over her head.

"Now it's time for bed. And do not forget, you are to rest all day tomorrow." Razvan regarded her with a forbidding frown as he turned down the bed. "If I catch you doing anything strenuous when I awaken…"

"What'll you do? Spank me?" she asked in a heavy, drugged voice.

A ghost of his old rakish smile crossed his lips, but it was tinged with something else. "Now that is an idea."

Once she was in bed, Razvan climbed in and pulled the covers over them both. There could be nothing more comforting than the feel of his arms around her. Still, the circumstances were nearly unbearable.

"I can't believe they killed Max," she said. Her throat tightened, and her eyes burned as the reality crashed upon her. The gruff, kind man that she had met was no longer here. He had never done anything to harm anyone, and yet he was dead because Razvan and Silas pissed some vampires off. He'd been like a father to Akasha. How would she make it without him?

"Poor Akasha," she murmured, head swimming with grief and the Valium's stupor.

"No more talking," the vampire commanded.

She opened her mouth to protest his bossy tone but fell asleep instead.

Chapter Twenty-one

When Jayden's breathing was smooth and steady, Razvan crept out of bed, then joined Silas upstairs. The vampire reclined on the living room couch, staring blankly at the television as he sipped a glass of scotch.

"May I have some of that?" Razvan asked.

Silas blinked at him as if he didn't recognize him. Then comprehension appeared to dawn, and he went to the sideboard to fetch the bottle and another glass.

When Razvan received his drink, he took a tentative sip and grimaced. "This brew is potent but rather unpalatable. I don't suppose you have any *palinka*?"

"What is that?" Silas asked idly.

Razvan sighed, giving up hope of ever tasting the delicious plum liquor from his home country again. "Never mind." He lit his pipe and regarded his friend. "Do you think Akasha will get well?"

Silas closed his eyes as if in a brief prayer. "I hope so. The only thing with which I am certain is that Selena must pay. I contacted my attorney, and after Max's will is read, I'll enlist his aid in preparing a case to submit to the Elders."

"Do you think that will bring any results?" Razvan asked doubtfully.

McNaught's eyes were tight from strain. "I don't know, but I must try."

"And when that fails?" He couldn't keep the sarcasm out of his voice.

Silas narrowed his eyes. "We shall punish her ourselves. Do not worry, old friend. Justice will be served. I know this situation is even harder for you since Selena is after your woman." He lowered his voice. "But you must know that Jayden will be much safer if we can secure a writ of execution for Selena and reinforcements from the Elders to aid in her arrest."

Razvan took a deep draw off his pipe instead of responding. Silas was right, but it didn't make their inaction any easier. He stood up and bowed stiffly. "I should go check on Jayden. I only hope her mind can bear this strain."

The other vampire smiled. "I think she is stronger than you give her credit for."

Razvan frowned. "I am not so certain, Silas. You didn't see her when I found her. Malnourished, psychologically tortured, and desperate to die."

Silas raised a brow and quoted, "*The best steel goes through the fire.*"

"Perhaps." Razvan shrugged noncommittally as he left Silas alone with his whiskey.

His brows drew together as he remembered the spy. That matter remained to be dealt with. Quietly, he made his way downstairs to the room he shared with Jayden. One glance at her fragile, sleeping form brought his rage back, a possessive roar trying to claw its way out.

With trembling hands, he took his pipe from his breast pocket and loaded it as he struggled to grasp control of his temper. As he ignited the tobacco and inhaled the cherry-flavored smoke, rationality gained a foothold. Such impetuous anger was unlike him, he realized with a pensive frown as he sat down in the chair across from the bed. Razvan normally faced problems with a cold calculation that Silas often called Machiavellian.

Lately, he'd been acting on whims. Why? Was it because of the Mark he placed on Jayden? He shook his head and took another deep draw from the pipe, idly chewing on the stem. No, his impulsiveness had begun the night he first laid eyes on the captivating clairvoyant.

That realization was more disturbing than enlightening, so Razvan shunted it away, instead, focusing on the issue with the spy. In a way, the postponement of his destructive rage had been a good thing, for he was forming a better idea.

Jayden awoke at two in the afternoon. She carefully extricated herself from the arms of the sleeping vampire and paused as she heard a thumping noise upstairs. She hurried up the steps, nearly tripping over her nightgown. Another thump came from the kitchen, followed by Akasha's voice, grumbling, and cursing.

A chill ran up her spine. If Akasha went into one of her rages, Jayden had no idea how she would deal with it alone. Very slowly, she walked towards the kitchen.

Akasha spotted her and her expression twisted into a sickly grin. "Jayden, thank God. Could you open a beer for me before I lose my mind?" she chuckled. "Oops, bad wording there." She held up her bandaged and splinted hands.

She nodded cautiously. "Sure.

So far, it seemed that Akasha was in an amiable mood, but if that changed…she suppressed a shiver.

Jayden stubbed her toe on a beer can on her way to the fridge. Another one lay on the floor, leaking through a fizzing hole. It appeared that Akasha had been trying to open them with her teeth. They must have slipped from her grasp. Jayden barely had one beer opened before Akasha sucked it down and asked for another one.

"Are you sure that's a good idea with the pain pills you're on?" Jayden asked worriedly.

"I don't give a shit," Akasha grumbled, a faint spark of rage flickering in her purple eyes. There would be no reasoning with her.

Jayden sighed in defeat. "Okay, I'll open one more for you. If you want any more after that, you'll either have to try your teeth again or take it up with your husband."

There was no more rest for her for the rest of the day. Akasha was a querulous patient. It enraged her that she couldn't use her hands, and the house echoed with her foul language. Jayden sympathized. She doubted that the woman had ever experienced helplessness before. Luckily Akasha's thumbs were okay, or things would have been a lot worse.

By the time they were curled up on the couch with a movie, Jayden was tempted to take another Valium. When Silas and Razvan rose for the night and returned from their hunt, she was happy to leave her charge in someone else's care.

The vampires brought home Vietnamese takeout and practically bullied the women to eat. Once that was finished, Silas gave Akasha another pain pill and tucked her into bed. Razvan didn't say a word to Jayden. He kept darting glances at the door and checking his watch.

The mystery was solved when the doorbell chimed just as Silas returned to the living room.

"Thank God," Silas said. "I was afraid he'd show up when Akasha was still awake."

"Who is it?" Jayden asked as he went to answer the door.

"It's Silas's attorney. He's here to read Max's will," Razvan said. "Akasha isn't ready to deal with this sort of thing."

Jayden agreed wholeheartedly. However, she didn't want her friend kept in the dark forever. "But she'll be informed when she's feeling better, right?"

"Of course," Silas assured her quickly, acknowledging her concern with a slight smile.

The attorney, who was also a vampire, apparently from the way he greeted Silas and Razvan, joined them at the table. Since Jayden was a mere mortal, she was ignored after the introductions were made, and he opened his briefcase and launched into his legal diatribe.

At first, she was able to follow the talk, with all the "whereas" and "bequeaths." Silas and Akasha would get all of Max's money and his share of Resurrection Wrenches, LLC. However, his music collection, which included some valuable records, went to Razvan. And, to everyone's astonishment, his '67 Dodge Charger also went to Razvan, along with a motorcycle that had been entrusted to a friend in California. Max's explanation was included in the will: "Because that son of a bitch needs to learn how to drive." The friend's contact information was included in the paperwork, and a copy of the will had already been sent to him.

Anthony Salazar, attorney at law, was apparently an expert in vampire law as well as human law. Silas explained the circumstances of Max's death to him and asked if there was any legal recourse. The legal jargon was even harder to follow then, but from what Jayden gathered, the lawyer wanted Max's medical records and autopsy report before he could put together the proper paperwork to submit to the Elders.

By the time Mr. Salazar had departed, Jayden's head was swimming from all the details. Apparently, in the vampire world death had just as much if not more red tape.

She was just about to leave to check on Akasha when Silas said, "Jayden, I was hoping you would be able to help me with something."

"Of course!" She was thrilled to have an opportunity to repay him for all he had done for her. It was like a weight off her chest she didn't realize she'd been carrying.

Silas smiled. "There were four cars in Akasha's shop. She's not going to be able to take care of them. I'll collect the work orders later tonight and call the customers. What I need you to do is to call the dealerships around town and arrange for the vehicles to be towed to them for repair. Thankfully, it is winter, and the sun is down before those places close." His eyes narrowed. "I would like you to do your best to be home before dusk. I will send some of my people to guard you when such is unavoidable."

Jayden realized that all of Akasha and Max's customers were vampires. On the heels of that thought came a revelation. Silas and Razvan now trusted her to be out and about alone… Or maybe Razvan just didn't care about her anymore. A lump formed in Jayden's throat before she resolutely forced the self-pitying thought away and returned her focus to helping her new friends.

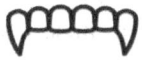

Razvan watched as the last of his vampires filed into the abandoned warehouse. A hundred pairs of preternatural eyes darted nervous glances at their surroundings. He did not have to be their lord to know what they were thinking: *What had possessed him to hold a meeting here instead of the usual plush hotel conference rooms?*

A venomous smile curved his lips. Soon they would rue their curiosity.

Foregoing greetings of any sort, he began, "As you know, matters with our enemy, the Lord of Post Falls, have escalated to most vexing levels, interrupting my business with the Lord of Coeur d'Alene."

After giving his subordinates a moment to digest the obvious, Razvan continued. "In fact, they have escalated so far that we now have a traitor in our midst."

Gasps and hushed whispers floated up to the rafters, but the spy gave no sign of alarm. Keeping his expression bland, he called, "Jake, Hilda, Sarah, and Trey, come forward. I require your assistance in this matter."

Shocked mutters broke out among the audience as the four vampires approached, only thin lines of tension in their spines betraying their trepidation.

Razvan surveyed them one by one. Jake, the Civil War veteran turned ranch hand, regarded him with a fixed green gaze. Hilda, the buxom beauty who was alleged to be German royalty, and served as amicable bed sport last year, stared at him, her eyes grey pools of lust. Sarah…he didn't know her origins, but she numbered among the most expensive assassins in the world. She met his regard unflinching. Though he had decreed all would come unarmed, Razvan would bet money she had a weapon stashed away somewhere on those luscious curves or within her dark silken mass of hair. He hid a wry grin. Sarah and Akasha would likely get along well.

Then there was Trey, a former Navy Seal. He would be as deadly as Sarah, had he her coldness and skills in subterfuge.

Without warning, Razvan seized Jake, sinking his fangs into the vampire's throat. At first, Jake struggled, but he quickly went limp, submitting to his master's authority.

After releasing him, Razvan licked the blood from his lips. "I have learned what I needed. Sarah, Trey, seize Hilda. Jake, you may return to the others."

The vampire's sigh of relief was palpable enough that Razvan's was undetected. Both Jake and Hilda had guarded Jayden and Akasha at the *Rage of Angels* concert. Now that he knew Hilda had been acting alone, he was willing to spare Jake from the carnage that would follow.

Trey and Sarah brought the struggling traitor forward. Razvan met Hilda's gaze, and the savage fury boiled up within him once more.

He had trusted her to guard Jayden, and she'd been acting for Selena all along. A low growl escaped his throat as he struggled to see beyond a red haze of anger.

Gaining control, he addressed the spy. "When did you join my enemy, Hilda?"

Her response was obscured by outraged mutters from the audience.

"What was that?" he asked mildly, an edge of menace creeping in his tone.

Hilda groaned in pain as her captors tightened their grip. "When you cast me aside for that human freak!" Her lower lip stuck out petulantly. "Selena wants her, so at least there will be a place for the girl when you are done with her."

Razvan's eyes narrowed. He'd made poor choices in bed partners before, but this had to top the list. Not wanting to discuss personal matters before his subordinates, he said coldly, "I *Marked* her. Surely you know that means I will never be done with her." He turned to Sarah. "Take out your blade."

Her eyes widened for a split second before she nodded and pulled out something resembling a small sword from a sheath on her spine. Razvan grinned and brought a six-inch switchblade from his pocket and tossed it to Trey.

"Now," he said to Hilda. "You will tell me everything you know about Selena's plans. You will also tell me if there are any more traitors in mine or Silas McNaught's territories."

"Why should I?" Hilda shrieked. "You will kill me either way."

"True," he said agreeably. "But how fast or slow that happens is up to you."

With a nod from their master, Sarah and Trey began cutting. At first, the wounds healed fast, but as the blood loss accelerated, they would mend at a human's rate. The audience shrank back in horror as Razvan questioned Hilda.

He didn't torture her for the information. He could have drunk all he wanted to know from her veins. He tortured her to make an example of her to his people.

Let them witness the results of betraying Razvan Nicolae. Let them see the consequences of endangering what was his.

The smell of blood and raw meat permeated the area, but it was unappetizing. Razvan looked at the babbling crimson-covered mass before him and suddenly thought of Jayden. He pictured her reaction to this interrogation. Her eyes would be huge and luminous with fear, and her lovely mouth would be thinned in disapproval. Crippling shame knotted his gut, making him feel like the monster he was reputed to be.

Razvan held up a hand. "Enough." His voice was raspy.

Trey and Sarah obeyed, blinking at him in curiosity.

"I have another appointment this evening," he half lied. There was much that he needed to tell Silas.

He seized Hilda's bloody wrist and plunged his fangs into the mauled flesh. In seconds, he received the rest of the scant information. In the next second, she was dead. Releasing Hilda's lifeless body, he ordered it disposed of and dismissed his people. They bowed lower than usual and departed with terrified glances and funereal whispers. This did not please him as much as he anticipated, despite his relief that Jayden's safety had marginally improved.

Now alone with his conscience, Razvan realized it would take more than a shower and Listerine to wash away the filth and the foul taste in his mouth.

Chapter Twenty-two

The next few days were hectic for Jayden. She spent long hours on the phone at Resurrection Wrenches, calling car dealerships and scheduling repair appointments, more hours waiting for late tow-trucks, and even longer fielding questions she had no answers for. She knew that Akasha and Max had dealt with ten times more every day on top of their actual duties, repairing cars and her admiration for them grew. On top of handling Akasha's business, she spent hours nursing the lady herself.

Fortunately, the doctor had been right. After three days, Akasha was healed. When the splints and bandages were removed, Jayden's jaw gaped as she stared at her friend's hands. They were wrinkled from the bandages but otherwise perfect. There wasn't even a scar.

Akasha made a beeline for the fridge to get a beer, shouting her thanks to Dr. Greenbriar over her shoulder.

Then came the night of Max's funeral. Jayden had no idea how much Silas had to have paid the preacher and funeral home staff, but it was beautiful. The Forest Cemetery got its name from the tall pines that filled the grounds, and each one was now adorned with gold Christmas lights. Christmas had been Max's favorite holiday. A dozen patio heaters had been arranged around the graveside pavilion to make the December air barely tolerable. Jayden huddled with Razvan, Akasha, Silas, a bunch of other vampires, and almost the entire crowd of the Powder River regulars. There would be a "wake" at the bar afterward.

The preacher swept the crowd with another odd look and opened his bible. Before the sermon began, the roar of motorcycles echoed through the cemetery. Thirteen men on Harley Davidson motorcycles drove slowly down the plowed drive and lined up along the graveside as close as they could go. In unison, they nodded at the preacher to begin. It was more like a ZZ Top music video than a funeral, Jayden thought wildly as she fought to keep her mental shields in place.

The preacher began, and either the standard sermon was not like in the movies, or Silas had twisted some arms to make it extra meaningful and poignant. Jayden struggled to breathe past the lump in her throat while simultaneously keeping her shields in place. The only tear-free face was Razvan's, but even he looked overcome with grief.

When the bible closed, the bikers revved their Harleys like a twenty-one gun salute. Cigarettes were lit, ghostly embers in the darkness. Akasha was surrounded by people offering condolences. She shook like a captive rabbit, and Jayden knew it wasn't just because of the cold. She remembered her friend saying she didn't like crowds. The shivering group dispersed quickly with promises to meet at the bar.

The oldest biker, a tall, slim man with a white beard and an aura of command, stepped off a bike that probably cost as much as a sports car. "Which one of you is Akasha Hope, and which one is Razvan Nicolae?" His voice was deep and booming.

Akasha approached them and lifted the hood of her heavy coat. Razvan followed behind, lighting his pipe.

The biker laughed, a rich bass sound. "You're exactly how Max described you, girl." Without warning, he wrapped Akasha in a bear hug and lifted her.

When he set her down, he turned her to face the other twelve bikers. "This is Akasha, the adopted daughter and business partner Max was always rambling about."

They greeted Akasha like long-lost relatives, embracing her and kissing her cheeks. Jayden watched with a smile, touched by their warmth. From her practice sessions with Max, she recognized nearly half the bikers from his memories. She also knew that he'd vowed never to ride again after his wife had been killed in a motorcycle accident. The leather jacket Akasha wore in the fall had belonged to Max's love.

The leader cleared his throat and turned to Razvan, as if noticing him for the first time. "And you're the man Max deemed worthy of his Harley?" His voice was laced with skepticism as he took in the vampire's urbane looks.

Razvan drew deeply on his pipe, blew out a cloud of smoke, and regarded the aging biker with a sinister gaze. "It would appear to be so." His accent was thicker than normal.

Jayden realized that he was nervous. Silas watched the drama with an amused smile.

The biker held out a leather-gloved hand. "I'm Rusty. Max didn't tell me much about you."

Razvan shook his hand. "Razvan Nicolae. I am a friend of Akasha's husband." He nodded in Silas's direction. "I am quite surprised at Max's gift to me, though I am honored."

Rusty smiled. "Max said you didn't know how to drive. Why is that? Too accustomed to having a chauffeur?" he asked, though not unkindly.

The vampire chuckled. “Something like that.”

“Can we go now?” Akasha said through chattering teeth. “I’m freezing my ass off, and I need a beer.” She turned to Rusty. “You guys are invited to the wake, of course.”

“Sounds good to us,” Rusty said. “We just gotta load up our bikes. The roads were too damn icy. We can show Razvan his new ride as well.”

Two RVs with trailers were parked in front of the cemetery gates. Silas introduced himself while the bikes were loaded. Then Razvan’s motorcycle was revealed. It was beautiful, sleek, and black, with flames carefully airbrushed on the gas tank.

“There she is,” Rusty said. “1976 Harley Davidson Ironhead XLH. You’d better take good care of her, Nicolae.”

“She is beautiful,” Razvan said reverently.

Mourners packed the Powder River. Akasha was offered more beer than even she could drink. The pool table was covered with a cloth, and food was served. Everyone’s love for Max was displayed in the telling of countless stories while his favorite songs were played on the jukebox. They played a dart tournament in his honor with the proceeds going to the college’s motorcycle repair program.

Jayden stayed as long as she could, but eventually, the smoke and noise gave her a splitting headache. She tapped Razvan on the shoulder to ask if they could leave. Before he could reply, Akasha yelled, “Turn the jukebox down!”

The bartender complied with a confused frown, and the bar noise died down to a hush. Everyone looked at Akasha as if she’d lost her mind. Akasha didn’t notice. She watched the TV with a look of horror growing on her face.

“The famous heavy metal band, Rage of Angels, has disappeared,” a news reporter said as photos of the band flashed on the screen.

Akasha gasped, and Silas's gaze jerked towards her, his green eyes filled with obvious terror that his wife would go into another rage. Akasha guzzled her beer and slammed the empty glass on the bar before grabbing Silas's beer and doing the same.

The screen returned back to the news anchor. "They were set to perform a charity concert at the Seattle Center Coliseum last night as a sort of preview to their upcoming tour of their new album, *The Roses are Bleeding.* The group was last seen together in their home in Queen Anne on the third. Their agent, Todd Williams, was the first to notify police when drummer Aurora Lee failed to appear for a commercial shoot for Sketchers Shoe Co."

Jayden glanced worriedly at Akasha, who had just seized her wineglass and sucked it down as if it were water.

The report continued. "Investigations of their home show no signs of forced entry. Anyone with information leading to locating any of the four is encouraged to call our tip line. Alan Winters is on the scene speaking with Dominic Slade, owner of Seattle's famous club, The Mortuary, and longtime friend to the group."

The screen changed to show a posh bar with a prominent Goth theme. Another reporter sat awkwardly at a crimson table as far away as he could be from the man he was interviewing. Jayden couldn't blame him. The owner of The Mortuary was an imposing figure. His tall, lanky form stretched out in the booth. His ears and face were covered in piercings, and his dark purple, well, it wasn't quite a Mohawk…was at least six inches tall. There was something familiar about his dark gray eyes.

"When did you last see any of the members of Rage of Angels," the reporter asked, nearly hyper-extending his arm to reach the club owner with the microphone.

Dominic's voice was stiff and formal despite the lines of worry in the corners of his eyes. "It was the Friday after

Thanksgiving. They played a show. They were supposed to do another one a week and a half from now, on the twenty-first."

"Did any of them give a sign that anything was out of the ordinary?" the reporter demanded eagerly. "Did they mention they have a trip planned?"

For a moment, Dominic looked like he was about to say something, but then he shook his head. The reporter's face fell, and he visibly struggled to focus on his next question.

Silas cursed under his breath. "I better call him."

Jayden realized what was "familiar" about Dominic. He was a vampire. She choked on a hysterical giggle. Perfectly fitting for the owner of a Goth club, albeit a little redundant.

The screen flicked back to the station anchor, and she flashed their tip line phone number once more before launching into the next story without taking a breath. Everyone in the bar began speaking at once. Everyone except for Akasha. Her face was as white as the falling snow outside, and she had a look about her indicating that she didn't quite know where she was.

Jayden's heart clenched in sympathy. It wasn't fair. After what just happened, now Akasha had to deal with this? Silas noticed his wife's condition, and picked her up off her barstool as he fielded questions. Akasha went without a protest.

"We don't know what happened," Silas said firmly to the crowd. "All I know is that I must get my wife home."

Razvan took Jayden's arm, and they followed Silas out the door. Rusty and his biker gang trailed behind. Jayden had forgotten about them and Razvan's bike.

When Silas had Akasha settled in the car, he gave Rusty directions to his home and offered to let them stay the night. The bikers declined, having already reserved an RV park for the night.

Akasha didn't say a word the whole way home. When they arrived, she shambled into the house like a zombie and headed straight to the kitchen to get another beer.

Silas looked like he longed to stop her. Jayden was helpless to do anything to help either. Razvan was outside, helping Rusty and his gang unload his new Harley.

When Akasha settled on the couch and reached for the TV remote, Silas found his voice. "They're not dead, Akasha."

Her head swiveled like a rusty hinge to meet his gaze. "What?"

"I said that they are not dead. But they are very far away from here, farther than I've ever sensed."

He turned to Jayden and explained. "Since I Marked them, I would feel it if any of them were killed or even hurt."

To their relief, a little color returned to Akasha's face.

"That's good," she murmured and began to flip through channels aimlessly.

Silas's eyes began to glow. He stalked towards his wife, suddenly looking terrifyingly dangerous.

Jayden froze to the spot, praying that he wasn't about to do something terrible.

Akasha looked up at him. "What?" she slurred.

"I am sorry, my love, but I must do this," he said roughly.

In a blur of speed, his arms locked around his wife, and his fangs sunk into her neck.

A scream tore from Jayden's throat, and she ran out of the room, heart pounding in her ears.

Razvan came in just then and caught her by the waist. "What is happening?" he demanded.

"Silas is attacking Akasha!" she gasped, unable to believe her words.

Had the entire world gone insane?

Razvan blinked at her panic-stricken face and made for the living room. Jayden took a deep breath and followed him, even as her instincts shrieked at her to get away.

Silas sat on the couch, holding Akasha in his arms. The savage predator seemed to have vanished, leaving in its place the usual, devoted husband.

"I thought she may have been close to alcohol poisoning," he said grimly. "I had to take some of it from her. I am sorry I frightened you, Jayden."

"Um, that's okay," she said lamely, still shaken from his actions.

"Would you please go get a glass of water for when she comes to?" he asked with his usual politeness.

Jayden nodded and rushed off to the kitchen, eager to escape the vampires long enough for her pulse to return to normal.

By the time she returned, and her heart had stopped pounding, Akasha was conscious. She reached eagerly for the water and guzzled the entire glass down in seconds. Unfortunately, it looked ready to come back up.

When Akasha bolted to the bathroom, one hand over her mouth, Silas moved to follow her, but Jayden stopped him.

"I'll take care of her," she told him firmly.

She didn't relish the thought of holding her friend's hair for the next few hours, but some sights were not meant for one's man to see. Jayden only hoped that if their positions were reversed, Akasha would do the same for her.

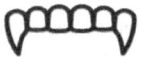

Razvan looked on as Silas put his face in his hands.

"I don't know what to do about her," he moaned. "She's suffered so much. First, Max dies, and now her best friends have vanished. I want to comfort her, but nothing seems to work. She's drawing further away from me every day. We haven't made love in nearly a month."

The confession seemed to suck the life out of Silas, and he slumped at his desk.

Razvan patted his friend's shoulder awkwardly. In the department of comfort, he didn't think he'd do any better. "You are doing your best. And Jayden seems to be helping her quite a bit."

His heart warmed as he thought of Jayden's concern for a woman she'd only met recently. It was hard to believe anyone could be so kind, and even more unfathomable given all the other things Jayden had to worry about…things that were his fault.

He changed the subject in hopes of easing Silas's mind.

"Do you have any idea where Xochitl and the others went?" he asked carefully, more in hopes of detracting Silas from his pain than care for the band. Razvan adored Rage of Angels, but in the face of Jayden and Akasha's plight, they could go to the devil.

The vampire sighed. "I called Dominic while you were unloading your motorcycle."

"And?" Razvan couldn't keep the admiration from his voice. Silas's ability to think and act under stress never ceased to amaze him.

"He said that Xochitl disappeared once before, on Halloween to be exact," Silas said, irritation and worry creeping into his tone.

Razvan blinked. "Why didn't he report the incident to you when it happened?"

Silas sighed in abject irritation. "He wanted to, but the Lord of Seattle dissuaded him because she returned a few days later. He didn't want to cause an unnecessary uproar." He leaned forward. "Here is what is interesting. The last few times she was seen, it appeared that she had a new boyfriend."

"What's so interesting about that?" Razvan asked. "It is about time, in my opinion, though I cannot fathom a man that could keep up with her."

"Dominic said that there was something very odd about him. Nothing could be read from him, and he smelled like power and unfamiliar things." At Razvan's perplexed look, he added, "Dominic couldn't explain what he meant, but he sounded really unnerved by the gentleman. I wish his lord would have let him call, although I wouldn't be surprised if he has more of an inkling as to what is going on than he cares to reveal."

There was a long silence as Razvan loaded his pipe and took a deep draw before regarding Silas intently. "But what do you think of the whole picture? Are they safe? Will they return?"

Silas sighed. "They are safe, and they will return. And when they do, their priorities will no longer be solely revolved around making music. Any more than that, I do not know. Although," he rose and fetched his Scotch from the sideboard, "I believe this incident may be why Delgarias has suddenly turned up missing again."

Razvan raised a brow. "You think he is involved?"

The Lord of Coeur d'Alene nodded and smiled thinly. "Up to his neck."

Chapter Twenty-three

Selena let out another infuriated shriek as she tore through the closet. The signed Rage of Angels tee-shirt had to be in there somewhere! What if it was the artifact with the most power? What if she couldn't find them without it?

Behind her, Rage of Angels memorabilia made a pile on the table, surrounded by burning candles like some sort of shrine to heavy metal. She would touch each item in turn while working herself into a trance in which she hoped to see where the musicians had disappeared to. But this last tee-shirt, which could hold the most of their essence being that all four had touched it, might be the key.

In a panic, she began tearing everything out of the closet. Dresses, scarves, and hats flew over her shoulder as a rhythmic mewling sound escaped her lips. By the time the area was empty, but for a single coat hanger, she was panting and quivering in impotent rage. Someone must have stolen it.

She surged forward to round up her followers and discover the thief, to punish them as she'd never punished anyone before. Then she stopped and cocked her head to the side in girlish confusion, suddenly remembering what she did with the shirt. Her hand crept up to grasp and tug on a lock of hair. The pain helped clear her mind a little more.

That shirt, as well as another, had been worn by the two members of her flock she sent to the Rage of Angels concert in October. The two that failed in their mission and gotten themselves killed by Razvan. She pulled harder on her hair. A hank of hair came free, and she dropped it to the floor indifferently, touching a finger to the bleeding wound on her scalp.

Had Razvan killed them? Or had they run away? They were not the first of her followers to disappear. Selena had assumed that Silas and Razvan had been killing them off…until now. Could it be that her flock was abandoning her? Or even worse, were they now plotting against her? Her eyes darted back and forth, searching for threats in every corner of the room as her fingers crept back up to her scalp to pull at her hair once more.

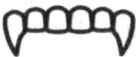

The next evening, the household of Silas McNaught awoke to discover five reporters camped out on their doorstep. Razvan and Silas had to sneak out the back door to get their first meal of the evening while Akasha and Jayden remained hidden in the house.

"This is bullshit," Akasha said for the tenth time. "Why don't they get the hint and leave us alone?"

"It's against the holy code of the press," Jayden quipped half-heartedly as she stirred a pot of beef stew for their dinner.

"Well, they need to leave soon. I'm almost out of beer," Akasha grumbled as she lit another cigarette.

Jayden frowned. "Don't you think you should cut back on the drinking?"

Purple eyes narrowed on her. "Who do you think you are, my mother?"

Jayden sighed and ladled the stew into a bowl. "At least eat something first before you tackle the media in your quest for alcohol."

Akasha rolled her eyes at her, but at least she obeyed and ate two bowls of stew.

The reporters followed them on their beer run. The stress of being tailed was so much that Jayden picked up a small bottle of wine for herself.

They spent the evening cloistered in the living room, drinking and darting annoyed glances at the reporters' attempts to peek in the windows. Akasha didn't mention a word about the disappearance of her friends, and Jayden left her to her silence.

The next afternoon, disaster struck. Silas had scheduled a contractor to assess the damage to the dining room. As Jayden opened the door to let him in, the reporters, joined now by the paparazzi, forced their way in.

Microphones were thrusted into her face. One hit her square in the nose. The reporter holding it was practically salivating.

"Who are you? What is your relationship with the McNaughts? What do you know about the disappearance of Rage of Angels? Where is Akasha McNaught?"

"I…I," Jayden swallowed, suddenly feeling very faint and queasy.

Akasha came down the stairs then, her eyes glittering amethyst flames of rage. "What the fuck are you people doing in my house?" she demanded.

They advanced upon her with their cameras and microphones. "How do you feel about the disappearance of your close friends, Mrs. McNaught? Do you know anything that could lead to them being found?"

"I don't know shit," she growled. "Now get the fuck out before I call the cops!"

Jayden danced back and forth behind her, knowing she would be helpless if Akasha decided to unleash her fury. People could be hospitalized...and Akasha could end up in jail.

To the contractor's credit, he ignored the chaos and headed straight for the dining room, taking notes and doing his job as if everything was normal. Unfortunately, one industrious cameraman snapped pictures at the hole-ridden wall.

Akasha pulled her phone from her pocket. "I'm calling the cops."

Reluctantly, the intruders departed, still calling questions over their shoulders on the way out. Akasha made a beeline for her beer like she was dying of thirst.

The next day, her grieved and angry face was plastered all over the media, along with the trashed dining room.

"*Friend of Missing Metal Band Smashes Wall in Grieved Rage*," the headlines read.

"Those sick bastards," Jayden whispered. Her heart swelled with pity for her friend.

"Yeah," Akasha said sullenly and tossed the paper in the fireplace.

The press continued to harangue them for the next week, which made things difficult, for vampire envoys began to visit Silas to go over the details of Max's murder.

Eventually, the reporters left. Whether it was because Silas threatened to press charges or because they finally believed Akasha didn't know anything interesting, Jayden didn't know or care. She was just happy to be able to go to the grocery store unmolested. They'd been out of cheese for three days.

Akasha didn't seem to care either way. She had fallen into a drunken void of despair.

When Jayden had returned and finished putting the groceries away, she heard Silas and Razvan talking in the office. Her stomach fluttered at the sound of the Romanian vampire's voice. She hadn't seen him for three nights. She hurried to the office and stopped when she heard another voice, this one with a thick British accent. They were not alone.

"I am sorry, Silas," the voice said. "I am afraid there is not enough evidence to prove Selena had a hand in your friend's demise. The autopsy report indicates that all signs point to a heart attack."

"But what about the signs of blood loss?" Silas protested. "Surely we all know what that means."

"All it proves to *us* is that a vampire fed from him shortly before he died. Being that he lived with a vampire, it is not unexpected…and to the mortal authorities, it indicates a sign of anemia, nothing more."

Jayden sucked in a breath. Was this one of the famous Elders Razvan had mentioned? She peeked around the doorway and saw that Silas and Razvan were alone in the room.

They spoke to the British vampire on the computer via webcam. He was startlingly handsome, with long black hair like Silas's and startling silver eyes. It must be a rule that most vampires had to be almost illegally gorgeous, Jayden thought with a small smile.

Razvan turned and glanced at her, unsurprised by her presence. His attention returned to the computer screen as if uninterested.

"I never drank from him, Ian," Silas remained fixed on the monitor, unaware of Jayden's arrival.

"Do you think anyone would believe that?" Ian countered, though not unkindly. "And from what the reports say, you had not Marked Mr. Gunderson, so it is irrelevant either way. They were not directly poaching your property by our laws. I do wish more could be done on our end about this unpleasant situation. Please believe that, McNaught."

"I do believe you," Silas said. "And I believe that things would have worked out better if I could locate Delgarias."

"You are probably correct about that," Ian replied. "But let me give you one more bit of advice from me and a few of the other Elders: You have immunity. Use it. Now I must go."

The computer screen went blank.

Silas sighed and leaned back in his chair as he turned to Razvan. "I figured that things would be this way. At least it sounds like you've made headway ferreting out Selena's spies in your territory. But we need to come up with another plan before the bitch sends us a third note or kills someone else."

Razvan darted another glance at Jayden and quickly looked away. Jayden suddenly realized why he had been spending so much time in Spokane. Relief that he hadn't been sleeping with someone else warred with anger at his lack of communication. She stormed into the room.

"Why didn't you tell me any of this before?" Jayden knew there was a hysterical note creeping into her voice but was helpless to stop it.

Silas looked away, but not before she caught a look of shame on his face.

Razvan was as calm and collected as usual, except that he was also avoiding her gaze.

He tugged on his goatee a little before replying, "I didn't think it was wise with the present condition of your mental state."

"My mental state?" Jayden nearly spluttered in shock as her rage and frustration seemed to boil over. "*My mental state*?" she repeated and stalked closer to the vampire, hands balled into quivering fists. "Your psychotic ex girlfriend just killed an innocent man because she's obsessed with some prophecy and you're concerned about *my* mental state?"

Razvan did not reply. His glittering black eyes were inscrutable and appeared to be focused everywhere but in her direction. The implied shame made an alien kernel of pleasure blossom in her breast.

Akasha came into the room for once without a beer in her hand. "What's going on?"

Silas said gently to Jayden, "Now, lass, we were only trying to protect you. You've been under enough stress, what with learning to control your visions and being exposed to our kind. We thought it prudent to—"

"To keep me in the dark lest I have a mental breakdown and slit my wrists?" Jayden cut him off, panting with rage. The Lord of Coeur d'Alene's discomfort was more obvious, making that inner imp within rejoice. "I think I have the right to know when someone's threatening to kill people because of me. Who the hell do you think you are to decide to keep that from me?"

"He's the Lord of this city," Razvan countered smoothly.

Jayden rounded on him, all pleasure crushed in a new rage of fury. The sanctimonious ass! "Oh, that's how it works. Never mind that he thinks I'm crazy, and his wife has a major drinking problem, but he keeps his head in the sand, refusing to see it!"

She clapped a hand over her mouth, but it was too late.

Silas rose to his feet. His eyes glowed neon green and his fangs bared in a mask of fury.

"You go too far," he growled. "Akasha does not have a problem. She's just been under a lot of stress lately."

"Silas, no!" Akasha spoke for the first time. She met her husband's eyes. Her pupils were dilated with pain and shame. "She's right," she said quietly.

Jayden was stunned silent as Akasha put herself between her and Silas, one hand on her husband's chest.

"I probably do have a bit of a drinking problem," she said, voice trembling. "And I think somehow you must have known that, cuz you've kept me in the dark with the Selena situation along with Jayden."

Silas's lips moved, but no sound came.

Razvan chuckled, but there was no humor in it. "I am surprised we have not yet been subjected to your wrath."

Akasha's cheek dimpled with a half-smile despite the tears in her eyes. "I thought Jayden was handling it just fine on her own."

Jayden's anger dissipated with her friend's obvious pain. Guilt struck her like a sledgehammer. All of this was happening because of her. Max had been murdered, Silas and Razvan's territories were in danger, and Akasha was nearly out of her mind with grief.

"Maybe I should just give myself up to her," she said softly. "Then Selena will leave you all alone."

Razvan's chair clattered to the floor. He bared his fangs and growled, "You will not be going anywhere!"

He charged forward, but Akasha seized his arm.

"Jayden, don't wuss out now. You belong with us," she said, ignoring Razvan though still gripping him. "Come with me to Max's room. We need to talk."

"O-okay," Jayden stammered. All of her courage had fled.

"She's not going anywhere," Razvan repeated with a low growl. "Not after speaking such foolishness."

Akasha turned cold amethyst eyes to him. "Do you want me to break your arm? Because if you keep being an asshole, I will do it. If anyone's mentally unstable right now, it's me…and I mean it. I will break your arm if you don't stop."

Her grip tightened on Razvan's arm, and he winced in pain.

"Akasha, lass," Silas pleaded.

"No," she said as if there were an unspoken argument between them. "Your love and kindness can't fix this." She turned back to Razvan. Her voice softened slightly. "I swear I won't let her go anywhere, so chill."

For a moment, Jayden thought that Razvan wouldn't back down, but there was some silent communication between him and Akasha, and he nodded curtly. Akasha released him and walked out of the room, nodding at Jayden to follow her.

Akasha led Jayden into Max's old room. She plopped on the bed and regarded Jayden with a determined look in her eyes. "You once told me that you wanted to be a counselor, so counsel me."

Jayden gaped. This was the last thing she expected her friend to say. "What?"

"I accept that my drinking is out of control, but hell if I'm going into a bible-thumping twelve-step program or checking into a rehab clinic with Selena's bullshit going on." Akasha lit a cigarette with shaky hands. "You mentioned that you took some college psychology classes, so you're the best shot at help I can get. Are you willing to try? Cuz it's taking all my willpower to stay here talking to you and not get a beer."

"Yes!" Jayden answered before Akasha could bolt from the room. "You just caught me off guard a bit. I'd be happy to help you, but I just don't know how well I'll do because I didn't get my degree."

"Did you drop out because of the visions?" The concern in her voice made Jayden's throat tighten again.

"Sort of. I was homeless and living in my car when the fall semester began, so by then, I wasn't even thinking of school."

Akasha nodded. "That's understandable. So can we start now?"

Jayden sighed. "I guess. Um, go ahead and get comfortable or something." She sat down in an easy-chair near the bed and did her best to look professional and welcoming.

Akasha lay down on the bed in a caricature of the typical Freud patient. "Now what?"

"Well, I think if we explored the reasons for why you drink when you're upset, we might be able to go from there," Jayden told her, hoping that she was doing the right thing.

At that thought, she added, "If I say anything that sounds like a load of crap, it very well might be, so don't be afraid to call me on it, okay?"

"Okay," Akasha said somberly. She took a deep breath and began. "I've been drinking since I was twelve or thirteen, I can't remember which, but I didn't drink to get drunk, y'know, or even to cope with a problem until a year or so ago."

Jayden nodded and did her best to keep her expression passive but welcoming. "Why do you think it started, then?"

"I dunno…maybe because I started to get lonely. I mean, Max was great company and all," she added defensively, "and Silas is wonderful. I mean, he's my life, but…I guess I missed talking with another girl, especially one who was different. Xochitl and the others practically lived with us before they moved to Seattle and made their big break."

Akasha sighed and shifted awkwardly on the bed. "Xochitl just had a way about making me feel better, about myself, about the world, whatever. Without her being around to comfort me when I had a bad day, I guess I turned to the next best thing: beer."

She snorted derisively. "Like that came any close. I was such an ass, I knew it, but I couldn't stop feeling that way."

The self-loathing in Akasha's voice brought tears to Jayden's eyes. She blinked them away and said soothingly, "You lost your best friend, your only friend, really. The pain was inevitable."

"But still, it wasn't like I was all pissy because she was gone. I knew she had to follow her dream and all, just as I did. I was so damn proud of her, still am. I mean, that girl had determination. When she said, 'I will,' she fucking *meant* it...and somehow that determination rubbed off on everyone around her. That's why Aurora's the world's fastest drummer, and Sylvis is the best guitarist to walk the planet."

She lit a cigarette and smiled, pride dripping from her voice.

"That's why three *chicks* and a *gay* guy were able to play with the big boys in heavy metal. Not only that, but I fucking know *I* wouldn't have been so successful at my business if *I* hadn't known her...and now look at me. I'm a fucking drunk who almost killed herself with alcohol poisoning the other day." Anger crept back into her tone, and she flicked her cigarette so hard that it broke.

"Don't be so hard on yourself," Jayden said softly. "You had just attended Max's funeral and then heard that your friends disappeared in the same night. Anyone would have reacted strongly."

Akasha laughed, but it was a harsh, brittle noise, like cracking marble.

"*That's* not what made me lose it," she said quietly. "Xochitl and the band are going to be fine. For one thing, Silas would have known if they were hurt because of Marking them and all, and I really think I'd know because, I dunno, but I think I would. No, I know they're okay. Xochitl's not afraid of anything and although

I don't know what she is, I know she can handle anything that anyone can dish out."

"Then what made you…lose it?" Jayden asked carefully, hoping she wasn't going too far for this first session.

Her "patient" took a deep, shuddering breath. "It was the way Silas looked at me when we heard the news. He was *afraid* of me. Afraid I'd freak out again and tear the place apart." Akasha choked on the last word, but continued speaking between growing hiccupping sobs. "He's my husband, the fucking love of my life…not only that, but he's a fucking five-hundred-year-old vampire! He's…not…supposed…to…be afraid of me!"

A keening wail escaped her throat, and she grabbed a pillow and buried her face in it to stifle the sobs.

With tears rolling down her own cheeks, Jayden crossed the small distance to the bed and took Akasha into her arms, not caring if the visions came back, only needing to comfort her friend.

The two women held each other and cried for what felt like an eternity.

When it ended, Akasha slowly pulled away and wiped her nose with the bottom of her shirt.

"Thanks," she said huskily. "I actually kinda feel better now. I know that sounds weird, but there it is."

Jayden squeezed Akasha's hand. She felt better too. Now that she'd actually helped someone, the healing light of purpose was a balm to her soul.

Chapter Twenty-four

Akasha's daily counseling sessions with "Doctor" Leigh continued…only from now on, they did them before sunset to avoid interruptions from the men. Akasha told her about her traumatic past. Besides the things that Max had narrated to Jayden, Akasha also had been abducted by government agents, experimented on like a lab rat, and almost killed just before her high school graduation.

When Akasha began talking about earning her college degree and opening Resurrection Wrenches, Jayden interrupted her.

"You never really had a childhood, did you?"

Akasha blinked at her. "Well, no."

It was then that they had another epiphany. Besides being her first and only friends, Xochitl, Sylvis, Aurora, and Beau had been Akasha's only link to a normal childhood. The same went for Max, as he was the closest thing to a father she'd had since she was eight.

Jayden had an epiphany of her own. With the suddenness of how she and Razvan got together, was it possible that her infatuation with him was childish? After all, he was technically her rescuer.

Maybe I should distance myself a little from him until I get it figured out, she thought. But figure what out? Razvan had never given a hint that he harbored any deeper feelings about her than lust and possessiveness… and aside from a few heated glances, the lust seemed to have vanished. She forced the thought away and focused on Akasha.

Their mock therapy was going pretty well. Silas installed a punching bag downstairs for anger management, and Akasha pelted it regularly. She was also down to an average of three beers a night instead of the usual half-rack, and she only got drunk one night a week instead of every day. Jayden wished Akasha would just quit drinking completely, but she supposed she'd have to be grateful for some progress, especially since, most important of all, Akasha finally reopened her shop.

The fact that she was ready to re-embrace her love of turning wrenches was a clear indication that she was healing. Jayden accompanied her to work every evening to hold the flashlight and continue with the counseling sessions.

Silas and Razvan were also making progress. They were confident that they had eliminated all of Selena's spies from their lands.

"When we get hold of her, she shall rue the day I Changed her," Razvan said with an evil smile.

A possible opportunity came on the evening of December twenty-first. Akasha and Jayden had just returned from Christmas shopping when there was a knock on the door.

Yet again, when Silas opened the door, no one was there, but a note sat on the stoop.

"This ding-dong-ditch thing is getting old," Akasha said.

Jayden nodded, but her pulse was in her throat. Who was Selena going to kill this time? Silas read the note, looked up, and smiled wickedly.

"Razvan, you'd better come here a minute," he called.

"What does it say?" Jayden asked.

Silas waved his hand dismissively as Razvan came down the stairs. He smiled at the other vampire and held up the note.

"It seems Michael wants to meet us in neutral territory. To 'negotiate peaceably,' he says." His brows rose in disbelief.

Razvan laughed. "How diplomatic of him. When will this meeting take place?"

"Tonight, at seven o'clock." Silas tore up the note and threw it in the wastebasket.

Underneath their banter, Jayden heard a hum in her mind. They were having a silent conversation along with their talk. She could almost discern the words, but it was as if they spoke underwater.

One thing was certain. They were hiding something from her and Akasha.

Again.

Well, this time, they're not getting away with it. She forced a compliant smile and turned to Akasha, winking at her as she hoped her friend wouldn't ruin everything by asking too much.

"Are you gonna kill him?" Akasha asked. "Please say you are."

Razvan chuckled. "If he gives us the opportunity, you can be sure of it."

"Cool. Can we come too?"

Silas sighed. "Unfortunately not. He only wants to talk with Razvan and me. Besides, it'll be more difficult for us to get our chance at destroying Michael if we're too busy keeping an eye on you both."

Akasha frowned. "I can take care of myself."

"We know that, but if you would please indulge us, I would feel so much better."

To Jayden's surprise, Akasha didn't argue further. "Fine. I have a lot of work to do anyway. Just don't get yourselves killed. It might be a trap." She headed out of the room. "Come on, Jayden," she called over her shoulder. "We gotta get ready for work."

Once Jayden joined her, Akasha whirled to face her. "You know something. Give."

She nodded and said quietly, "They're hiding something from us…again."

"No shit, Sherlock. Do you have any clue what it is?"

"I only know they were having a silent conversation over the one they had aloud." Jayden paused. "I do have an idea on how I might be able to find out more. Do you think you can get the wastebasket out of the living room without them noticing?"

Akasha nodded. "You bet. Are you going to try using your psychic mojo on Michael's note?"

"I sure am," Jayden said with a grin, for once grateful for her freakish ability.

Akasha was back with the wastebasket in less than five minutes. "It was easy. They were shut up in Silas's office so they can conspire in peace."

Jayden rifled through the trash. It was mostly paper waste, thank God. As she gathered up the pieces of Michael's note, brushing away cigarette ash from the paper, flickers of thoughts and images teased at her mind. This was going to work.

She clutched the shreds in one fist, shut her eyes, and focused.

When she'd gleaned all she could, she opened her eyes. "You're right, Akasha. There will be a trap. But it's not for Silas and Razvan. It's for us."

Akasha raised a brow and lit a cigarette. "Talk."

When Jayden finished explaining, her friend laughed with such sinister evil that she could be competition for Razvan. "I have a plan."

Chapter Twenty-five

Razvan's heart lurched painfully as the ladies left for work. Instead of a kiss or at least a warm smile, Jayden gave him an indifferent wave and a muttered goodbye.

It had happened already. Jayden's affection for him had passed. At first, he'd hoped she had merely been preoccupied with helping Akasha, but now Silas's wife seemed better off than ever, and Jayden was still distancing herself from him.

He cursed Selena and her cult to the foulest pit of hell. If the bitch hadn't launched her obsession with his woman and killed Max, perhaps he could have had more time with Jayden.

Silas interrupted his thoughts. "The guards are already in place near the shop to keep an eye on our women. I'm going to make some calls. If this is a trap, it would be good to have backup nearby."

Razvan grinned at his friend. "We think alike. I already called my best vampires. They'll remain hidden unless we need them."

A few minutes later, they were in the car and headed to State Line Showgirls.

"I really hope there won't be a battle," Razvan said. "I think a bloodbath would frighten the poor dancers."

Silas laughed as he navigated the icy roads like an old hand. "I'm more afraid of Akasha's reaction if she finds out where this meeting is taking place. She can be a jealous woman at times."

"You have a point there." Razvan frowned as he gazed out the window.

He couldn't let Jayden go this easily. He pictured her statuesque beauty, remembered the feel of her warm, soft skin, the silk of her hair through his fingers, the way her eyes grew wide with surprise before he stole a kiss. The thought of returning to a life without her was unbearable.

Silas guided the car into the crowded parking lot. The ice crunched under the tires. "I cannot fathom that so many men risk their lives to come here in this weather." He gestured at a group of men laughing jovially as they approached the front door. "All for the sight of a pair of likely false breasts."

Razvan chuckled. "Actually, I had one of my subordinates investigate the place beforehand. He says that the majority of the dancers have natural endowments, just little to speak of. But then, I believe he admires the falsies. Many young ones do."

"Are your people in place?" Silas asked as they got out of the car, pulling their coats tight against their bodies to ward off the cold.

"Yes, I sensed their arrival a few minutes ago. I only wish Sarah could have come. She would be invaluable if it comes down to a fight." He opened the door and surveyed the all-male clientele. "Alas, she would stick out like a sore thumb in a place like this."

Silas nodded. "I am only now getting petitions from females with any sort of fighting ability. Before Akasha, the only ones interested in joining me were those escaping a cruel master or hoping to sleep their way into a position of power."

Razvan snorted. "I assume your bride frightened those away? Really, you need to develop a mean streak before you're stuck ruling over a populace of weaklings."

They settled at the bar. Immediately a waitress dressed in a scrap of shiny fabric that could hardly be called a dress made a beeline for Silas and Razvan.

"What can I get you this evening?" she asked, bending low to display her cleavage even as she eyed their designer clothes with undisguised enthusiasm.

The vampires ordered hot drinks to warm their hands and did their best not to encourage her flirtation. She left, trailing a noxious cloud of perfume behind her.

"It seems we are early," Razvan said, looking at his watch. "My people have just arrived." He nodded at the door where two large vampires were being checked in by a bouncer. "Jake and Trey are going to be close by in case Michael plans to start a ruckus. The rest will remain outside with your people."

"Speak of the devil," Silas said as Michael entered the club with his usual arrogant sneer plastered on his narrow face.

Michael grinned at them, barely concealing his fangs. He seemed genuinely happy to see them and that made Razvan extremely nervous.

Selena's head "apostle" sat down next to them and pulled out a sheaf of five dollar bills. "Nicolae, McNaught." He purposely omitted their titles. "It is a pleasure to renew our acquaintance! I hope the roads weren't too bad this evening."

"We have little time for small talk," Silas said brusquely. "Tell us what you hope to gain from this meeting."

Razvan leaned forward. "Because if you think to convince us to spare your worthless hide for the crimes you and your mistress have committed, you are wasting our time and your breath."

Michael waved his hand languidly. "Please, have some patience and indulge me. I do not have the pleasure of getting out much." He waved his money in the air to beckon a dancer before they could protest.

The dancer gave him a false smile as she came forward, and Michael ordered lap dances for the three of them.

"You fool," Razvan growled. "What are you playing at?"

"Come now, Nicolae," Michael said with a leer. "Don't you want to enjoy some feminine charms after being stuck guarding your new pet for so long? Although I do hear she is a rather exquisite thing."

To hear the bastard speak of Jayden as if she were to serve just an object designed for a man's pleasure, to hear him, in fact, call her a "thing," made Razvan quiver in fury.

The dancer saw his reaction and, mistaking it for arousal, strutted over to him and began wriggling her derriere mere centimeters from his groin to the tuneless music. The scent of baby powder and perfumed oil was cloying to his sensitive nose.

"No thank you, Madam," he said, nearly choking on the miasma of her odor.

She moved away, wide-eyed in surprise, whether it was because of his refusal or his polite manner of addressing her, Razvan didn't know or care, for he just realized something that made his heart cringe in abject shame.

He *had* treated Jayden like an object. In fact, his words to her the second night they were together were, *"Sometimes my kind will keep a human companion. We call them 'pet mortals.' I think you'd make a nice one."*

And then, the night Selena had first demanded he turn over Jayden, she had thanked him for refusing to give her up. "*You are mine,"* was all he'd said, as if she were a fancy piece of furniture.

It was no wonder she'd gotten over her infatuation with him so easily.

But he couldn't let her go. He had to try to win back her affection. He must speak to her as soon as possible. He had to tell her he was wrong. He had to tell her that…he loved her.

"My God," he chuckled, overcome with the irony that it took this many centuries and this gaudy locale for him to realize his foolishness.

"What is it?" Michael asked suspiciously.

Was it Razvan's imagination, or did the bastard look worried? It was hard to tell with the stripper writhing all over him.

Silas thrust his hands in his pockets and frowned at them both. He suspected something as well.

"Oh, nothing," Razvan said nonchalantly. "I just find it amusing that your mistress keeps you on such a tight leash that you use this meeting as an excuse to seek such cheap titillation."

The stripper gasped in outrage at his remark, but he had to speak crassly. It was Michael's reaction that he wanted to see. The sooner they discovered his motives and the sooner Razvan was back with his love, the better.

Michael's eyes spat daggers. "You know nothing of our relationship or my sacred duties." The dancer stood, and he pulled out another fistful of money. "I didn't tell you to stop."

As the woman sighed and put the money in her G-string, Razvan met Silas's gaze. They came to the same conclusion. Michael was using her as a shield.

"Enough of your delays," Silas said. "Tell us why you have arranged this meeting, or we leave."

Michael smirked at that, confirming their suspicions that something was off.

"Is that one of your enforcers, I see?" He nodded over at Trey, who was shaking money at another dancer with an eager grin that didn't reach his eyes.

"Enough stalling," Razvan said with a glare.

The music, which was supposed to sound provocative, was starting to annoy him.

The dancer's gestures had gone from seductive grace to a half-hearted sway. Her eyes darted nervously around the room and her lips moved as if she were on the verge of calling for aid from the hulking bouncers.

Michael laughed, his posture oozing triumph. "You brought most of your people here, haven't you? Or at least, the very best?"

"You should keep that in mind in case you consider trying something foolish," Silas whispered, low enough that only the vampires could hear.

Razvan gripped his coffee cup so tightly that the handle snapped off, and the beverage slopped over onto his hands. Something was wrong.

"You *did* bring them. Splendid!" Michael clapped his hands, still wearing that infuriating grin. "That means your women are quite alone, doesn't it?"

"Dear God!" Silas gasped and leaped to his feet.

His eyes went distant as he sent out a call to the vampires who were supposed to be guarding the women.

The Lord of Coeur d'Alene grimaced and Razvan knew the guards were dead.

They had to leave now.

Michael glanced at his watch, unperturbed as he spoke too low for the dancer to hear. "Oh, I am certain you are too late. By now, Akasha will be dead, and the seeress will be safe in the hands of the high priestess."

Razvan bared his fangs.

Michael grinned at them over the dancer's shoulder. "Go ahead and try it. Then you will have to contend with them."

He nodded at a pair of nearby bouncers standing with their arms crossed under a sign reading, *"Don't touch the dancers, or you will be escorted from the premises."*

Ah, so this was why he was using a shield. Razvan smirked. That could work both ways.

With a silent apology and a blur of inhuman speed, he grabbed the stripper's breast and squeezed just enough to cause pain. Guilt pierced him along with the squeak of silicone He rubbed his hand on his pants as if he could wipe away the unnatural sensation and the stain of his crime.

To mortal eyes, he looked as if he hadn't moved. The dancer shrieked and jerked away from Michael, cupping her breast, and pointing an accusing finger at the vampire. The bouncers marched forward and seized Michael by the arms.

"The rules are posted, asshole," one of them said. "Time for you to go."

Michael turned bright red with impotent rage as he spluttered, "But I didn't touch her!"

"Yes, he did!" The stripper cried, clutching her breast. "He squeezed my tit!"

"The lady speaks truly," Silas added, suppressing a smile.

The other bouncer nodded. "Now, how about that," he said coldly. "Don't come back here again."

The two dragged a still protesting Michael out the door as Razvan handed the flustered dancer some hundred-dollar bills, needing to atone the only way he could.

"I'm very sorry, Madam," he said as he and Silas left the club.

By the time they got outside, Michael had fled, no doubt back to his insane mistress.

"Do you think he spoke truly?" Silas asked, practically vibrating with panic. "Could we be too late?"

Razvan's stomach plummeted at the possibility, but he refused to entertain it.

"Perhaps not." He tried to sound confident. "If I fly, I just may get to them in time."

The vampires gazed up doubtfully at the rapidly falling snow.

"It will be dangerous in this weather," Silas said. "You could be blown clear to Canada.

"I must try." Razvan rose in the air and flinched as the icy wind tried to carve up his cheeks. "Drive as fast as is safe, my friend," he called over his shoulder.

His voice was swallowed in a snowy gust.

Chapter Twenty-six

"I can't believe they're going to a strip club," Akasha growled, slapping a wrench on her palm. "But what pisses me off more is that they didn't tell us. I really don't like the idea of another woman in my man's lap, even if it is just for money…"

"We'll take it up with them if we survive this," Jayden said. Her eyes darted back and forth from the service doors to the grimy windows.

From the vision she received from touching Michael's note, Jayden learned that Selena had organized the meeting with her head goon, Michael, as a distraction to get Silas and Razvan out of the city so Lionel could return to Resurrection Wrenches and take Akasha and Jayden.

They'd decided to keep that information from the men and go to the shop to offer themselves as bait. Akasha was eager to reap her revenge upon Max's murderer.

Jayden was now unsure of the plan. So much could go wrong.

Before she could worry anymore, she sensed the vampire's approach. Lionel's thirst for their blood and his lust to strike terror in their hearts rivaled his fervent desire to please his mistress.

He was close.

Too close for them to get away.

"He's coming!" Jayden cried. Her heart hammered in fear.

They were all alone. Silas and Razvan couldn't protect them.

"How long?" Akasha was all business, her voice cold and eager.

"Any minute," Jayden said.

A cylindrical object was shoved into her hand. She looked at her friend questioningly.

"Take this and get onto the alignment rack," Akasha commanded. "When I say go, turn the knob."

Jayden got on the rack and crouched as Akasha headed to the lifting lever, still blinking at the odd tool she held. "What is this thing?"

The mechanic explained. "It's an oxyacetylene torch. If he gets too close, blast him in the face with it."

She showed her how to work it, blasting blue flame.

"What about you?" Jayden wasn't sure if she liked where this was going.

Apparently, she was to be the bait.

Akasha's smile was terrifying to behold. Her eyes were twin lavender pyres of hatred. "Oh, I can't wait to take him down."

Akasha pulled the hydraulic lever and pressed the lift button. As the rack shuddered and rose, Jayden wobbled for a second and caught her balance. The lift shuddered to a stop at about eight feet in the air.

"What if he can fly?" Her voice quivered with growing terror.

"Then we'll have to be faster," Akasha replied, unconcerned.

The door slammed open so hard that Jayden nearly dropped the torch. The bell crashed to the floor with a demented clang.

The lanky vampire who'd murdered Max came into view. "Turn over the Seeress, General, and I'll leave you unharmed."

"Fuck off and die, prick," Akasha hissed and flicked her cigarette into his face.

The burning ember struck him on the cheek. Lionel howled in enraged agony before charging.

The tiny mechanic was ready and caught him with an uppercut that sent him flying backward. His ankles caught the lift arm behind him, and he was knocked to the ground. Lionel's head struck the concrete floor. For a second, he lay stunned.

Jayden blinked and saw that the vampire had regained his footing. He struck Akasha's face with a swift backhand.

"Go!" she shouted as she flew through the air and slammed against a car.

The vampire moved too fast for Jayden to see. Frantically, she turned the knob and gasped as the torch came to life with a blue flame. The moment Lionel came into range, she scorched him in the face.

He screamed and darted back and forth below her perch. Jayden swung the torch in a frantic arc, trying to catch him with the flames.

Akasha threw a jack stand at his back, and he crumpled…for a second.

"You and I have unfinished business," she said. "So ignore the damsel and fight like a man…unless you're too much of a pussy."

"I'll kill you slowly, bitch." Lionel hissed, and lunged at her.

The vampire was fast, but Akasha nearly kept up with him in a blur of inhuman speed, punching kicking, ducking…

Jayden winced at every blow Akasha took and gasped every time she retaliated. Though the fight seemed to go on for ages, Jayden knew only seconds passed.

Akasha thrust her torque wrench through his chest and through the cinderblock wall. Lionel's shriek shattered glass and popped Jayden's eardrums.

"I told you, you'd pay," Akasha told him as his breath slowed to thirty-second pants.

The vampire writhed against the wall, struggling to pull the wrench from his chest.

He whimpered in agony for what felt like hours, though Jayden's glance at the clock confirmed that the death throes only lasted about five minutes.

At last, Lionel's muddy eyes stared at nothing, and his body slumped against the wall. The hand gripping the torque wrench handle slid off to dangle alongside the dead form.

"Should I get down?" Jayden asked, turning off the torch.

"No, I'm not done yet." The doll-like girl got into a car and drove it into the wall, squishing the body into the concrete.

She picked lit another cigarette and rummaged through her toolbox until she pulled out a hacksaw.

The torch fell from Jayden's hand through bloodless fingers as she realized Akasha's intention.

"This is for Max, you asshole." Akasha put the saw against Lionel's neck and began to cut.

Jayden turned away with a gag.

In minutes the crunching and sawing noises ended. She chanced a glance.

Akasha carried the vampire's severed head to her cylinder head straightening oven. A trail of blood splattered the concrete with every step.

"I think two hours at four seventy-five should do," Akasha said. "At least I hope so, since that's as hot as that bitch gets."

That was enough for Jayden. She leaned over the lift and puked all over the floor.

When Jayden was reduced to dry heaves, Akasha lowered the alignment rack back to the ground.

"Don't worry about the mess, Jayden. I got a pressure washer." Akasha told her before running to the bathroom and throwing up as well.

The smell of burning hair and baking flesh permeated the shop.

Jayden stepped off the lift with rubbery legs. Willing herself not to look at the corpse, she headed over to turn off the "Open" sign.

Akasha emerged from the bathroom, lighting another cigarette. "Good call. I should have done that sooner. I can't even imagine what would have happened if a customer walked in."

"Thanks," Jayden said, voice still shaking from the unreality of it all.

"Does that new phone Razvan bought for you have a camera?" The mechanic asked as she headed over to the industrial size sink to wash the blood from her hands.

Jayden nodded carefully. Her head still spun. "I think so."

Akasha giggled. "Excellent. Then I got something to send to Selena."

Jayden's gasp seemed to echo off the cinder block walls. "You have her number?"

"Yup," Akasha replied, grinning like a lunatic. "I got it from Razvan's phone when I was getting the trash can for you. He leaves that thing lying around all the time. I'm surprised he hasn't lost it yet."

Jayden handed over her phone and watched in morbid fascination as Akasha snapped pictures of the headless corpse of the vampire impaled against the shop wall.

"This will show you, you psycho bitch," Akasha muttered as she uploaded the picture and pressed the send button.

Just then, the bells on the front door jangled.

"Fuck! I forgot to lock the door! Still, can't the dumbass read?" Akasha said, "Stall 'em, Jayden, so I can cover up the body."

"That won't be necessary." Razvan's form darkened the doorway. He didn't sound happy.

Chapter Twenty-seven

Selena's brows rose at the unrecognized address on her phone. Who would send her a picture at this hour?

She almost deleted it, but then a sudden thought made a thrill rush through her breast.

Perhaps Lionel had confiscated Akasha's phone and used it to photograph her dead body.

She licked her lips and pushed the button to open the file.

At first, the image was just a jumble of shapes and colors that made no sense. Then Selena blinked, and the details became apparent.

A headless corpse was impaled on a cinderblock wall with a metal tool. Its legs were pinned by a smashed car. Blood soaked the clothing, making the body unrecognizable…until she noticed the ruby on the pinky finger of one dangling hand. She had given it to Lionel when he became her apostle.

A shriek built up in her throat, escaping at the same moment she tore another hank of hair from her bleeding scalp. Footsteps sounded on the stairs, but she hardly noticed.

Selena continued to scream. Her lips trembled as she struggled to form coherent words to justify her fury.

The door flung open, and her faithful followers filled the room.

"What is it, my lord?" Their voices formed a perfect echo.

A few looked away when she met their gazes, and her eyes burned at the sight of their evasion. Yet more were thinking of betraying her.

"Lionel is dead." She shifted her gaze over all of them.

She allowed them to murmur comforting words to her, whether genuine or feigned she was past caring.

When her flock grew carried away with their condolences and questions, Selena rounded on the vampires.

"Which one of you told them? Which one of you is a traitor?"

Every single one of her followers shrank away and cowered in abject submission. The sight usually pleased her, but tonight she was implacable. One of them had betrayed her. Perhaps more than one…she paced back and forth in front of the vampires like a caged animal. She struggled to read their minds, but their thoughts were an endless cacophony, each one drowning out the other.

Were her powers weakening? Or were *they* doing it on purpose?

Selena tugged a lock of hair, welcoming the surge of pain as she looked at the terrified faces of her order. She stopped with a frown. A few were missing.

"Where are Adam and Collette?"

The answering silence was like a pressure on her skull. They looked back and forth at each other and then to her as if they were characters in a comical play. Selena scrutinized each of them, bile rising in her throat as she noted that terror seemed to outweigh devotion in their expressions.

Though perhaps fear could be more useful.

She seized a vampire who appeared to be on the verge of wetting himself; he was trembling so much. Was his name Jeffery or Justin? Her hand reached up for her hair, then fell back at her side. His name didn't matter. Getting information and setting an example was what was important.

"Where are they?" She grabbed him by the hair and threw him down on his stomach.

The sound of his breath being knocked out of his body gave her a tingling satisfaction.

"I- Aaaargh!" Jeffery/Justin wailed as she yanked his head back and stomped on his spine. It crunched like pieces of dried wood beneath her feet.

Selena breathed in his pain as if it were an elixir. It felt so good, but she would have to stop before she was unable to glean any information from him.

She removed her foot and knelt beside him to whisper in his ear. "Where are Adam and Colette?"

His eyes glazed over as if he were delirious with fever. "R-ran…a-away…," he whispered before he lost consciousness.

"Mephistopheles damn them!" she roared before turning back to the others. "Find a doctor! The Lord of Coeur d'Alene has one. Why don't I?"

Her audience froze.

"Does anyone here have any medical experience?" Selena's eyes searched the terrified faces of her subjects.

If anyone lied, they would get more than a few broken bones. She reached up and gave a lock of her hair a satisfying tug.

A young female raised her hand. "I was a nurse in my mortal days," Jessica said with a quavering voice.

After a moment, Selena remembered her name. "Very well, Jessica. Tend him."

As the female and a male carried Jeffrey or Justin off, a voice called from the doorway. “What has happened, my lord?”

Selena’s heart surged at Michael’s beloved form, and she ran into the welcoming circle of his arms.

“Michael, oh, Michael,” she murmured, stroking his hair. “They killed Lionel!”

He growled at the news, and a thrill ran through her as the sound reverberated against her ear. “Impossible! They couldn’t have gotten back in time.”

With a shaking hand, she pulled her phone from her pocket and showed him the image of the apostle’s corpse. Michael’s eyes narrowed as he dialed the number from which the picture came. Selena felt a wave of fury and self-loathing that she had not thought of it.

A tinny, unmistakable feminine voice came on. “Hello?”

“To whom am I speaking?” Michael demanded.

Frantic whispering could be heard over the phone before another woman came on the line. “Hello, Michael. Did you and Selena enjoy the picture? I think your turn is next.”

Michael hissed. “Oh, no, Akasha. It is your death that will be soon, and it will be slow.”

The low laughter was like shards of glass. “Funny, Lionel said the same thing shortly before I staked his ass. Broke my good torque wrench, but it was worth it.”

Selena couldn’t hold back a shriek of outrage. “How dare you! You mutant abomination!”

“Oh, hi, Selena.” Akasha’s dripped venom. “Fuck off and die, you crazy bitch.”

The phone went silent.

Silas’s pet mutant had killed her dear apostle. She should have known.

That little monster was more than capable of such an atrocity. She turned back to Michael.

"Find them," she hissed, quivering with rage.

The apostle flinched. "But if Silas or Razvan catches me, they will kill me. Please, my lord, you've lost Lionel. Do you want to lose us both?"

"Do you dare question my orders?" Selena flexed hands that were eager to tear flesh and draw blood.

He shook his head fervently. "No, my lord, I merely—"

"Surely you can handle two mortal females?" she said silkily, toying with the lapel of his jacket.

"Akasha isn't your typical mortal," Michael protested.

Selena backhanded him, sending him crashing into the mass of vampires, still on their knees. She blinked at them in surprise, having forgotten about them completely.

"I will tolerate no more of your insolence, Michael!" she screamed. "Now get out of here and don't return without the freak, Akasha, or the Seeress!" She paused and adjusted her skirt. "You can bring me Akasha's dead body if you so desire, but I need the Seeress alive! Do you understand?"

Michael sat up and wiped the blood from his lip. "Yes, my lord."

After he bowed and left the room, Selena turned to regard the rest of her followers. They were cringing on the floor, trying to make themselves look as small as possible. Pathetic.

"What are you looking at?" she demanded. "Get out, all of you! In the name of Mephistopheles, give me some peace!"

When at last she was alone, Selena collapsed on her knees and seized her hair. "Oh, Mephistopheles, creator of us all, please help me regain control!"

Control of what, precisely? A little voice in her head asked. *Over her people, or herself?* She didn't know. Selena gasped as another lock of hair tore free.

For the longest time, Razvan stood before Lionel's body. His hands clasped behind his back as if he were viewing an art exhibit.

"Very good work, Akasha." He seemed to mean it, though there was something off in his tone.

"Hey," Jayden protested. "I helped too."

He turned to her, and his smile dimmed. For a moment, she thought she'd said something wrong.

Then he put his arm around her and pulled her close. "I am so sorry I wasn't here to protect you, Jayden. Were you frightened?"

The feel of his touch and gentle comfort was almost enough to undo the horror of the past hour. Jayden leaned into him, eager to express her gratitude, but before she could reply, the door banged open.

Silas burst into the shop. "Akasha, are you alright?"

Akasha launched herself into her husband's arms just as he saw Lionel's headless body pinned against the wall.

Silas managed a weak laugh. "I should have known you could handle things on your own. Still, I wish we had been here." His expression sobered. "The guards are dead."

Razvan interrupted. "Dear God, what is that smell?"

Silas frowned and wrinkled his nose. The odor of burning flesh and hair was getting stronger.

Akasha smiled. "I put the head in my cylinder head straightening oven. Gotta make sure he stays dead."

Her husband smiled and shook his head. "That was likely more than necessary, but very creative all the same." His eyes turned more serious. "Were you hurt?"

"No," she replied. "I had it all planned out." Her eyes widened, and her mouth snapped shut.

Jayden met Akasha's apologetic gaze and cringed, but it was too late. The truth was out.

Silas froze, and his head swiveled to look at Jayden.

Razvan gripped her arm and pulled her around to face him. "Oh, really?" he said silkily. His gaze wasn't so soft and kind anymore.

Akasha's husband stalked toward Jayden, his eyes beginning to glow green fire. "I presume you were responsible for the foreknowledge of Lionel's attack?"

Jayden swallowed and nodded. Her stomach seemed to be sinking into her feet. She was surrounded by two angry vampires. This was bad.

Razvan seized her shoulders, his eyes gleaming like molten obsidian. "Why didn't you tell us? What the hell were you thinking to put yourself in such danger?"

Akasha stomped forward. "If we'd told you, Lionel would have been called off and I wouldn't have had my shot at him!"

Both vampires rounded on her. "You risked yourself and Jayden for revenge?" Silas said incredulously. "Dear God, woman, what possessed you to do such a foolish thing?"

"It was my idea!" Jayden blurted and cringed as the censure was back on her.

"I am not so certain I believe that," Razvan said with a raised brow.

His skeptical tone infuriated her. He'd been practically ignoring her for the last few months, and he thought he knew her?

"Why are you so surprised?" she asked. "Did you think I was some weak damsel that would be content to wait for Prince Charming's rescue?" She couldn't keep the sarcasm from her voice any more than she could hold back the bitterness in her heart as she realized that was exactly how she'd been acting since she met him.

Razvan sighed. "Actually, I did," he said quietly.

Before she could attempt to decipher his tone, Akasha leapt back into the fray.

"What about you two?" she demanded. "Why didn't you think to tell us that you would be off getting lap dances during your meeting with the enemy?"

Silas stepped back and held up his hands. "Now, lass, we did not…"

Jayden didn't hear the rest of his protest. She was looking at Razvan's face, which had colored bright red. He was hiding something. In a flash, she seized his hand and speared his mind before he could throw up a mental shield.

She saw an incredibly beautiful dancer swaying hypnotically, she heard the thumping music. Then she saw Razvan's hand reach out to caress the woman's breast.

"No!" she gasped, thrown from the vision. "How c-could you," she choked, feeling like she swallowed a stone. The smell of baking flesh was suddenly overpowering and she fought not to gag.

"Jayden, I—" he began.

"Don't bother lying to me. I saw you!" She swallowed burning tears. "I-I saw you touching her."

The pain and humiliation threatened to drop her where she stood. What was worse was that she had no real justification for it. Razvan hadn't made any commitment to her. But it still felt like she'd been stabbed through the chest.

Before Akasha or Silas could say anything to further her mortification, Jayden fled the shop, thanking the fates above that she had taken her car.

Razvan moved to go after Jayden, but Akasha blocked him.

"What the fuck did you do?" she demanded, voice trembling with suppressed fury.

He sighed. "It wasn't what she thought."

Silas nodded. "I have a guess on what Jayden saw," he explained to Akasha. "Michael was using the dancer as a shield. Razvan touched her, but only to trick her into thinking that Michael was the culprit so that he would be thrown out and we could deal with him."

"Ah," Akasha said, satisfied with the explanation. "And did you deal with him?"

He shook his head, overcome once more with bitter regret that he didn't so much as touch Selena's obnoxious apostle. "Unfortunately not. We had just learned of Lionel's intentions to attack you, so we hurried here instead." His expression softened. "You are more important."

Razvan interrupted before the couple could get too wrapped up in one another. "I am glad the matter is cleared up for you, but now I must find Jayden and explain…also, the smell of Lionel's head cooking is getting to be a bit much."

Akasha nodded. "You're right. But first, could you help me dispose of the body? Then we can all go find her. I doubt she went far. I'll even back you up if you need it."

Razvan sighed. "Very well, I suppose it wouldn't do for someone to happen upon this thing." He gestured in the direction of the corpse. "And perhaps Jayden will be home by the time we are finished. After all, she doesn't have anywhere else to go."

Chapter Twenty-eight

Jayden cursed as she reached another dead-end street and cranked the wheel into a U-turn. Max had done a beautiful job with her Camry. It drove like it was new… but there was nowhere for her to go. The thought brought forth another surge of hot tears. She dashed them away with her fist. Her uncontrollable crying was the reason she kept getting lost on the back roads to nowhere in the first place.

The first bout of sobbing nearly caused her to crash into a pickup only four blocks from Akasha's shop. The icy roads and constant barrage of falling snow didn't help matters. She reached for the defrost lever and sighed. It was already turned to the max.

More tears welled up, burning her eyes as she fiddled with the radio. As if the fates were mocking her, it seemed like every break-up song ever written was playing on every radio station.

Why the hell am I crying over him anyway? She'd known he hadn't had any feelings for her. And his subordinate vampires confirmed that he was a man-whore. Besides, she'd made peace with the fact that she had a childish infatuation with him for saving her life.

"If that's true, why are you still crying, you moron?" Her voice sounded hollow in the dark car. She bit her lip before another pathetic sob could escape.

Christmas lights gleaming from the houses lining the street reflected in her tears, edging her vision with a nauseating kaleidoscope of color.

"Oh, God." Jayden gripped the wheel tighter and attempted a hiccupping laugh. "I still love him. I can't believe it. I'm a bigger moron than I thought."

She took a deep, shuddering breath and swerved to avoid a cat crossing the dimly lit road. She needed to get control of herself before she killed herself or some other poor creature.

The '80s station started playing an old favorite, and she cranked up the volume, hoping to focus. But even a good classic couldn't ease the turmoil. She needed to go somewhere safe where she could think.

Blinking back the remaining tears, Jayden made a right turn, hoping to end up at the Denny's on 4th Street.

In one blink, the road was dark and empty.

The next revealed a man in front of the car.

Jayden screamed as she struck him. The body bounced on her hood and rolled halfway up her windshield before she slammed on the brake pedal. The abrupt halt sent him flying back onto the pavement.

"Oh God, Oh God, Oh God," she whimpered as she turned off the engine and opened the door.

The high beams shone down on a prone figure lying on the ground.

He wasn't moving.

She reached into her pocket for her phone. It wasn't there. After fumbling with her coat and hurriedly searching her car, she realized that Akasha still had it.

Jayden bit her lip and looked at the nearby houses. All the windows were dark except for a few lit Christmas trees.

She wondered how many would answer their doors at two AM.

Or what if they'd seen what she did, called the police, and were now peering at her through the curtains?

An obscenely large Santa Claus statue seemed to leer at her from the lawn to her right.

Her eyes strayed back to the still body on the ground. At least she should see if he was still alive.

What if he wasn't? Her heart thudded in her ears at the likely possibility.

She would go to jail for vehicular manslaughter. She would be handcuffed, manhandled, stripped, degraded, and thrown in a cell. The visions would assault her from everyone who touched her. She would go insane and die locked up, just like her mother.

The Santa statue seemed to grin in agreement. No presents for her this year.

Pain screamed in her hands where her nails bit into her palms. Jayden shook her head and forced her feet to take shuddering steps towards the man. If she kept thinking like that, she would go crazy.

She had control of her powers now. And she wasn't alone anymore.

Akasha or Silas would bail her out so she could say her goodbyes. Maybe Silas would hire a lawyer for her. Did he know any human attorneys? Or did he have enough clout to make sure her trial was scheduled at night so that Salazar could represent her?

As she drew closer to the man's crumpled form, she saw that a thin layer of snow was already beginning to cover him. Her stomach roiled in guilt. Did he have a family? Suddenly she imagined herself on trial, facing the man's crying wife and his family's accusing stares.

Walking those ten feet felt like ten miles. By the time she reached the man, her legs were quivering and threatened to collapse under her weight. Her knees creaked as she knelt beside him. Slowly, she reached out a trembling hand to touch his neck and check for a pulse.

The body jolted underneath her fingertips, and the man's breath puffed out in a December cloud as he rolled over. Jayden was dizzy with relief.

"Oh, thank God," she babbled hysterically. "I'm so sorry. Are you okay? I'm going to help you, alright? We'll get you to a hospital…or we'll call someone."

The man sat up.

"I am sorry," Jayden repeated. "I'll help you. I'll—"

The man's face came into view. His lips curved up in a wide smile.

The light from the Toyota's high beams reflected on his fangs.

She gasped and stumbled backward, slipping on the ice and falling on her rear. Freezing slush soaked her pants.

"It took you long enough to identify me, Seeress." His cheery tone was incongruous with the nightmarish scenario. "My mistress will be disappointed that you are not as powerful as she thought."

A scream built up from her toes but never escaped. Michael's hand crashed into the side of her face before she could make a sound. Then all was blackness.

When Lionel's body had been safely disposed of, Silas, Akasha, and Razvan returned to Resurrection Wrenches, hoping Jayden had come back. But the parking lot was still empty. After everyone's hands were washed in the gargantuan shop sink, Razvan cursed.

"Jayden's Mark is fading. She knows better than to leave this territory." He pulled out his phone and dialed her number. "If she doesn't get back here right away—"

Immediately, Alice Cooper's "Poison" trilled from Akasha's pocket.

"Damn," Akasha said, pulling out Jayden's phone. "I forgot to give it back to her after we sent the picture to Selena."

"Is that song just for me?" Razvan asked, forcing casual amusement into his voice. The thought of Jayden assigning a song for his calls brought a pleasant rush of warmth to his flesh.

She looked at the screen, oblivious to his inner triumph. "Yep."

"Excuse me," Silas interrupted. "Did I hear you say that you and Jayden sent a picture to Selena?"

Akasha nodded with a malicious smile that was incongruous with her doll-like features. "I wanted her to see the consequence of her stupidity."

Razvan chuckled. "I would have liked to see the look on her face."

Silas cleared his throat and pushed off the car he was leaning on to pace in front of them. "I imagine she was quite infuriated." His expression was grave. "Perhaps even infuriated enough to send immediate retaliation… and Jayden is out there somewhere on her own unprotected."

The vampire's words were like a spear through Razvan's heart. He closed his eyes and opened his mind wider to the Mark between him and Jayden.

It was faint and thready like a weak pulse. He turned to the others and saw his panic reflected in their gazes.

"She's unconscious," he whispered, "and maybe hurt." He slammed his fist into the cinderblock wall, crumbling the concrete. "Damn it! I knew I shouldn't have let her go!" Rage and anguish warred within him until he was ready to explode.

"Maybe she got in an accident," Akasha said. "I mean, that wouldn't be good either, but she'd be safer in the hospital than with Selena."

Silas shook his head. "That would be too nice of a coincidence." He pulled his phone from his pocket. "I think we'd better assume she's been taken. Our only condolence is that Selena will want her alive."

"What are we waiting for?" Razvan said, heading for the door. "Let's go get Jayden."

Silas grabbed his arm. "For one thing, it'll be dawn in a little over four hours. And for another, I think we should gather a few reinforcements and come up with something at least slightly resembling a plan."

Razvan opened his mouth to argue, but then he stopped. Silas was right. Selena was a devious bitch, made even more dangerous by her insanity. "You're right, damn you. Who are you going to call?"

"Everyone," Silas replied, texting a message on his phone with lightning agility. "I will take the first five that volunteer. Any more would draw too much attention from the humans in the area. This invasion will be a high risk to any involved, so it is only fair that I allow the opportunity to refuse."

Razvan shook his head. “You are far kinder a master than I.” He withdrew his phone and sent out his own message to five of his strongest vampires. Unlike Silas, he gave them no opportunity for refusal.

As the vampire lords awaited replies to their summons, Akasha went to the gas station across the street to fetch a map of Post Falls. Thirty minutes later, the small parking lot of Resurrection Wrenches was full. A dozen vampires gathered inside the shop. They huddled around one of the smaller hydraulic lifts, studying the map.

“I can fit four in my van, maybe five,” Jonathan Greenbriar said. “But I would like to leave some extra room in case I need to haul a patient.”

At first, Silas was reluctant to allow Jonathon to accompany them, for he was still fairly young, but Razvan and Akasha insisted that it would be useful to have a doctor with them. It was a done deal when Jonathan revealed that he had a pistol and a license to carry a concealed firearm. With him, that made five vampires that were shooters. Razvan was one of the five. His second in command had brought him his gun.

“I should have known you’d go all ‘Scarface’ on us,” Akasha said, watching him stroke the barrel of the submachine gun. Her face had gone chalk-white.

“That’s a Tommy gun,” Silas said with a slight smile. “Scarface had an M-16 with a grenade launcher.” He raised a brow at Razvan. “Although it fits you, I don’t think you’ll be able to use that with so many neighboring humans around.”

“Her main lair is underground,” he replied as he savored the mental picture of cutting Selena in half with a hail of bullets. “Akasha, what is the matter?”

Akasha had flinched when he moved to tuck the gun inside his coat. A fine tremor overtook her small form.

Silas growled a Gaelic curse. “I had forgotten about that issue.”

He took his wife into his arms and looked down at her. “Do you want to tell him, or should I?”

The tiny woman who was the strongest being Razvan had ever encountered leveled her amethyst gaze on him with an unmistakable challenge. “I have a bit of a phobia with guns, okay? It’s got something to do with my parents being shot down in front of me when I was little…but…I can handle it. It’s just a stupid phobia,” she repeated, sounding more like she was trying to convince herself.

Razvan wasn’t so sure from the panic written all over her face and body. Silas reinforced his opinion.

“I’m not certain she can fight in such a state,” he said quietly.

Silas had been teaching Akasha to fight with a Claymore. It was a formidable Scottish battle sword. With her superhuman strength, she would be an invaluable asset in this battle…but not if she became a quivering mass of terror.

Razvan placed his hand on her shoulder. “Which bothers you more, the sight of the guns or the noise they make?”

She looked up at him with her eyes full of self-loathing. “Both, but the noise is worse.” She took his hand, something she’d never done before. “Quit worrying about my bullshit. We need to get Jayden back and kill Selena. I’ll handle my issues, okay?”

Her cheeks flushed as she looked at the vampires, although they were all too well trained to acknowledge hearing the exchange.

Never before had she looked so vulnerable. Normally, Razvan would have been fascinated, until Jayden came into his life. Now there was no room for petty fascination with human weaknesses, no room for games. The only thing that mattered was having his love safe in his arms.

He and Silas exchanged a look before he replied, “I will only use my gun if I need to.”

That seemed to be good enough for Akasha, for she nodded, and the cold look of intent to murder returned to her eyes.

They went back to their planning. The vampires with guns, except for Razvan, would ride in the van with Jonathon while the rest followed in other cars. Firepower would be needed to gain entry to their enemy’s lair.

Aside from Jonathon, the other three shooters were Razvan’s. Two even had guns equipped with silencers. Sarah carried a sleek Beretta while Jake and Trey toted their favored Glocks. With hope and luck, they could take out whatever guards Selena might have in place.

“You should be ashamed,” Razvan teased Silas. “We’re in northern Idaho, for God’s sake. I would have thought your people would be better armed.”

Silas shrugged. “If rifles and shotguns weren’t so hard to conceal, I’m sure they would be. I just don’t want to risk it. It will be hard enough to explain the swords.”

Shen Li, one of Silas’s oldest vampires, smiled at Razvan. “Thanks to my teachings, most of us need no weapons to kill.”

He nodded at Jonathon, who tossed a block of wood straight at his face. In an indecipherable blur, Shen split it in two.

“Hey, watch it!” Sarah snarled as she ducked to avoid the half flying at her.

Trey gaped at the vampire and whistled. “Man… that was incredible! Did you do that with your hand?”

Shen nodded before turning to Silas and bowing. “It will be an honor to assist you in this mission, my lord.”

Razvan stroked his beard and observed Jayden's rescue party. There were twelve vampires, five with guns, and the rest with either swords or skills in martial arts. And there was Akasha, the military-engineered killing machine.

Perhaps there was hope that this mission would be a success, despite being outnumbered at least four to one.

Then again, perhaps someone should have brought a grenade launcher.

Chapter Twenty-nine

The left side of Jayden's face throbbed like an infected tooth. As she surfaced into wakefulness, the pain intensified, and she let out a pitiful moan.

"She's regaining consciousness," a soft feminine voice said, burgeoning with relief.

"Splendid," another woman answered in a voice that seemed vaguely reptilian. "We may begin preparations, then."

There was a rustle of fabric, and the click of a lighter, before the pungent aroma of incense flooded her nostrils. Jayden tried to turn her head away, but it seemed to weigh two hundred pounds.

"If you please, my lord," the first woman's voice quivered in barely checked fear. "I would like to see if she has a concussion." Her cool hands touched Jayden's face, and a little more confidence seeped into her tone. "I wish we were able to get her an X-ray. Her cheek is swollen, but I can't tell if it's broken or not."

The other woman growled. "She better not be too damaged, Michael, or you will suffer the consequences."

The voice of her abductor answered. "Yes, my lord. I did not mean to hit her so hard."

The memory of hitting the vampire with her car came back to Jayden with sickening clarity.

It had been a trap…a good one, too. She couldn't think of any other way she could have reacted.

The woman's fingers slid up her face, and her eyelid was gently coaxed open. A flashlight beam pierced her eye like a thousand needles, making her brain scream in pain. Jayden whimpered and tried to close them.

"I'm sorry," the female vampire said, looking at her with compassionate brown eyes. "I need to examine your pupils. I'll get it over with quickly, I promise."

That piercing light came back, spearing her skull and blinding her.

"They look to be the same size," her nurse said. "I can't tell."

Jayden dropped her shields and tried to read the vampire's thoughts. Nothing came.

"You cannot read Jessica either then?" The reptilian-voiced vampire stepped forward. "That is very interesting."

It had to be Selena. As she came into the light, Jayden choked back a horrified gasp.

The woman's head was covered in bloody scabs and bald spots. The little hair she had left hung in stringy unwashed strands the color of a sickly pumpkin.

Before Jayden could wonder about that, Selena's hand crept up to tug on a lock of dirty hair as her cloudy gray eyes darted about the room as if invisible imps were capering about.

"You are far prettier than I expected," Selena crooned and took Jayden's chin in her other hand. "What is your name, Seeress?"

Jayden swallowed. Revulsion knotted her belly at the sensation of the vampire's fingers so near her mouth. She could almost smell the torn flesh under her nails.

"My name is Jayden," she replied, desperate for that sickening touch to go away.

Selena's mind pressed against hers. It was powerful but full of madness, imbued with stinking slithering things and an abyss where screams never died. Jayden knew that if she spent too long here, she would tumble into its depths and be swallowed up by the terrible insanity.

"Jayden," the vampire seemed to taste the name. Her lips screwed up as if she'd sucked on something sour. "Do you know why you have come here to us?" Those fingernails scraped against her skin.

Jayden shook her head. She didn't think that there was an answer that would appease the mad goddess.

Her feigned ignorance seemed to pay off, for Selena withdrew her hand and smiled as rapturously as a televangelist. "You have been chosen, Jayden. I have deemed your powers worthy of The Order of Eternal Night, and I welcome you into the fold with a special task which you will perform. If you please me, I shall reward you with eternal life."

The news didn't bode well. As Jayden searched for a reply, her eyes took in the rest of her surroundings. The other vampires, Jessica and Michael, were on their knees on either side of their lord. Their twitchy, submissive postures indicated that Selena's temper was unpredictable and formidable. Things were looking worse by the second.

The room was not what she expected the headquarters of a vampire cult to look like. Clothes and bits of paper were scattered everywhere. If a few beer cans were added, it would be the very image of a college dorm room. Candles and incense burners were arranged haphazardly on tables and shelves, giving no sign of ceremonial order.

"Are you not going to express your honor of being chosen?" Selena demanded and moved as if she were going to touch her again.

Jayden shrank back in her seat. "I am sorry…um…Ma'am. I'm very dizzy. Wh-what um…task do you want me to perform?"

As if a switch were thrown, Selena's face warped into an expression of exaggerated maternal concern. "Oh, you poor thing," she crooned. "You are still recovering from your ordeal at the hands of the terrible Lord Nicolae." She turned to the vampires on the floor. "Jessica! Bring our new acolyte something to drink."

"Yes, my lord." The vampire scrambled up and fled from the room.

"Michael, leave us," Selena commanded.

Her abductor departed with a bow.

Once they were alone, Selena returned to her side and stroked Jayden's hair. Her head ached as she fought to keep her shields in place. But the vampire's mind was like a battering ram, and it was only a matter of time before her will would collapse.

"Do not worry, Jayden. I will take good care of you, and you shall be recovered in no time," the madwoman crooned.

It would be a good idea to pretend to be more hurt than she actually was. The dizziness had faded, and besides the throbbing of her face and her stomach clenching in terror, Jayden felt relatively okay. Still, she let out what she hoped was a convincing moan of pain.

Selena clucked like a mother hen. "You will be safe with me. Razvan can never touch you again."

It was funny how she didn't acknowledge that it was *her* vampire who had injured Jayden in the first place. However, she didn't dare mention that thought aloud.

As she looked at the scabbed and balding vampire with her bloodshot eyes and maniacal grin, it was hard to believe that both Razvan and Silas had slept with her. Then again, with her lush curves and classical features, she had likely been beautiful before her madness had taken over.

Instead of the expected pang of jealousy, Jayden felt pity for Razvan. He must have once felt deeply for Selena to have Changed her. And it must have traumatized him deeply when he saw what she had become. No wonder he was so distant with women.

Did Razvan know that she had been captured yet? She knew that he'd Marked her, but he'd never explained how that worked. Jayden had no doubt that he would come for her. She closed her eyes and prayed that he would come in time.

"No, no!" Selena tugged on Jayden's hair, inciting a sliver of pain. "You cannot go to sleep if you have a head injury. "We must keep you awake."

"Could you tell me more about your order?" Jayden asked. Maybe she could keep Selena talking long enough for her rescuers to arrive.

The evangelical smile returned. Selena lit a few nearby candles, and to Jayden's dismay, rekindled the cloying incense. Apparently, she wanted to add ambiance to the story.

"Eons ago, the dark god Mephistopheles created his own world. To expand his kingdom, he created an army of powerful blood-drinkers who could live forever and replenish themselves by creating more. But somehow, they displeased him, and he banished them to Earth. Only one of those first vampires still lives, and I learned the truth when I found his writings."

Jayden suppressed a smirk. Silas had told her that Selena stole them. "His name is Delgarias, right?"

Selena nodded approvingly like a teacher with a difficult pupil. "Yes!" Her brow furrowed in a frown as she toyed with the thread of smoke from the incense. "The years have not been kind to Delgarias. He is weak and misguided. He could not grasp the significance of his own writings."

"What do you mean?" Jayden asked, eager for her to keep going.

"I had long prayed for a sign that our kind could regain Mephistopheles's favor," the vampire continued with breathless zeal. "My prayers were answered when I gained Lordship status and found the scrolls. Besides proving the truth in the old legends, they spoke of another world in which the sun would die. A world which will be a haven for our kind…" Her eyes narrowed. "Unless *she* ruins everything for us."

"Who?" Jayden wondered whether she was getting sucked into Selena's insanity already or if the vampire was just that good of a storyteller.

Selena bared her fangs in a hideous grimace. "Xochitl Leonine is the daughter of Mephistopheles and the one who is prophesied to bring back the sun and thus destroy our nocturnal paradise. You must find her for me so that she may be stopped."

Jayden couldn't help her gaping disbelief. "What?"

Selena nodded solemnly. "You have been in her presence, Jayden. You have felt her power. Surely you knew that Xochitl was no ordinary musician?"

"Well, yes, but…" Jayden stopped. It was true that Xochitl wasn't human…but the daughter of a vampire god and prophesied savior of another world? It was ridiculous.

Where was Razvan? Her longing for him and the sanity that he'd brought back into her life was an unquenchable ache in her heart.

Before Jayden could form a response, Jessica opened the door. "I am sorry I took so long, my lord. We had no human sustenance, so I had to go to the store." She held a steaming cup.

"Very well," Selena said, waving a dismissive hand. "I must prepare for the ceremony. Attend to our new member. If something amiss happens, I will tear out your heart and feed it to one of those incessant yapping dogs outside." With that stomach-churning remark, she swept from the room, muttering under her breath.

"H-here," Jessica said, handing her the cup. "It's spiced cider. I hope it's to your liking."

"Thank you," Jayden said and took a sip before blurting, "How did you get mixed up with her?"

"Shh!" Jessica admonished with wide eyes. "I was a nurse during the second world war. One of the soldiers got a little…over amorous with his thanks for my treating him. Selena saved me, and I've been with her ever since. I don't know anything else."

"What do you think of her…um…beliefs?" Jayden asked.

Jessica sighed and ran a hand through brown hair that looked like it had been hacked up by a two-year-old. "At first, it seemed harmless, but now…"

She didn't get a chance to answer. Michael thrust open the door. "Justin is screaming for you again. He says his legs hurt. I will take over here."

Jessica nodded and hurried out of the room, casting Jayden an apologetic look over her shoulder.

"Tell me," Michael said as he plopped down in a chair nearby. "Do you think Razvan and Silas will come to rescue you? I think they will try. I do hope that Akasha will come." He bared his fangs in a parody of a grin. "I have special plans for her."

Jayden glared at him. "I think it's the other way around."

Michael hissed, but his retort cut off abruptly.

Selena had returned. "Come, Jayden. All is in readiness."

She scrambled out of the chair and followed the Lord of Post Falls. Her head spun dizzily, and she nearly fell.

Michael leered at her as she passed him. "I advise you to do your best to please her," he whispered.

Selena led her down a dark hallway. The air had a faint familiar mildew odor that made her realize that they were underground. Panic ate at her throat. Would Razvan know where to find her?

They passed through a gaudy bead curtain and into a large chamber that looked a little more like a setting for a cult. Around fifty folding chairs were arranged in a semi-circle facing an ornate hand-carved throne. On the other side of the room sat what looked like a shrine dedicated to Rage of Angels.

Candles surrounded a table full of concert tee shirts, CDs, magazines, guitar picks, and other memorabilia. Posters and photographs covered the wall behind it. Jayden shivered and wondered if John Lennon's killer had incorporated similar décor in his home.

Selena led her over to the shrine. "Touch everything," she commanded. "Feel her essence and find her."

Jayden hesitated. She didn't want to drop her shields, didn't want to drown in Selena's madness. The vampire grabbed her wrist and jerked her forward. "Quit shielding and do it!" she hissed.

Jayden's mental barriers crashed down, and she almost fell to her knees at the onslaught of the vampire's mind. Desperation, fury, and paranoia flooded over her head in a chaotic tide.

Desperate to find the equivalent of a psychic lifeboat, Jayden seized the first thing her fingers reached. It was the neck of an autographed guitar.

Immediately she was thrown into a vision.

Chapter Thirty

The rescue party parked on the side of the road across from the borders of Selena's lair.

"How long do we have?" Razvan asked, surveying the cluster of nearly identical ranch-style homes close by.

Silas checked his watch. "About two hours, maybe two and a half. We should be thankful that tonight is the Solstice, the longest night of the year."

Razvan nodded and turned to Akasha and the other vampires. "Her four houses are at the end of the cul de sac on Riverview Terrace. I am sure all four contain passages to her underground lair, so we need to get inside only one. All are likely guarded. We're going to split into two groups, led by Trey and Sarah. If all goes well, they will be able to kill the sentries quietly with none being the wiser."

Trey and Sarah nodded.

Razvan continued relating the plan. "Since my gun is too noisy, I will fly above and serve as communication between the two groups as well as keep an eye out for mortals."

Silas stepped forward and regarded them all seriously. "Remember, if a mortal sees you, you must clear their memories right away. Our immunity is null and void if there is exposure to human eyes."

Razvan took to the air, and the two groups split up. Sarah, Silas, Akasha, and Salazar piled into Jonathon's van while the rest approached the housing development on foot.

The aerial view wasn't as good as he hoped. The slanting snow blurred the houses, making them almost unrecognizable. There was no way to read street signs either. His gun swayed on its ill-fitting strap, and he reached with one hand to steady it. Another thought struck him suddenly, making him lose altitude.

Could any of Selena's vampires fly? With this weather, he did not know how well he'd handle an attack from the air.

Flight was a rare power, and Selena did not enjoy the company of those who possessed what she lacked. Still, it would be best to be aware of the possibility.

By the time Razvan saw Jonathon's van ease to a stop, his eyes throbbed in their sockets from darting around in all directions while being pelted by snow.

The quartet of houses below were the only ones on this street without Christmas lights. They sat cloaked in darkness without even the illumination of a porch light. The curtains were drawn, giving no view of the menace inside.

He watched Trey circle around the easternmost house, gun drawn. The remainder of his party fanned out behind him. Two kept a lookout for spectators.

Trey made it five feet before the front door opened, and a vampire launched out. At the same time, two others came from around the sides of the house.

Trey dropped his attacker with two bullets to the heart. Shen seemed to materialize out of nowhere, breaking one vampire's neck with his hands and catching the other in the throat with a roundhouse kick.

Another vampire came out the front door in a blinding rush, and Trey shot her in the head before going in. The others picked up the bodies and followed him inside. Razvan smiled in approval. Things were progressing well on this end. He flew to the westernmost house. It was time to check on Silas's party.

Sarah had shot three of Selena's vampires. Jonathon and Salazar were gathering up the corpses, and Akasha studiously covered the bloodstains with snow while avoiding looking at the guns. The blood would disintegrate when the sun rose.

Razvan, Silas spoke in his mind, *we have a witness. I am going to take care of him.*

A car had turned onto the street, illuminating the fight in its high beams. The driver gaped dumbly at them like a landed trout. Razvan blinked, and then Silas was beside the driver's door.

By the time Sarah was leading her party into the westernmost house, the human was driving away, gazing forward with a dreamy look on his face. His memory of seeing them had been obliterated... And likely, McNaught had gotten a snack for the trouble.

Akasha and Silas drew their swords as Razvan landed beside them. He unfastened his gun from the strap and partially drew it from his coat. The handle was so cold that he wondered if his skin would stick to the metal.

Using the blood bond he held with his subordinates, he sent a thought out to Trey: *what is happening at your end?*

Trey sent him an image of a living room that would resemble the set of a television sitcom if it weren't for the raucous bloodbath.

The group fought about six vampires. Four others were down on the floor, possibly dead. One of Silas's vampires had a gash on his forehead, but he appeared to be the only one on their side who was injured... So far.

I gotta let you go, boss. Trey's voice sounded in his head, *it's hard to shoot like this, and I need to reload.*

Very well, Razvan replied. *Let me know when you find the underground passage.*

He came back to himself and followed Silas and Akasha into the house.

Ten of Selena's guards were already in action. Sarah crouched behind an overturned sofa, firing at whatever came into range. Jonathon had a large male in a headlock as he sliced his throat open with a scalpel. His gun was at the small of his back, undrawn for now.

A female ran at Akasha with a kitchen knife. Akasha decapitated her in a smooth swipe of her sword. Silas saluted a male who had his own sword before their blades met in clanging combat. Razvan was beginning to think he wasn't going to get any action.

He caught a flash of movement at the corner of his eye and spun in that direction, fangs bared and eager to devour his enemy.

A bedroom door was open a crack, and to his disbelief, a hand had emerged, waving a white pillowcase. With wary steps, he went down the hall and crouched, aiming his gun at the center of the door.

"Tell me who you are and what you want." His voice rang out in command. "Or I will shoot through this door and blast you through the heart and whatever else I can hit."

"My name is Jessica. I am with another vampire who is badly hurt," a quavering voice replied. "I hear you have a doctor with you. We would like to surrender if you help him."

Razvan cursed under his breath. He hadn't expected to take prisoners. "I assume you are referring to only yourselves. The ones out here do not seem to be in a surrendering mood."

He heard a defeated sigh and a moan of pain from further in the room.

"Open the door, and we shall negotiate," Razvan said, writhing with impatience. "And make it quick."

Before the door opened all the way, he bolted inside and seized the female by the throat. A quick glance around the small bedroom assured him that she was telling the truth. A male lay on the bed in a contorted position, panting in agony.

"What happened to him?"

The scrawny female struggled to take a breath, and he loosened his grip slightly. "Justin displeased our lord, and she broke his back. It's healing wrong and pinching his nerves. He needs treatment."

"And what of your mistress?" Razvan asked silkily.

Jessica shuddered. "She's gone mad. We just want to escape, don't we, Justin?"

Justin whimpered in what sounded like assent.

"Tell me how to get to Jayden and how many more of Selena's minions lie in wait, and I'll think about it," he told them.

"But you said," Jessica protested, but he cut her off, tightening his fingers around her throat once more.

"I am the one in power here. It would do well for you to obey me, girl," Razvan hissed and released her.

The female shivered. "Jayden is in the chambers below. Selena is seeing if she can locate the missing band. Michael bruised her a bit, but she is otherwise unharmed." She smiled weakly at Razvan's relieved sigh and continued. "The last time I saw, there were about fifty members of the order down there."

The door slammed open, and a large male burst into the room. "Traitor!" he growled at Jessica, "You are an abomination, you are—"

Razvan seized him and sank his fangs into his throat. When Jessica gave a mewling gasp, he noticed how emaciated she was. He lifted his face from the vampire, noticing how her pupils went dark with hunger at the sight of the blood.

"She starves you, doesn't she?" he asked, trying to keep the pity from his voice.

The female nodded. "She calls it 'fasting.'" Her lip screwed in disgust.

That explained why the vampires they fought had been so weak.

Razvan grabbed the vampire's head and bared his neck. "Feed, then. It's not much, but it should give you the strength to help carry your friend out of here when I fetch the doctor."

Her fangs bared, and she was on her former comrade in a second. Now he was just a meal. Her lack of loyalty to Selena had been proved. Razvan shook his head and wondered when he'd become so soft as he contacted Silas and informed him of this new development.

By the time Jonathon arrived to load up his first patient, Silas's group had slain the rest of the guards upstairs. He checked on Trey's group. All enemies lay dead there as well. Best of all, they had located the passage on their side in the underground chamber.

"Something must be going on downstairs," Jessica said worriedly. "There should have been more coming up to fight… or maybe they have a trap lying in wait. You must all be very careful!"

Razvan nodded as Jonathon helped her carry the wounded vampire out of the house. Now the rescue party was down to twelve, but they had some useful information. He reached out to touch his Mark with Jayden. It felt faint, as if she was on the other side of the world rather than right below him. His pulse leapt into his throat. Whatever Selena had done to her could not be good. *I am coming, Jayden!* He called, although he doubted that she could hear him.

Jayden watched Xochitl Leonine being led up stone steps to what looked like a giant gallows. She was resplendent in an ethereal white gown, but she was in chains. Two moons; one silver and the other gold, shone full and bright in the night sky, bathing an enormous crowd of witnesses with their opulent light. Multitudes of cats wove in and around the audience's feet, and dragons flew in lazy circles above.

"Ladies and gentlemen," a man in blue robes called out. "I present to you—"

The sound of machine-gun fire, impossibly loud, yanked her from the vision like an uppercut to the chin.

Selena's shrine and the reek of incense slammed into view as gunfire roared in her ears. Thumps from upstairs shook the ceiling.

"My lord," a vampire shrieked. "We're being attacked!"

Jayden's heart leapt. Razvan was here with major firepower. If she could hold on a little longer, perhaps this insanity would end.

Selena waved an impatient hand. "Then kill them! I am busy here. If you interrupt me again, I shall break every bone in your body." As the vampire hurried out of the room, she grabbed

Jayden's hand and forced it back onto the guitar. "Go back!" she hissed.

Jayden tried to keep her shields in place, but Selena's mind and will crashed over her like a tidal wave. For a moment, she felt split in two as the vision of Xochitl in that alien world played tug-of-war with Selena's all-consuming madness.

Jayden screamed from the pain of it and focused on the eerie twin moons. The oddest feeling came to her as she succumbed to that other world. It felt like the drama she was seeing was happening right now.

The blue-robed man was locked in combat with another garbed in black. Fire and balls of colored light shot out of their hands like missiles.

Another black-robed figure approached Xochitl and snapped her chains with his bare hands. He lifted his hood, and Jayden saw a familiar vampire. His skin was luminescent as the surface of a pearl, and his hair was like spun obsidian shot through with starlight.

"Uncle Del," Xochitl murmured, "Thank you."

Delgarias looked past Xochitl. His eyes seemed to meet Jayden's, and he nodded.

"I knew it!" Selena shrieked. "He wants to betray us all!"

For a moment, her mad fury sucked at Jayden, pulling her from the vision and into the chaotic chasm of her mind. Then she heard music, and the other world coaxed her back.

The crowd parted to reveal a crudely erected stage. Sylvis, Aurora, and Beau came into view and exchanged smiles with Xochitl as they began playing their instruments.

A man on the gallows pulled a guitar from the folds of his cloak and handed it to Xochitl. It was a twin of the one Jayden held. Xochitl watched with tear-stained eyes as Delgarias plugged the cord into an amplifier powered by a glowing crystal.

Xochitl struck the first chords on her guitar and took in a deep breath.

"Noooo!" *Selena's shriek echoed aloud and into the vision simultaneously.*

Jayden's skull exploded in pain, and in that other world, Xochitl faltered. *A frown of confusion marred her brow. Somehow, Jayden and Selena were affecting her. From a world away, they were affecting her.*

"Do it!" Jayden urged Xochitl.

The singer's eyes widened, and she looked for the source of the thought.

Selena broke through, trying to silence her. Jayden forced her back while mentally shouting to Xochitl, *"Do it! Do it!"*

Though it only lasted milliseconds, the battle seemed to last forever. Her brain felt as if it were being pulled out of her nose and ears as Selena fought to gain her hold. With one last desperate thrust, Jayden threw her back. Xochitl's eyes cleared and her voice, clear as spring dawning, rose into the night.

Selena's scream catapulted Jayden back into her body. "You filthy blasphemer!" the vampire roared. "I'll kill you!"

The door burst open, and a mass of vampires poured into the room. Razvan leveled a wicked looking gun at Selena. Jayden leapt out of the way.

"I think not, bitch," he said and pulled the trigger.

Chapter Thirty-one

Razvan smiled in satisfaction as he awaited the sight of his former protégée being sliced apart. But in a split second, another vampire launched in front of Selena. Its body danced and jerked as the bullets tore through it. And then his gun clicked empty. He threw it down with a virulent curse.

Selena cackled. "You cannot harm me. Mephistopheles protects me."

He shook his head ruefully. Her obsessive zeal had worsened over the centuries. "Your people protect you. But not for much longer." He met Jayden's eyes, and the bruise on her cheek filled him with remorse.

"I have been trying to tell you that I love you, but we keep getting interrupted," he said idly before he moved forward.

Jayden gasped, and her eyes widened in the most adorable manner. He nearly reached her, his hand grasping for hers—then he was thrown to the ground by a pile of vampires. As Razvan's entire body was pierced by multiple sets of fangs, he thrust out his hand and yelled, "Silas, save her!"

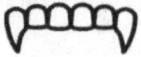

Akasha huddled behind an overturned bureau. The sound of gunfire still echoed in her head, freezing her as panic thrashed through her chest like a captive bird. She was a little girl again, watching mommy and daddy dying under a hail of bullets. She had to get away, or they would shoot her too.

"No, no," she muttered through gritted teeth.

This wasn't happening. After everything that Jayden had done for her, she wasn't going to wuss out now.

The gunfire passed, and the sounds of the fight moved farther away into another room. When Akasha heard Jayden scream, she scrambled to her feet, gripping her sword until her knuckles ached.

"Time to kill some more cult members," she hissed and ran after the fight.

She charged through the door in time to see a bunch of Selena's vampires dogpiling onto Razvan, biting at him like hyenas on a wounded gazelle.

Another vampire stalked behind them and raised his sword over the writhing mass. Akasha roared and brought the flat of her blade down on the back of his head. He crashed to his knees but was not out.

"The mutant!" Selena shrieked, pointing at her. The bitch didn't look good. Bald patches and bloody scabs covered her head. It looked like she'd been tearing out her own hair. What was left hung in grimy orange tangles.

"Fuck you." Akasha raised her sword to spear Razvan's attacker.

Her blade clanged against the steel of his as he whirled to his feet to meet her strike.

"Why hello, Akasha," Michael said with a grin. "I've been looking forward to this."

All was chaos.

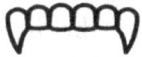

Jayden watched with her heart in her throat as a mass of vampires attacked Razvan.

He'd throw aside one, and another would take its place.

When Michael raised his sword and Akasha beat him down, Jayden cried out in triumph and stood up on shaking legs.

Selena jerked her back by the hair. "I am not finished with you!" she hissed.

Let her go! Silas's voice echoed in her mind. From Selena's startled gaze, she heard him too.

Silas, my love, you've come back to me! Selena's face had transformed into girlish adoration.

The Scottish vampire walked forward. He had lost his sword, and Jayden wondered for a moment how he expected to fight Selena when the force of his mind crashed over them both.

Break free, Jayden! he commanded.

For one terrifying moment, it seemed impossible. The two ancient minds threatened to drown her, and it felt like she was tied down with lead weights. But then, Razvan's last words echoed in her mind.

He *loved* her, and she would not disgrace him. With an agonizing pull, her mind wrenched free.

Still, Jayden could feel the magnetic currents of the telepathic battle between the two ancients. The veins stood out on Silas's temples in sharp relief, and his eyes glowed like emerald stars. He trembled, and beads of sweat gathered on his upper lip. It seemed that Jayden's release had strengthened Selena, and she was getting the upper hand.

Then it happened. The hazy red tinge overlay returned to her vision just as it had the night of the Rage of Angels concert. Jayden could suddenly see the insides of everyone around. Razvan was weakening as the blood drained from his body.

Get back! She screamed into their minds.

Selena's vampires froze and obeyed like puppets.

Razvan rose in the air with Silas's fallen sword in his grasp. He spun like a dervish and sliced the nearest vampires in two.

How dare you? Selena's gaze focused on her.

Jayden saw that one of her pupils was slightly smaller than the other. She probed deeper with her inner vision and saw the cause. Deep inside Selena's brain was an unmistakable bulge in one of the arteries. She had a brain aneurism. It was probably from when she was mortal. Razvan likely saved her life when he changed her into a vampire.

That alien force inside Jayden reached for it and wrapped invisible fingers around the delicate bulb.

This time, she didn't shrink in terror at the destructive urge. She gathered that strange force and squeezed with all her might.

The result was instantaneous.

Selena's pupils doubled in size before her eyes rolled up into her head, and she dropped like a stone.

Razvan swung the sword in a shining arc and chopped off her head, sending it rolling towards the feet of her remaining followers.

All dropped to their knees, except for Michael. Selena's favorite apostle spun on his heel, his mouth gaping in shock. Akasha decapitated him in one swipe. His head flew from his shoulders and rolled next to that of his mistress.

"Jayden." Razvan dropped the sword and swept her into his arms.

His skin was cool, clammy, and deathly pale. Blood ran freely from what looked like hundreds of bite marks. If he didn't feed soon, he'd die.

She brushed her hair from her neck and grasped his face, drawing him closer. "Drink and heal," she whispered.

As his fangs penetrated her flesh, they stumbled into the makeshift altar of Rage of Angels memorabilia. Thankfully, a pile of tee shirts cushioned most of her fall. Jayden's hand reached out for balance. As she touched the autographed guitar, she once again sank into the world with two moons.

Dawn broke forth, chasing away the darkness with crimson and purple light. The vampire Delgarias looked at her and began to speak. His words came from her lips as if she were his amplifier.

"And the queen shall seek seven nightwalkers with seven brides to lead their brethren to battle the unholy father," Jayden gasped. "And they will be joined by kin of the queen and those from allied worlds that hear her call."

She breathed the last words in a sigh as darkness flooded into her eyes and she sank into unconsciousness.

Chapter Thirty-two

Razvan released Jayden gently. He didn't mean to take so much, but he'd been so weak. As her blood coursed through his veins and healed his injuries, tears rose to his eyes. Again she had sacrificed herself to him, and again he had hurt her.

"What the hell did she say before she passed out?" Akasha's voice intruded.

"It was a prophecy of some sort," Silas said. "Delgarias sent it."

Razvan raised a brow. "What are you talking about?"

Silas's eyes widened. "You didn't see him when you fed on her? From the remainder of my connection, I saw everything. It should have been vividly clear to you."

He shook his head. "I had my mind closed off to protect her from further psychic intrusion, as I always do. Is Jonathon still here? I think I took too much from her."

The Lord of Coeur d'Alene smiled gently and held out his arms. "Let me see her."

Reluctantly, Razvan handed over his burden.

Silas inspected her for what seemed to be an eternity. Razvan gnashed his teeth in impatience.

"She's going to be fine," he said finally. "I think she passed out more from psychic overload rather than from blood loss. Still, you should be sure she eats a hearty meal when she wakes up." He handed Jayden back to Razvan.

"What about this prophecy?" Akasha interrupted.

"Yes, yes, the Prophecy!" The remainder of Selena's cult murmured.

Silas looked at them and rolled his eyes before he turned to his wife. "Delgarias was right. It seems that when Xochitl returns to this world, we are going to fight a war."

"You seem awfully calm about that," she retorted. Still, a smile of adoration hovered on her lips.

"When you've lived as long as I have with powers like mine, little will surprise you." He looked at his watch. "It's only an hour until dawn. We need to feed and get home so I can make out a report to the Elders."

"The Elders!" One of their captives exclaimed with zealous fervor. "They will punish you when they hear what you've done."

Razvan laughed. "We have immunity. Didn't your former mistress inform you of that?"

The vampire shrank back. Her eyes bulged in horror.

"Dear God," she whispered. "If we had known, we never would have fought you! Please, have mercy!"

"Speaking of," Trey said, reloading his gun. "What *are* we going to do with them?"

Razvan raked the six remaining cult followers with a furious gaze. "Give them a choice. They can surrender to us as prisoners or perish in the fire."

"Why Razvan, you've grown soft in your old age," Silas said with a grin.

"What fire?" a small male asked.

"We can't leave any evidence for mortals to find. Surely you knew that?" He glared down at the youngling until he was reduced to a mass of quivering flesh. Then he turned to the rest and asked cheerfully, "Now, who is surrendering?"

All six hands came up.

"Whose prisoners are they?" Shen asked. "Yours, or Silas's?"

Silas answered, "It was Razvan's woman they took, so they should be Razvan's captives."

"Except for the injured one and the nurse," Razvan said. "If you do not mind, Silas, I would like them to remain with your doctor. He could use a nurse."

Silas nodded. "Since they did not fight us, I thought of them as voluntary transfers, probationary, of course. I think the nurse will be agreeable, and we shall see about the other one when he is healed." He took out his phone and called Jonathon. "You may bring the gas cans down now."

Trey and Sarah took charge of the six prisoners. Razvan doubted that they had enough bullets left between them to take care of all six, but no one had to know.

Minutes later, they drove off in their vehicles before the first tendrils of smoke became visible from Selena's soon-to-be-former compound.

Since they had nearly double the passengers, many volunteered to take taxis and score a convenient meal while they were at it.

Razvan looked down at Jayden's slumbering form. Her head lay on his lap, and she was curled up on the backseat of Jake's car. There was virtually no traffic on I-90 at this hour, and they were making good time.

"Would you please stop at the nearest restaurant that is open?" Razvan remembered Silas's admonition that Jayden needed to eat. "Pick up the most fattening meal you find on the menu…and get yourself a quick bite if you are able," he added.

Jake raised a brow at the "please." "Sure, boss."

Razvan settled back against the seat and ran his fingers through Jayden's hair. Silas had also said that physical activity would help bring Jayden back into the world and keep her visions at bay. He looked forward to that.

Jayden awoke slowly, reluctant to abandon the sensation of safety. Her cheek was pressed to something warm and firm. The smell of food and the soft sound of a television newscast reinforced the instinct that everything was okay.

Her stomach growled and the surface cradling her shifted.

"Good morning, Jayden," Razvan said.

She rolled over to face him and nearly fell off the couch. He steadied her and smiled down at her. "How are you feeling?"

"Starving." She didn't mean for it to come out so bluntly, but the smell of the food was driving her crazy. She sat up. "Is that chicken fried steak?"

"I have no idea." Razvan grabbed a paper sack from the arm of the couch and pulled out a to-go box. He opened it, frowned, and handed it to her. "I hope that will be enough for you. There is orange juice in the refrigerator as well."

It was chicken fried steak. There were also hash browns, bacon, sausage, and two fried eggs. Jayden salivated as she reached for the bag, hoping it contained plastic utensils. Not only were there utensils, but the bag was stuffed full of napkins, little pats of butter, salt, pepper, and ketchup packets.

"I think it'll be plenty," she said as she grabbed a fork and dug in.

Jayden's cheek hurt as she chewed the steak. As she reached up and touched the bruise, the night's events came back to her.

"Selena's dead," she said.

"Yes," Razvan replied agreeably.

"Is everyone safe? What happened afterward? I must have passed out when I saw—" The memory of that strange world with the two moons came back, and she felt a twinge of pain in her head.

"Eat," he commanded. "We'll have plenty of time to discuss that later."

His tone, along with her hunger and the almost headache, decided the subject, and she returned to the food. But halfway through her meal, she stopped.

"Where are we?"

The air didn't have the stale cigarette odor of Silas and Akasha's house, and yet the lack of the aroma of pungent incense indicated that they weren't in Selena's abode either. The walls were bare of typical hotel room décor…or any décor, for that matter, and the couch and TV were old and well worn.

Razvan gave her an enigmatic look. "This is my home." At her incredulous expression, he added, "I told you it was empty."

Jayden dropped her fork and gazed around. The room was large, verging on cavernous. An old wooden elevator sat at the far end near a shadowy staircase. The drywall only extended so far before abruptly cutting off to reveal ancient brick walls.

Razvan touched her shoulder. "I will give you the full tour if you finish eating," he said. "I took more blood from you than I'd intended."

He sounded so guilty that Jayden hid a smile and returned to the food. Did he really mean it when he'd told he loved her earlier? Or had he been performing to piss off Selena? The sincerity of his tone then gave her hope.

When there was only a scrap of egg and a few bites of potatoes left, she pushed the Styrofoam container away. "I can't eat anymore. Where do I put this?"

Razvan took the container and put it back into the bag. "We should save it. I'm afraid I don't have any more food here."

The news came back on, and he grabbed the remote and turned it up.

"An update in our latest story: a group of houses in Post Falls, Idaho, caught fire at approximately six AM this morning. It's reported that no one was believed to have been in any of the homes at the time. Police and firefighters suspect arson." The reporter looked up at the camera with an almost salacious smile.

"We have just received information that all four houses were registered to the same owner. The police have been unable to reach her, and a neighbor has stated that the owner owed back property taxes."

The camera cut to an elderly woman bundled up in a warm scarf and cap. "There were always people going in and out at odd hours of the night," she said with a disapproving frown. "But nobody was around during the day. And then those tax notices began coming in. I got one at my address by mistake," she said defensively. "I think drugs were involved."

The camera cut to the charred remains of the four houses and the reporter. "As police attempt to contact the homeowner, anyone with any information leading to the cause of the fire is encouraged to call our crime hotline."

Jayden smiled. "So you guys burned it down?"

He nodded. "It was the only way to destroy evidence of the bodies." He turned the TV off and chuckled. "That was quite convenient about the taxes. They will think she did it herself."

"That had to be the most insane night of my life," Jayden said. "I can't believe that Xochitl and the others are in another world.

But what did Delgarias mean when he said there's going to be a war?"

Razvan shook his head. "I'm not certain, but I suppose we shall find out when they return." His brows drew together. "I think it best if we do not talk about it for now. Why don't we begin your tour of my home instead?"

Jayden grinned and stood up. The world tilted for a moment before the dizziness abated. "About that orange juice?"

Razvan smiled again. "Follow me."

The carpeted area ended shortly, and their boots echoed on cracked concrete flooring. The place had a basement feel to it, and yet not.

"This isn't a house, is it?"

He shook his head. "We're in the lower level of the old Sal's Warehouse."

Jayden gasped. They were only half a block from where he had first taken her. The crumbling red brick monstrosity had been a usual sight in her days of homelessness.

She had once considered breaking into this place for shelter when the weather got cold. With a wry smile, she wondered what would have happened if she did. Maybe then he would have killed her for real…or would he?

The kitchen area was bleak and dim, with a low-hanging bulb casting shadows in the corners. An ancient stove sat in one corner covered in dust and cobwebs. The hot plate and coffee maker on the counter appeared to be used more often. Razvan opened a fifties-style fridge and placed her leftover food inside before he took out a large Styrofoam cup. She took it and sat in the only chair at the cracked table.

"I take it that you don't have company often." Jayden was still in awe over the revelation of his home.

She'd expected a chic bachelor's residence with top-of-the-line everything, hot tubs, and scantily clad women running around. Hell, she'd expected the Playboy Mansion.

Razvan smiled slightly at her tone. "I am not often at home."

Probably because it's too lonely. The thought struck her, and she had an urge to take him in her arms and vow that he'd never be alone again. She blushed and sipped her juice.

"Well," he said after an uncomfortable silence. "Would you like a tour?"

Most of the rooms were empty, though a few contained stacks of unpacked boxes. One room made her breath catch in amazement. The walls were lined with shelves of records running from the ceiling to the floor. A gorgeous wooden console stereo dominated the room, and an enormous La-Z-Boy recliner sat nearby, inviting the listener to relax.

"Wow," she whispered. "You must have thousands of dollars-worth of vinyl in here."

"I like music," he said simply.

Another long, awkward silence ensued as she burned with a thousand questions. A strand of hair fell on her face, and she smelled Selena's incense. Her stomach roiled.

"I need a shower," she said.

"There is one in the bedroom. Shall we go there now?"

Her curiosity rose to a fevered pitch, and she tried not to show her eagerness. "Sure."

The bedroom was a little homier than the rest of the rooms, perhaps because the bright splash of color of the fluffy quilt on the bed detracted from the blank walls. The wood from the antique dresser and wardrobe gleamed warmly when he turned on the lamp.

"I had a bathroom installed, and there is a shower," he said stiffly. "No tub, I'm afraid…"

She realized then that he was embarrassed.

"Your bed is very nice," she offered. And it was. The king-size colonial, covered with the elaborate quilt, likely cost a fortune. "I love the quilt."

"It is from my home country." He looked down at her, his dark eyes inscrutable. "Jayden, after your shower, I would like to talk with you about…well… I would like to talk."

He was so stiff and formal, with no sign of his usual mocking demeanor in sight. Though Jayden wanted to scream with the suspense, she knew it wouldn't work to press him.

"All right."

He didn't offer to join her, and she realized he must have cleaned up when she'd been asleep.

"Should I turn up the heat?" he asked. "These old baseboards never seem to provide enough warmth."

This new, insecure Razvan was unnerving.

"Sure," she said and fled to the bathroom, hoping he would be more himself when she came back.

The bathroom was cold and full of antique, worn fixtures. The bare hanging bulb did little to lighten the gloom when she pulled its chain. But the water was hot, and the shampoo and soap were luxury quality. She frowned at the stubble on her legs and grabbed his razor, hoping he wouldn't mind.

When Jayden emerged from the shower, Razvan reclined on the bed. The lamplight cast half his face in shadow and highlighted the chiseled beauty of the rest. His eyes glittered like pieces of onyx. She trembled as she remembered the first time she saw him, looming over her like a dark god.

He stood up and handed her a red velvet smoking jacket. Suddenly shy, she removed her towel quickly and put it on, her face flaming.

With his indrawn breath at her brief nudity, the air became charged with electric sensuality. Her legs trembled as she walked to the bed to sit next to him.

"I don't have any clothes for you," he said suddenly. "I'm sorry, I didn't think this through. I just wanted—" His fingers gripped her shoulders as he looked into her eyes. "Jayden, I love you. I want you to stay with me and help me make this place into a real home. Please, be my girlfriend or wife, or whatever title you desire. I only want to wake up each night with you by my side."

Warmth curled from her head to her toes at his awkward declaration. Jayden swallowed a lump in her throat and took his face in her hands.

"I love you, too," she whispered and kissed him.

Razvan devoured her lips like a man starved. She reached for the buttons on his shirt, eager for the touch of his skin. In seconds they were both naked. Razvan worshiped her body like he'd never get to hold her again. When he slid inside her, they both sighed in ecstasy. He made love to her slowly, torturously, bringing her to climax again and again until they collapsed in each other's arms.

As he tucked the quilt over them and cradled her from behind, she whispered sleepily, "'Girlfriend' sounds nice for now. And I hear that sort of thing sometimes leads to 'wife.'"

Razvan pulled her closer to him. "I believe this will be a pleasurable courtship."

Epilogue

Six Months Later

Jayden and Akasha sat at Silas's dining room table, huddled over the latest issue of Elle Décor magazine. She and Razvan were staying in Coeur d'Alene while the warehouse was being renovated. Jayden was happy to be back with their old friends and ecstatic at trying her hand at interior decorating.

"What do you think of these drapes?" she asked.

Akasha frowned and lit a cigarette. "You don't have windows in your place."

Jayden sighed. "But they're so pretty."

Her friend's expression was unyielding. Akasha wasn't the best at giving opinions on paint swatches or carpet samples, but she was good with practicality.

"Why don't you get some of those cloth hanging…things?" the mechanic suggested.

"Tapestries?" Jayden's eyes widened at the thought. "That's brilliant!"

"Whatever," Akasha replied. "I'm just glad my house already came furnished. You better put that away and get ready for your date with Razvan. Didn't you say you think he might propose?"

Her heart fluttered with excitement. "Shh! They might hear you!" Then she thought of Akasha's earlier words. "Wait, so Silas decorated this place all by himself? Maybe I should ask him for advice."

Akasha shrugged indifferently. "I guess so. Maybe you can pick his brain after you show off your rock."

Jayden narrowed her eyes. "Don't jinx it!" she called over her shoulder as she headed upstairs to dress.

When she came back down, Razvan's eyes raked her up and down, appreciative of her long slinky black dress and upswept hair.

"I guess we shall have to forego the motorcycle," he said with a touch of regret.

Silas came into the room and chuckled. "I am certain your Charger will be enough to garner envy."

When he opened the car door for her and got into the driver's seat, Jayden fought back her usual nervousness. She had taught him to drive, and besides that first mishap with the mailbox, he had done well, though he sometimes drove too fast.

He took her to Cedar's, Coeur d'Alene's famous floating restaurant. As she dug into her Seafood Pappardelle, almost moaning with delight, Razvan fidgeted with the tablecloth and gazed out the window at the lake.

He seemed almost as nervous as he'd been the night he first declared his love. Jayden hid a smile as she chewed her delicious food.

Soon afterward, the waiter appeared with two glasses of champagne and a knowing smile on his face.

"A toast," Razvan said. "To the woman who has made my life complete."

She took her glass and clinked it against his, pretending not to notice the glint of metal in the bottom. But after she sipped her champagne, her cry of surprise was genuine. It was the most beautiful ring she'd ever seen.

After she fished it out with her butter knife, she examined the ring with wide eyes. It was platinum embedded with gold filigree, centering a diamond that likely had cost the earth.

Razvan left his seat and sank down to one knee before her.

"Jayden Leigh, will you marry me?"

She nodded, tears welling up in her eyes as she threw herself into his embrace. "Yes!"

The restaurant broke out in applause. Apparently, they had an audience. Jayden dabbed at her eyes with her napkin, hoping that her mascara hadn't run.

Razvan slipped the ring on her finger. At his touch, she was suddenly thrown into a vision.

Radu Nicolae was awake. The vampire reclined by the fireplace in the stone chamber beneath the ruins of his family castle. He felt her watching and looked up, meeting her gaze with eyes eerily similar to Razvan's.

"You," he whispered and stood up.

Without warning, he plunged into her mind. She felt him tear the knowledge of her location from her head like a sort of rape. Mercifully, he withdrew and stepped back, his lips twisted in a bitter smile and he turned his back to her to address someone else.

"We are going on a little trip, my pretty," he said. His Romanian accent was thicker than his brother's. His voice was harsh as if hadn't spoken for ages.

Jayden saw a cage in the far corner of the chamber. A woman was inside, clinging to the bars. Her strawberry blonde hair was tousled, and bite marks were starkly visible on her pale neck. She looked at Radu in fearful confusion.

Razvan's twin said one last thing before he thrust Jayden out of the vision. "I am coming, brother."

A cool breeze bathed her face, and her eyes fluttered open.

"Are you all right, my love?" Razvan asked.

She struggled to sit up. He had taken her outside to the patio overlooking Lake Coeur d'Alene. The moonlight reflected on the gently lapping water, a calming sight.

"I didn't embarrass myself, did I?"

He shook his head and smiled. "They assumed you fainted from surprise. One woman thought it was very romantic." His gaze turned serious. "Now, what did you see? Was it that other world again?"

Jayden shook her head. Dread filled her gut.

"Your brother is coming here…and I think he's still mad at you."

I hope you enjoyed Ironic Sacrifice! Keep reading for a teaser of Conjuring Destiny

Teaser of Conjuring Destiny

Xochitl

Halloween. This was *my* night, and nobody would fuck it up. Determination coursed through my veins for tonight's show to be our best damn performance ever. I owed it to my friends.

I opened the closet door and took out my costume, a wedding dress, dyed black. Sylvis, our guitarist and my best friend, chose this year's costume theme to be obscure horror movie characters. With an upside-down cross earring, tiara, and poofy '80s hair, I hoped some people would recognize me as Angela from *Night of The Demons*. If not, at least I'd still be seen as classically goth.

When I met Sylvis in the hall, I grinned at the sight of her blonde wig and pink baby-doll dress. The sloppy crimson lipstick lines drawn down her cheekbones and over her eyebrows in the shape of a heart were a dead giveaway. She'd also picked a character from *Night of the Demons*: Suzanne, who'd had an iconic scene with a tube of lipstick.

Neither of us told each other about our costume choices. The coincidence had to be a result of us being inseparable since the third grade.

Her blue eyes swept over my costume with an appreciative grin. "Great minds, Xochitl. Great minds."

She drew the syllables of my name out. *So-She*.

Aurora and Beau took forever to join us downstairs, both dressed as cenobites from the *Hellraiser* movies. The only reason I could tell them apart was that I'd never seen Pinhead with breasts before. Beau, our bassist, dressed up as the female cenobite…who's depressingly known just as "the female cenobite" in the film credits. Beau loved doing drag, but he rarely did it when we played gigs.

Sylvis frowned at them. "I said the theme was obscure horror films, not famous classics!"

Beau waved her off with a hand worthy of a pageant queen. "We're not as creative as you two. Besides, we look fabulous."

I nodded, admiring them both. The vinyl outfits were custom or tailored from expensive S&M store attire. Beau's sexy dress, complete with a realistic breastplate, was to be envied, but Aurora's makeup job with the meticulously placed "pins" blew my mind. So that's who'd been spray painting toothpicks.

"How did you get the pins to stick?"

Aurora grinned, her smile at odds with the creepy black contacts and white face paint. "Liquid latex. Beau has a lot of tricks."

"You didn't cut your hair, did you?" I asked with alarm. She had gorgeous hair.

Beau shook his head. "Of course not! I let her use one of my bald caps. The rest of it is tucked under the high collar in back."

They'd out-Halloweened me, I realized with a twinge of envy. I always rocked this holiday…until this year, when I somehow forgot about it. What was wrong with me? The blow softened as they admired mine and Sylvis's costumes.

"You guys nailed *Night of the Demons*. I wish we'd thought of it." She pulled out her phone and glanced at the time. "We better hustle if we wanna make it in time for load-in."

When we formed our band, Rage of Angels, it became our tradition to do a concert every Halloween. Our first ones were at keggers in the backwoods of northern Idaho. Nowadays, the most exclusive venues would pay us a fortune to grace their hallowed grounds. But we still played the annual show at the club that gave us our start: The Mortuary in Bothell. Though in the middle of nowhere, the club remained popular because it was near a reputed haunted cemetery.

"You look out of it," Aurora commented as we hauled our instruments out to the van. "Are you burnt out from the tour?"

I nodded, trying not to trip over Isis, my blue point Siamese cat who wove around my ankles. "I think so. When I woke up this morning, I didn't even know where I was."

Sylvis carried her guitar case. "That's understandable since we just got back from our tour. I think rock stars see more hotel rooms than hookers."

I laughed, then flinched as raindrops pattered on my head and shoulders. Isis growled and darted back into the house.

"I fucking *hate* rain." My voice came out harsher than I intended, due to lack of sleep.

Aurora raised a brow. "We're in Seattle. I figured you'd be used to it by now."

We packed our gear into Aurora's van and were off. As I watched misty raindrops hit the back window, a strange sense of foreboding washed over me.

My best friend leaned over to whisper in my ear. "You're having the dreams again, aren't you?"

I nodded, the back of my neck prickling. "Every night."

They'd started when I was seventeen, right after my mom died. Almost every night, I walked in a garden of dying black roses. Two moons shone in an alien sky as a shadowed man in a black cloak beckoned me. His presence filled me with unfathomable longing, doing strange things to my insides. I always awoke before I reached him, covered with goosebumps and a need for something I couldn't identify.

The more I had the dream of the shadowy man and the world with two moons, the more disoriented I became.

I shook my head; the cross earring slapped my cheek. I tried to convince myself my imagination just ran wild…that I was only pissed because it was raining on my favorite holiday, but my foreboding refused to abate. I clutched my guitar as if it were my baby blanket.

Beau admonished Sylvis not headbang too much and dislodge her wig, but I barely heard a word he said. However, when we arrived at The Mortuary, and I saw everything decorated for Halloween, my spirits lifted.

Taffeta, velvet, plastic, and other various materials rustled around us as we waded through the crowd, hefting our instruments. The breathtaking array of colors and textures made me giddy. On an average day, people who frequented The Mortuary dressed weirdly, but tonight, on Halloween, few even looked human. Faces under glowing masks and elaborate makeup gazed eerily at us under the red and black lights. Even now, the spooky ambiance of the holiday made me feel like a kid playing hide-and-seek with the boogeyman.

Dominic, the club owner, greeted us while his house crew took our gear and readied the stage. While Aurora chatted with him over the night's setlist, I scanned the crowd once more as if I expected to see the shadow man. His words in last night's dream echoed in my head.

I'm coming for you.

My stomach tightened. Had he said that before in the other dreams?

Irritation chased off the unfamiliar sensation. Determined not to let him distract me from my favorite gig, I straightened my spine. This night was *mine*, damn it.

Zareth

Zareth Amotken, high sorcerer of Aisthanesthai, wove through the crowd of jabbering mortals, his lip curled in scorn at their lack of magic. With such tepid fare, his hydra would starve if he remained too long in this desolate world. Already, his power dwindled. Disdain faded to unease at that prospect. Zareth quashed the debilitating emotion. He would secure Xochitl and be back in his own world tonight.

The mortals stepped warily to the side as he passed, either intimidated by his height or because they sensed that he was other. He wore a hooded cloak to conceal his luminescent hair, even though unnatural colored tresses swarmed his vision. He likely didn't need to worry about anything except for his hands, which he kept in his pockets.

Delgarias had been right. Locating Xochitl Leonine had been simple.

"She shines like a beacon," the Keeper of the Prophecy had told him. "And she'll smell like a banquet to your hydra. Even if she didn't, she'd be easy to find."

"Why is that?"

"She's the lead singer of a world-famous heavy metal band. They call themselves Rage of Angels."

Zareth had gaped at the faelin high sorcerer in disbelief. "She's a troubadour? The bastard daughter of Mephistopheles and the princess of Medicia, the one who will save our world, is naught but a minstrel?"

"Think about it, Zareth. What else would she be given the words of the Prophecy?"

"'With her triumphant roar...'" His eyes widened at the implication. "You can't be serious."

"Has the prophecy ever lied?"

Now, here he stood, in a raucous Earth realm tavern on the Spirit Feast—what the people here called Halloween—to at last lay eyes on the woman he'd been dream-summoning for the last four years.

As he wove through the costumed masses, he detected several non-human presences. One could be Xochitl, though it was doubtful as the stage remained empty. Strengthening his shields, Zareth surveyed the crowd.

His breath caught when he glimpsed two dark-haired men. They were Mephistopheles's fallen monsters.

Two millennia ago, the would-be god created some metaphysical mutation, which morphed humans into blood-drinking monsters with unnatural strength. They'd acted as his foot soldiers until they'd displeased him, forever banished to Earth, punished to live in a world free of magic.

Zareth couldn't think of a worse punishment.

Eyeing the creatures, who the people here called vampires, he wondered if they had a connection with Xochitl. After all, she was Mephistopheles's daughter. Zareth prayed they were only here for the music. He had no wish to interact with those abominations.

The lights dimmed, and all went still as a vampire appeared on the stage. His fangs gleamed in the stage lights. The humans grinned in admiration, assuming the teeth were part of his costume.

"Welcome to the annual Mortuary Halloween bash!" the vampire shouted. "As many of you know, tonight's honored guests got their start in my club. Some of you even saw them doing covers of Megadeth, Iron Maiden, and my personal favorite, Metal Church."

The creature owned this establishment. Zareth ground his teeth in disgust.

"Despite landing a major record deal and recording two platinum albums, they've never forgotten us. Every Halloween, they perform a concert, and all the proceeds go to a charitable cause. This year your cover charge and drinks will help homeless veterans." The vampire spread his arms wide. "Without further ado, I present to you, Rage of Angels!"

Zareth felt her before she emerged. Once again, Delgarias had been correct in his assertions. Xochitl's radiant presence and effervescent power washed over him like a force that made his knuckles tighten.

He cursed her inwardly. Foolish creature. Hadn't her mother taught her to shield properly? His hydra, a bodiless demon that gave him immortality, roiled with hunger for her essence.

The audience erupted into a cacophony as Rage of Angels came into view. Zareth's breath caught at his first sight of the savior of his world. Delicate and ethereal, her fine-boned features and pearlescent skin made the humans around her seem coarse by comparison. Her black and purple waist-length hair gleamed under the stage lights. Unbidden, his gaze swept across her firm, lush breasts, and exquisitely curved hips, drinking in the sight of her like a man starved.

Lust, hot and immediate, surged through him in a relentless wave. Zareth sucked in a breath. That wasn't what he was here for. She was an imperative means to a crucial end. Still, the intensity of his unexpected desire caught him off guard. He'd been too busy with his studies to crave female companionship often. He shook his head. Maybe it had been too long since he'd shared pleasure with a woman?

So captivated with her beauty, he hadn't taken notice of her costume. The full-skirted black taffeta dress at first resembled a ball gown, but the lace veil on her head clarified its true purpose. Many of his people also wore such veils for the same occasion.

It was a wedding gown.

The realization gave him a twinge of unease. Could her garb be an omen? The foreboding dissolved into fury when she hugged the vampire. Zareth's fists clenched in an effort not to charge forward and tear her from the monster's embrace.

A red haze obscured his vision, even after the vampire left the stage and Xochitl addressed her audience. Outrage kept him from hearing her words. What did she think she was doing, consorting with those things? Protective rage coursed through him, making his shadow spell waver.

His hydra roared in protest. *No! She is mine!*

A memory froze him. He'd uttered those words in a dream-summoning mere years ago. Something had intruded upon Xochitl's dream. Had it been a vampire?

Every fiber of his being longed to incinerate every blood drinker in sight. Only the dangers of revealing himself stayed his hand.

The other vampires congregated at the base of the stage, scanning the crowd with narrowed, watchful eyes.

They'd positioned guards. Have they sensed me? Zareth held his breath, poised to fight if necessary. So they meant to protect Xochitl and the others. A slight measure of his hostility waned, though his distrust remained.

Music filled the air and banished all thoughts of the loathsome creatures.

Heavy metal was an explosion on the senses. The wailing guitars, throbbing bass, staccato drums, and the vocalist's enraged screams evoked a primal life force within its listeners. A force that had them thrashing and jumping with exhilaration…a force that stirred his hydra into a frenzy. It spread its invisible form outward, opened its mouths, and fed. Zareth closed his eyes in pleasure, rejuvenated from his exhausting effort of coming through the portal to this world.

Zareth had heard electric guitars before, but he'd never heard the instruments distorted and played in such a blistering style. Leaning forward in fascination, he tried to decide whether or not he liked this music. Either way, it had power.

An impossibly fast drumbeat pounded through his consciousness. Whipping his attention to the source of the sound, Zareth studied the drummer. This one wore a costume even more elaborate than the singer. Her face was covered with white face paint, a cap to make her appear bald concealed her hair, and silver pins protruded from her face and skull like a pallid pincushion. But the odd costume wasn't what captured Zareth's attention. This woman held a glimmer of magic. Humans of that ilk were rare on Earth, descending from the time when mages, faelin, and luminites dwelled here until they were persecuted by non-magical humans. However, he was unsurprised that Xochitl and this woman had become friends. They must have sensed their kinship, as Zareth could.

Guitars joined the rhythm, and he shifted his scrutiny to the other minstrels. The bass player also held power…and so did the guitarist. They all did.

"How in the realms?" he whispered, staring in shock.

For two of them to meet was probable, but four?

His speculation broke off as Xochitl's voice permeated his consciousness. Rich and operatic, punctuated by bone-chilling screams of rage, it was more than pleasing to his ears. Her voice was thick with power, which imbued its listeners with pure, unadulterated emotion.

Zareth closed his eyes and pictured the people of Aisthanesthai hearing this voice…their passions renewed, their magic rejuvenated enough to bring forth the dawn of their salvation.

Xochitl

By the time Dominic mounted the stage and introduced us, I was ready to rock.

The audience roared as Sylvis and I picked up our guitars and waved. Beau slipped the strap of his bass over his shoulders, and Aurora sat down before her drum kit.

"It's All Hallows' fucking eve!" I screamed into the microphone as the crowd cheered. "The night of tricks, treats, witches and Sabbats! So tonight, we're going to have our own Sabbat. We're going to rage and have a hell of a night!"

Applause filled my ears, silenced as I struck the opening chords on my guitar and shrieked the first words of the song. The people in the mosh pit thrashed and jumped. The notes on Sylvis's guitar ripped the air. Aurora's drums pounded, and Beau's bass reverberated through the floor as he roared the background lyrics.

The moshing masses below became a blur, fading from my awareness as the song progressed. I concentrated on nothing but the soaring notes of my voice and playing my guitar, going through the process of losing myself to the music once more.

Nothing else mattered. Nothing existed but the pulsing rhythm of the drums, the deep vibrations of the bass, the soul-piercing melody of our guitars, and the resonance of my voice rising out of my being, lightening my spirit and celebrating everything.

My soul throbbed in intoxicated ecstasy. I felt alive, pure, at peace. But most of all, I wasn't lonely. I belonged.

Beau strummed the rhythm to the next song, and my attention returned to the music. I straightened my spine and willed my mind and body into the power stance I used on stage and…if the situation merited, a potential fight. I watched the crowd's eyes widen and knew I looked bigger now. My cat taught me the trick.

As we finished the song, the audience held its breath in collective anticipation as Sylvis's guitar breathed its last vestige of passion. My best evil grin spread across my face. This was my favorite part. I clenched my fists and gathered the inhuman force within. It built in the center of my chest, shot down my arms and out of my hands. Twin purple fireballs raced over the heads of the crowd, curving upwards at the last second.

I basked in the applause of my "special effects," doing my best not to bust out with a *Beavis n' Butthead* laugh and shriek, "Fire! Fire!"

As the fireballs climbed toward the club's high ceiling, their reflection flickered in the eyes of a man…black eyes, rimmed with silver. My heart stopped, my legs turned into pudding. A black hood obscured his features, but not enough to hide those eyes. It was *him*.

His eyes catapulted me back into the dream.

I walked through the garden of black roses. My hair lay like a heavy blanket over my back and shoulders, a welcome warmth against the cool wind whispering through the thorny bushes. Goosebumps rose on my skin. It shouldn't have been cold enough to dispel my magic, but this place rendered me as powerless as the human I'd once believed myself to be.

I looked up at the sky, frowning at the two moons, one a silver crescent amongst the stars—not silver like poets say Earth's moon is, but true silver like the finest jewelry. The other was gold as Egyptian treasure.

A rustling sound pulled my attention back to my surroundings. All around me, roses withered and died. The petals shriveled until they resembled flattened prunes. They dried with a crackle and fell to the ground. Dead leaves rained upon the garden. Thorny branches curled in upon themselves like gnarled, arthritic hands.

I pulled my robe tight across my breasts and shivered. I hated this part. Something pulled in my chest as I watched things die in fast-forward. Fog poured in with the speed of stage effects.

Shadows slithered through the air. Darkness flowed around and through my body to converge around a figure gliding toward me. He towered over me like a movie villain. Face obscured by the night and the cowl that covered his head, only his eyes were visible. They glowed in the moonlight like lightning-struck obsidian. His power thundered through my being, almost bringing me to my knees.

I resisted. No one would bring me down. I'd die on my feet, or stand triumphant.

I turned to run, and the branches of the rose bushes reached out. Thorns caught my clothes, trapping me until I whirled back around to face the shadowy man. He opened his arms as if offering a safe haven in the velvet folds of his cloak.

"Come to me." His voice was deep, rich, decadent.

Unbidden, my lips parted, and my belly tied itself in knots. My skin tingled, my heart pounded. Part of me longed for the warmth of his embrace, the feel of his lips on mine. The other part resisted the consuming power of my attraction, reluctant to give up my sense of self. I'd never been so affected by another person before. Only he made me feel this way.

Unable to resist the compulsion, my feet waded through the fog that curled around him like something alive, bringing me closer.

Awareness returned as the audience murmured in confusion. How long had I been zoning out? Sylvis met my gaze, eyes full of concern. I looked back at the crowd.

The shadowy man remained in place.

He mouthed his command once more. "Come to me."

Either I was going crazy, or the man of my dreams was real.

Zareth

He stared at the twin bolts of fire that Xochitl shot over the audience. Such power, such control…such irresponsibility.

"The little fool," he muttered.

Oblivious to his scrutiny, Xochitl's lush lips curved in a blissful smile that filled him with heat, despite his chagrin. Then, her honey-brown eyes met his and lit with recognition. Zareth sucked in a breath as electricity jolted between them. That sweet mouth opened, and time froze for an indeterminable instant before she turned her attention back to the microphone and thanked the audience.

Zareth smiled in triumph. She recognized him. His dream magic *had* worked after all. The question was, how much of his communication had she understood? Did she know that his world was dying, that it was her destiny to save it? Or had her dreams of him been as indiscernible and fleeting as his?

He shrugged. It didn't matter anymore. Soon he would learn everything she knew.

As Xochitl sang along with a blistering guitar riff, he closed his eyes…and released his hydra again. He fed until sated. Magic coursed through his veins with more power than he'd had since the sun vanished from his world.

Power that would sustain him until it was time to take her to his realm.

About the Author

Formerly an auto-mechanic, Brooklyn Ann thrives on writing romance featuring unconventional heroines and heroes who adore them. Author of historical paranormal romance in her critically acclaimed "Scandals with Bite" series, urban fantasy in the cult favorite, "Brides of Prophecy" novels, the award winning, "Hearts of Metal, and the "B Mine" series, horror romances riffing on the 1970s and 1980s horror movies.

She lives in Coeur d'Alene, Idaho with her gamer son, rockstar/IT Guy boyfriend, and their cats.

She can be found online at https://brooklynannauthor.com as well as on twitter and Facebook.

Keep in touch for the latest news, exclusive excerpts, and giveaways! Sign up for Brooklyn Ann's newsletter!

Books by Brooklyn Ann

Series by Brooklyn Ann

B Mine

Horror Romance

HIS FINAL GIRL

HER HAUNTED HEART

HIS SCREAM QUEEN

HER HALLOWEEN PARTY

~~~~~~

Brides of Prophecy

(Paranormal Romance/ Urban Fantasy)

Also don't need to be read in order until book 5...kinda

Prequel: Tesemini

Wrenching Fate

Ironic Sacrifice

Conjuring Destiny

Unleashing Desire

Pleading Rapture

Melding Souls

Reclaiming the Magic

Leaving the Shadows

Bewitching the Vampire

Redeeming the Angel

~~~~~~

Blood Prophecy (*standalone Brides of Prophecy spinoffs)*

To Tempt a Sorcerer

To Wed a Warrior

Hearts of Metal

Contemporary Romance

Standalones that intertwine

Kissing Vicious

With Vengeance

Rock God

Metal and Mistletoe

Forbidden Song

Tempting Beat

Heart Throb

Scandals With Bite

Regency paranormal romance

Books do not need to be read in order

Bite Me, Your Grace

One Bite Per Night

Bite at First Sight

His Ruthless Bite

Wynter's Bite

The Highwayman's Bite

For excerpts and special content,

visit BrooklynAnnAuthor.com

I love hearing from readers! If you have any questions or comments, feel free to send me an email!

Contact@brooklynannauthor.com

www.ingramcontent.com/pod-product-compliance
Lightning Source LLC
Chambersburg PA
CBHW011431240626
47153CB00011B/2933
* 9 7 8 0 6 9 2 2 3 6 1 3 0 *